SHOTGU
BELLS

BOOK #11 IN
THE KIKI LOWENSTEIN MYSTERY SERIES

Joanna Campbell Slan

~Spot On Publishing~

Joanna Campbell Slan
Spot On Publishing, a division of Luminary LLC
9307 SE Olympus Street
Hobe Sound /FL 33455 USA
http://www.SpotOnPublishing.org

Book Layout © 2016
http://www.BookDesignTemplates.com
Covers by Dar Albert, Wicked Smart Designs
http://www.WickedSmartDesigns.com
Editing by Wendy Green.

Shotgun, Wedding, Bells: Book #11 in the Kiki Lowenstein Mystery Series -- Joanna Campbell Slan. – 2nd ed.
ISBN-13: 978-1547199464
ISBN-10: 1547199466
Revised 10/30/2017

SHOTGUN, WEDDING, BELLS

BOOK #11 IN THE
KIKI LOWENSTEIN MYSTERY SERIES

Includes Bonus Excerpt
from

GLUE, BABY, GONE

BOOK #12 IN THE
KIKI LOWENSTEIN MYSTERY SERIES

Our wedding day dawned like a scene from a fairy tale. Frozen rain coated the freshly fallen snow. The glassy surface glistened like a million tiny diamonds. Icicles hanging from the eaves of our house formed natural prisms, casting rainbows across the blanket of white. Sunlight transformed the long dead banks of mums into mounds, like glittering pillows under a white duvet. The scene before us was beautiful, but treacherously slick. This overnight winter storm had paralyzed travel throughout the St. Louis area. All the salt and sand we'd tossed down on the walkways hadn't done much good.

Our friend Detective Stan Hadcho guided me along the flagstones, by means of a good grip on my elbow. He escorted me from the back door of our house to the gazebo. As we walked, Leighton Haversham, our former landlord and dear friend, snapped photos so I could make a memory album. That's what I do. I'm a scrapbooker and owner of a store called Time in a Bottle.

At the stairs to the gazebo, I stared up into the smiling faces of the people so dear to me: my newly adopted son, Erik; my daughter, Anya; Erik's aunt, Lorraine Lauber; our nanny, Bronwyn Macavity; my fiancé, Detective Chandler Louis Detweiler; and of course, our animal friends, my dog Gracie and Lorraine's dog Paolo. They'd all stood there patiently in the cold, waiting for me to arrive. Detweiler reached down to take my gloved hand so I could step up and join him. His eyes were warm with emotion, and his gaze was steady. Moist clouds of exhalations floated around all our faces, forming gossamer veils of moisture. As we turned to face Lorraine, who would be conducting the ceremony, Detweiler wrapped an arm around my waist.

Correction: A small portion of my waist.

At eight-and-a-half months pregnant, I'm the size of the Goodyear Blimp. Or at least that's how it feels. But Detweiler loves me. I'm carrying our baby, and our other two children are happy and healthy. Even though the overnight storm was keeping much of our extended family from joining us today, our wedding would be a joyous event.

Detweiler's shoulder brushing up against mine, so strong and solid, augured a good start to the rest of our lives. We stood side-by-side, exactly the way we intended to go through life, as friends and lovers.

"Not too bad for a wedding thrown together in forty-eight hours," he whispered in my ear as Lorraine (aka "Aunt Lori") opened her prayer book. There was a chuckle in his voice.

I tried not to giggle. Although I have been dreaming about marrying Detweiler ever since I met him nearly three years ago, this day was a long time coming. Even though I kept telling myself that a ceremony was only a formality, deep down I really wanted to wear a wedding band again—as long as it was his! The legalities of our relationship might not matter much to Detweiler and me, but they could matter terribly to our two kids and to the baby who was kicking imaginary field goals inside me. I'd learned the hard way that the legal system can be your best friend and your worst enemy.

Initially I'd planned for us to get married in the gap between Thanksgiving and Christmas. Detweiler and I had even talked about flying our whole family to Las Vegas and visiting the wedding chapel inside a Denny's. The kids would have loved that combination, wedding bells and pancakes. But my friend Clancy Whitehead reminded me, "You're eight months along. They don't allow women that pregnant on a plane."

Oops. Who knew?

I'd tabled that project, and made a notation on my calendar to revisit our wedding plans after December 25th. I would have hurried through the holiday season and put the idea out of my head, except for something unsettling that happened to my son.

My sisters, Amanda and Catherine, had asked if they could spend a Saturday baking cookies with my kids. Of course, I said yes. Anya and Erik were delighted. From the big smiles on their faces, they'd had a wonderful time.

"Look, Mama Kiki," said Erik, as he offered up a small shopping bag. Inside were two shoeboxes and two Pringles cans filled with yummy treats.

"I've got one too." Anya grinned at me. "We'll have plenty to share with Aunt Lori and Leighton." After thanking my sisters profusely, I hustled my children out to the car.

My mouth began to water as we were pulling away from the curb of the rental house my sisters share with my mother. The car's interior smelled wonderfully of butter, sugar, and vanilla. Now and then, I caught a whiff of cinnamon.

Sometimes playing chauffeur is a drag, but there's an undeniable magic that happens when you're looking out the front window and your children are in the back seat. Remember Art Linkletter? How he said that kids say the darned-est things? Something about car rides encourages that. Especially longish car rides.

We were merging onto the heavy traffic on Highway 40 when Erik explained to me that because Detweiler and I weren't married, our new baby would be a "littermate."

"A littermate?" I adjusted my rearview mirror so I could look at him. My son's solemn face stared back at me. His chocolate brown eyes, his mocha-colored skin, and his red hair testified to his biracial heritage. He might not be the child of my womb, but he's certainly the child of my heart. From the moment I set eyes on him, I fell in love with that little boy.

"A littermate? I don't understand what you mean, sweetie."

Anya rolled her eyes and explained, "He means i-l-l-e-g-i-t-i-m-a-t-e."

It took me a while to put those letters into a word. When I did, I nearly drove off the road. "Uh, Erik, honey? Who was talking to you about the baby being a ...littermate?"

"Grandma Co-wins," he said, mangling my mother's last name, Collins.

My mother. That paragon of parenthood.

I gritted my teeth. "That figures." Although she didn't know it, my Mom had just moved one step closer to an apartment in assisted living. Mom wasn't aware yet, but the rental house was going up for sale. My sisters and I had several meetings, trying to decide how to cope with our aging parent. In the end, we decided to wait until after the holidays were over.

Calling my child "illegitimate" marked a new low, even for her.

I told myself to shrug it off. To consider the source. But Anya turned her denim blue eyes on me and said, "She's right, Mom."

"Don't worry," I said. "Detweiler and I still have plenty of time to tie the knot."

Two hours later, the contractions started.

CHAPTER 2

Brawny, which is the nickname of our Scot nanny, handles everything with aplomb. "Braxton-Hicks," she said, after she timed my contractions by watching the second hand on her watch make its rounds.

"Who is Braxton-Hicks and how do I phone him?" Detweiler waved his cell phone in one hand. At the first sign of my distress, he had jumped up from the dinner table and run to my side.

"Braxton-Hicks means false labor," said Brawny in a soothing voice. "Of course, you'll want to take Kiki to the hospital to be sure, but I'm fairly certain that our wee lad isn't coming yet."

"Of course I'll take her to the hospital." Detweiler looked at Brawny as if she'd suggested we sacrifice a lamb on our dining room table. "Help me get her to the car."

Brawny grabbed my woolen cape and draped it over my shoulders. "Anya? Stay with your brother, please. I notice you haven't touched those peas. Eat them or there's no dessert."

The nanny wrapped an arm around my waist and pointed me toward the door. Detweiler proceeded to run around in circles trying to find his car keys (in his pants), his utility belt (locked in the gun safe upstairs as always), his cell phone (also in his pants), and his wallet (in his hand). Brawny and I hobbled through the kitchen and down the hallway toward the garage. As we did, our harlequin Great Dane, Gracie, started whining. But not because she was worried about me. She loves Detweiler best, even though I'm the person who adopted her. Her canine sixth sense informed her that if I was leaving, he was taking off too.

"I'm sure you're right about it being a false alarm. I've got almost a month to go."

"Twenty-five days!" Detweiler yelled from inside the house.

"It's not so bad for him to do a trial run to the hospital,"

Brawny whispered. "Let him get the kinks out. Prepare him for the real thing."

"See you in a couple of hours." I slid into the cold passenger's seat of the police cruiser.

"I'll have Erik in bed and Anya hard at her studies. Don't worry about a thing."

Detweiler raced into the garage and around his car clockwise, then counterclockwise to check on me, then clockwise to open his door, and then counterclockwise to make sure my seat belt wasn't too tight across my belly. With lights and siren blazing, we sped off into the night, alarming all of our Webster Groves neighbors in the process.

He tried talking to me, but the result was gibberish. I covered my mouth to keep from laughing. Considering that he's a homicide detective who copes with tragedy and high drama on a daily basis, you'd think he would have handled my impending delivery in a calm, cool, collected manner. But here's his secret: The one thing that Chad Detweiler has wanted, his whole life, has been to have a family. Even as a little kid, he'd tell his mother, "When I get married and have my own children..."

Thelma Detweiler thought it an adorable trait. I agree.

We broke speed limits right and left. I smiled to myself. Chad Detweiler was going to make a wonderful father to our son. He'd already proven that by how he acted toward Anya, and Erik. As long as he didn't crash the car on the ride to the hospital, we were well on our way to fulfilling his dream.

With one little hitch: We weren't officially married.

CHAPTER 3

Standing there in the gazebo, a wonderful sense of peace descended on me. Leighton kept snapping photos, which would make a beautiful wedding album. I was wearing a heavy white gown, thick with handmade lace. Leighton had donated his mother's damask and lace tablecloths so that Brawny, that marvel of domesticity, could whip up a special gown for my wedding day. The long sleeves came to a point at my wrists. The high waist reminded me of the gown of a medieval princess I'd once seen in a painting. Brawny even managed to concoct a sort of cape with a hood to keep me warm. It was a kind gesture. Even though pregnancy had cranked up my natural thermostat to a near feverish pitch, my ears still got cold.

To my left stood Erik and Anya, bundled up in their winter coats, scarves, gloves, and hats, and with solemn expressions on their faces. To my right was Detweiler in his navy blue dress uniform. Hadcho had taken his place at Detweiler's side. Brawny stood stoically at the far left, helping me bookend the children. She was wearing her "uniform," a tartan skirt, knee socks, brogues, and a woolen cape. Next to Brawny stood Gracie, shivering in the cold.

I turned my attention to our minister, Lorraine, a stooped figure in a full-length black mink coat. Because of a recent flare up of her MS, she was leaning hard on her walker. Leighton was at her elbow to steady her. Her guard dog, Paola, a Giant Schnauzer, scooted to one side to give the man access.

As Lorraine found the correct page in her prayer book, I drank in my surroundings. The world was achingly beautiful. Yet another layer of snow had been falling all morning. The large oak tree never wore such a splendid white mantle. A serene silence reigned, broken only by the occasional tinkle of the wind chimes that Leighton had hung at various locales. It was music so dear to me, as I'd heard the bell tones daily for years now. But this morning, they seemed particularly celestial as they chimed from every corner of Leighton's Webster Groves estate.

Except that this wasn't Leighton's Webster Groves estate. It was ours. Detweiler's and mine. When Erik first came to live with us, we were living in the tiny cottage on the edge of the grounds. The place had been a large garage until Leighton converted it into an oversized writing studio. But the building didn't work for him, so he'd rented it to me, back when it was just me and my daughter, Anya. As Detweiler joined us, and then Erik and Brawny, the tiny space became far too crowded for three adults and two children. Not to mention a big dog, and two cats. Meanwhile, a change in his finances forced Leighton to put his big family house up for sale. Like a fairy godmother, Lorraine waved a magic wand and—presto, change-o! In a move worthy of reality television, we had effected a house swap.

It all worked out perfectly, especially because in the meantime, Leighton and Lorraine had fallen in love. She agreed to move in with him. The big old Haversham mansion, with its multiple floors and stairs, was too cumbersome for a woman with MS, but the cottage suited her down to the ground. So we gained the space our growing family needed, and they doted on their cozy nest. Best of all, the close proximity encouraged Lorraine to take on the role of "Aunt Lori," while Leighton was already an ersatz uncle to the children. I couldn't have been more pleased. Hillary Clinton was entirely right: It does take a village to raise a child.

As Lori read our vows from her *Unity Book of Prayer*, Erik hopped up and down, catching flakes on his tongue. Because he'd lived his whole life in California, Erik had never seen snow. Each snowflake offered new temptation. At first, Anya tried to stop him. They were holding hands, so she simply gave his a tug, but Erik proved more determined. She's an indulgent big sister, so she let him have his fun. Meanwhile, I listened to the words that would officially make me Mrs. Chad Detweiler, and I agreed to take him as my husband.

"I now pronounce you man and wife," said Lori.

Erik jumped up to catch a snowflake. I reached for him, worried that he'd topple off of the gazebo.

Then came a loud *crack*—and a bullet tore a hole in the hood of my cape.

"Get down!" Throwing myself at the children, I pushed them off the gazebo and into a snow bank.

"Shooter! Two o'clock!" screamed Detweiler.

"I'm on it," responded Hadcho.

I glanced up to see Brawny cock her arm and let something silver fly.

Simultaneously, Gracie streaked past as she went running toward the shed with her leash trailing behind.

Detweiler and Hadcho jumped awkwardly off the gazebo and ran after Gracie.

Leighton must have knocked Lorraine off the side of the structure, as I had done with the kids, because I heard her metal walker clank against the wooden frame. Hot on Gracie's heels, Paolo flew past, barking up a storm.

"Anya? Erik? You okay?" I stared into the wide eyes of the kids.

"Uh-huh," said my daughter. Erik's lower lip quivered, but he nodded in agreement.

"Stay here." I crawled on my elbows around the back of the gazebo. Lorraine was blinking up at the sky. Leighton was on all fours, talking to her.

I glanced into Leighton's wide eyes. "You two okay?"

"I think so. Lorraine?" He brushed snow from her hair.

"Y-yes. I'm fine." She began babbling. "Kiki? Anya? Erik? The baby?"

"Right as rain. The snow cushioned my belly. I'm going to

check on the kids—"

Two more loud cracks followed.

Brawny appeared out of nowhere. She flew through the air and landed next to me in a crouch reminiscent of Superman arriving to save the day. "Anyone hurt?"

"I don't think so."

"Split up! Leighton, grab Lorraine and come with me. Kiki, take the kids and run to the shed! Stay there!"

Why the shed? I wondered as I pulled up Anya by the hand, and she helped me with Erik. We hustled awkwardly toward the wooden structure. Glancing over my shoulder, I saw Brawny working with Leighton to carry Lorraine toward the big house.

Of course.

Brawny had thought this through. If we'd all headed the same way, we would have jammed up at the door. That would have left me and the kids exposed while we jostled to get inside. Cunningly, Brawny had split us up to keep us safe.

Erik was too confused to cooperate, so Anya and I each took a hand and lifted him so that his feet skimmed the surface of the snow. When we were close enough, I used my foot to give the side door to the shed a mighty kick. It clattered open. Our eyes adjusted to the dark. Monroe, the donkey, nickered a greeting. He loves my kids, but has little patience for most people.

"Go get behind Monroe," I told the kids. "You first."

Luckily for us Brawny had mucked out his stall just a few hours ago. It's a chore she loves because it reminds her of the farm she grew up on near Aberdeen. The small shed smelled like fresh hay, leather, and donkey.

They wriggled their way past the surprised animal. His soft lips grabbed at them, searching for bits of apple. Anya always keeps pieces in her pockets, so she transferred hers to Erik. The familiar task of feeding Monroe seemed to calm the boy down.

"Get down low, in the straw," I said, heaping it up and over them. "I want you to hide. Stay there."

On the other side of Monroe's pen was a pitchfork. Against a shooter, it wouldn't do much, but it was better than nothing. I grabbed it. A smaller shovel with a pointed blade was also on the organizing hanger. That would work for Anya, so I took it, too.

"If the shooter comes in," I said, "we don't want him to know we're here. But if he advances on us, if he looks like he wants to hurt us, I won't hesitate to use this. Anya, you do the same."

"What about me?" asked Erik. "I'm strong."

I grabbed a small bucket next to the tool rack. "This can hurt if you have to hit someone in the head, okay?"

"Uh-huh."

We settled in, my two little soldiers and I, as sirens wailed in the distance.

CHAPTER 4

Monroe loves us. I hated to think that I was putting him in danger, but I knew that if asked the stalwart donkey would give his life for my children. Or at least, that's what I told myself.

The shed is about twenty by twenty-five feet with two "people" doors, one facing the house and one facing the cottage. There's also a larger garage-door type of opening that leads from Monroe's pen into his tiny fenced-in pasture. The floor of the structure is poured concrete. The whole building is covered by an overhanging tin roof so Monroe can get out of the sun, but still enjoy the fresh air. His stall takes up most of the back half of the shed on the left side. The right half of the shed houses Leighton's gardening tools, plus bins for Monroe's food. When you step inside from either door, there's a sort of foyer, room where you can stand and pet Monroe. The sides of his stall are about three feet high and solid. An intruder couldn't immediately see that my kids and I were hunkered down.

Brawny had instinctively directed us here, giving her time to get Lorraine up the back stairs and into the big house. In retrospect, her choice had made sense. The house was warm, and Lorraine couldn't handle chills. We'd been pushing our luck having the ceremony outside. Brawny had also recognized that the kids and I could hide under the hay, something that would have been infinitely harder for Lorraine and Leighton.

As I settled down to wait for the all clear, Erik started to cry. Little sniffles, but enough to alarm me. "Hey, sweetie. This is like a game. It's kind of fun to be hiding down here with Monroe, isn't it?"

"I wet my pants. I'm cold."

Oh, dear.

"Can you pull them off? I'll grab Monroe's blanket over there on the wall." Of course, I'd have to totally expose myself again, but what choice did I have?

"I'll help him get his clothes off," said Anya.

"Anya, have I ever told you that you're an angel?"

"Remember that the next time I want to go to the mall." In a matter-of-fact way, she tugged at her brother's sodden britches.

After looking both ways to see that the path was clear, I snuck around Monroe and out the swinging door to the stall. I could vaguely make out the whoop-whoop-whoop of a distant siren. That gave me comfort. But I knew better than to depend on the cavalry coming. I needed to keep my children safe until I was sure the situation was under control.

"Let's wrap you in this." I held up Monroe's blanket after grabbing it from its accustomed spot on the far wall. Is there ever a sight more endearing than the naked backside of a child? Despite the gravity of the situation, or maybe because of it, his sweet little behind tickled me. I choked back laughter.

"I am a big boy and I wear pants!" Erik turned an angry face on me.

"Shhhh! Of course you are. I'm dressing you like Brawny. This will be your kilt, sir. What a fine Scot you'll make."

He gave me a dubious look much at odds with his bare skin.

"Aren't you cold?"

That reminded him that he had more at stake here than his honor. I wrapped him tightly in the blanket, tucked it in at the waistband, adjusted his coat over the kilt, and then we settled back down. If I'd had my cell phone, I could have called Detweiler to see if he was okay. But my bridal finery did not include pockets. There was nothing we could do but to hide and wait.

"Mom? There's a hole in the hood of your cape." Anya fingered the fabric. "That bullet was really, really close."

If Erik hadn't jumped up for that snowflake, if I hadn't bent slightly to make sure he didn't topple off the gazebo, the bullet would have hit him.

CHAPTER 5

I knew we shouldn't even try to leave until Detweiler arrived. Erik was warmer now that he was wearing the blanket, so we hunkered down and played "I Spy." Monroe tolerated us, but I wasn't sure how long he'd be on his best behavior. Leighton had adopted Monroe after he was booted out of a petting zoo. Seems the quadruped took exception to anything pint-sized and wearing a diaper. Since most of the visitors to a petting zoo happen to be less than two feet high and incontinent, that presented a huge problem. Shortly after the donkey chased down his fourth toddler, the folks at the zoo decided they needed to make "other arrangements" as in "final arrangements" as in "they're coming from the dog food factory to take you away."

Fortunately for Monroe, Leighton was a board member, and when he heard of the animal's plight, he intervened. Thus Monroe became the only donkey in Webster Groves. Oh, I'm sure we have our share of jackasses like every other town, but as for quadrupeds, Monroe is our one and only.

Anya had just guessed Erik's "I Spy" target, the broom hanging on the far wall, when Monroe's whiskers twitched nervously. Snuffling, he tossed his head and stamped his feet. His eyes showed their whites, and his ears pricked at attention. I figured this was donkey-language for "get out of my crib," so I scratched him under his chin, in an attempt to make him happy. But he jerked his head out of my reach and brayed at the door pointing to the cottage.

A split-second later, it flew open.

I caught a glimpse of a man who came skidding inside. I pushed Erik and Anya down deeper into the hay. Then I joined them, as best I could. The intruder panted loudly, but he gave no indication that he'd seen us. Coming in from the bright outside light had temporarily blinded him. To find us, he'd have to get inside the stall, get past Monroe, and dig in the hay. But first, he'd have to realize we were hiding.

I was feeling kind of smug, although scared, when Monroe nickered angrily at the man.

Drat.

I could hear the intruder but not see him. The way he huffed and puffed suggested that he had been running. But was he the chased or the chaser? Could he be an undercover cop? Had he come in a police car with its sirens blazing? I couldn't risk getting this wrong.

His breathing became more even, and I heard his shoes slap the concrete.

"I know you're in here. Come on out. I won't hurt you."

Right.

He certainly wasn't a cop. I shook my head at the children and put a finger to my lips, warning them not to respond. But Erik whimpered softly. Anya wrapped her arms around him, shielding the boy with her body. Her troubled eyes turned to me for guidance. Patting the air, I hoped to reassure them that everything was fine, but Erik responded with a loud hiccup.

"I hear you," said the man. His footsteps came closer to the pen. "I'm not happy that you're hiding. Come on out or else."

I shook my head no, vigorously, warning the kids.

Monroe stomped his feet and did the iconic, "Eee-yore," his breed has perfected.

Instinctively, Anya flattened herself and her brother against the back wall. Erik burrowed his face in her neck. His cries were softer, but the damage was done. That's when I realized that unwittingly, I'd chosen to make us easy targets. True, I'd chosen the only hiding place, but I'd also backed us into a corner. How could I have been so stupid?

I gritted my teeth and reminded myself that a mama bear protecting her cubs is never an easy target. To get at my kids, this jerk was going to have to go through me.

And past Monroe, who was clearly not happy with our visitor.

The donkey kicked at his stall.

I heard a click, as the hammer was cocked on a gun.

"Come on out or I'll shoot this big ugly hunk of carpet. See if I don't!" yelled the man.

Anya's eyes grew big as half-dollars. Again, I used my hand to make a "stay calm" motion, and I slowly pulled the ribbon out of my hood and tied it to Monroe's harness. Then I pulled. This forced our pet to lower his head. Now, shooting Monroe wasn't the visitor's best option because the donkey's face was hidden by the pen. To get off a good shot, the intruder would have to move closer and lean over the side of the stall.

I planned to take advantage of his dilemma.

First I motioned to Anya to grab the ribbon and keep it taut. Crawling on my knees, I eased over to the gate at the side of the stall. By quietly collecting spit in my hand, I greased the latch. This allowed me to slide it open without a sound.

The feet shuffled nearer.

When the man's breathing sounded like he was almost on top of me, I threw open the gate.

It caught him in the gut.

He staggered backwards. I got a good look at him. Middle-aged, paunchy, sallow complexion, thinning hair, a face like an ugly bulldog, and tiny little eyes. His nose was bent to one side. He had a scar where Marilyn Monroe sported a beauty mark, near his mouth.

I lifted the pitchfork as if it were a javelin. Unfortunately, I am not a javelin thrower. Even my extra dose of adrenaline couldn't keep the pitchfork aloft for long. I brought it down with all my might, aiming at the center mass, the man's chest.

He twisted away.

The prongs tore into his sleeve. The pitchfork bounced after hitting him, clattering as it hit the floor. The intruder managed to keep his grip on his gun, but his attention turned to his wound. While he was distracted, I kicked at the hand holding the weapon. My foot connected, and the gun went flying.

He grunted in pain and tried to sit up.

I scrambled for the gun, cursing the size of my belly. Try as I might, I couldn't reach the floor. This was not how Laura Croft foiled bad guys! In a desperate attempt to grab the weapon, I resorted to scrambling around on my hands and knees. The concrete floor was rough and frigid. It ripped off a layer of my skin, but I stayed focused. If I got the gun, my kids were okay, if not...

All this happened in the space of a heartbeat.

As my fingers seized upon the cold metal, I rolled onto my back, fully prepared to shoot the bad guy.

But he was already gone.

CHAPTER 6

"Mom, you okay?" Anya raced to my side. She reached out to help me up.

"Fine. Go take care of your brother."

From his spot in the stall, Erik had burst into noisy sobs.

"But you're hurt!"

"It only looks bad." The palms of both of my hands were bloody. Warm trickles down my shins confirmed that both my knees were bleeding.

Anya stared at me as I checked the magazine of the gun. Two bullets.

"Enough to defend us," I told her. She nodded solemnly.

I grabbed the pitchfork in my left hand and carried the gun in my right. "We'll be fine now. Get back inside the stall with Monroe."

But in response Anya only stared at me blankly. Then she started laughing, hysterically. Erik quit crying at the sound of her chuckles. He got to his feet and came out to see what was so funny. By now, Anya was sagging against the back wall because she was laughing so hard.

"Anya? You okay?" As I queried her, I used the pitchfork to shut the door our intruder had used. It wouldn't offer much protection, but it would make us harder to target.

Anya was doubled-over with laughter.

I worried that she was going into shock. She gasped between giggles, trying to catch her breath.

"You look like a whacked-out version of *American Gothic.* You know, the painting by Grant Wood? We're studying it in art history."

I couldn't help but smile myself at that comparison.

Unable to curb his curiosity, Erik bolted out of the pen to see what was so funny.

One look at her brother in his makeshift toga, and Anya dissolved into more hysterics. Shaking my head, I handed her the pitchfork and lifted Erik onto one hip. It wasn't easy, because he couldn't use his legs to wrap around me. Not with the blanket he was wearing. Instead of hanging on, he slid back down onto the floor.

"Is it okay now? Did the bad man go away?" Grabbing my sleeve, he turned troubled brown eyes on me.

The sight of him wearing that stupid blanket made me giggle.

The excitement that follows a near-death experience will do that to you. Make you laugh unpredictably or sob wildly. But despite how funny Erik looked, I sobered up fast enough. We weren't entirely out of harm's way. "Okay. You two need to hunker back down. We can't be sure we're in the clear until someone from the police department or Detweiler comes to tell us that everything is fine."

"Yeah, yeah," said Anya, waving her hand at me. "Erik, as long as she's got a gun, we're fine, because my mom won't hesitate to use it on a creep."

"Really?" His eyes were round as donuts in his head.

"Really. Mom's actually a very good shot. Have I ever told you about the time that—"

"Anya? That's enough. Not now, please." Erik didn't need to hear how I killed a man. Not today of all days.

I limped over to the stall. My knees were tightening up as the scabs formed. Walking stung like crazy.

"Are you sure that the baby is all right?" My daughter guided Erik inside the pen again, so they could hide. She was busy heaping fresh straw over their legs. Monroe seemed fine now that the intruder had been chased away.

"I'm sure he'll be okay." I hoped I was right. Even if I went into labor this far along, my child would have a good chance of survival. A tiny kick under my ribs echoed my optimism.

I was joining the children in their cozy nest when sounds

from outside warned that someone was coming. "Get down!" I whispered. At least I still had the gun in my right hand. Then I got to my feet and stood with my back to the children, my weapon trained on the door.

It flew open.

But I didn't shoot.

In walked Detweiler.

CHAPTER 7

"Are you okay? Whose gun is that?" He rushed over.

"I kicked it out of the hands of the intruder," I said. My husband took the gun from me, emptied the magazine, and shoved the weapon into the back of his belt, under his jacket.

Some newly minted couples share a first dance. Here we were, trading off weapons. Oh, well.

"Dad?" Erik's piping voice came from inside the stall.

"Detweiler?" Anya's followed.

"It's all right. You can come out." My husband turned and opened the stall door.

"There was a man with a gun!" shouted Erik, as he hurled himself at Detweiler and caught the man's knees.

"But Mom bested him. She's so tough," said Anya, wrapping her arms around me. We did this sort of group hug routine, exchanging kisses and hanging on to each other, tightly.

"Mama Kiki throwed that big fork at the man. She hit him! He ran off!" said Erik.

"Yeah, Mom's going to try out for the javelin-throwing competition at next year's Olympics," giggled Anya.

"What's happening outside?" I asked my husband.

"Two squad cars setting up crime scene tape. One of the creeps was hit—" he hesitated, and I realized that he meant "hit" as in "dead," but then he continued, "—Brawny's knife-throwing skills are impressive. Stan took a bullet in the shoulder."

"No! Is he okay?"

"Other than a ruined cashmere coat?" Detweiler arched an eyebrow at me. "The whole time the EMTs worked on him, he was going on and on about how sick he felt that his coat had a hole in it."

That made me laugh. Hadcho is part Native American and all clothes horse. He turned a bedroom in his apartment into a huge walk-in closet. Not only is he Detweiler's partner again, after a brief hiatus, but he's also become a good friend to me.

"But Stan just got clipped. Nothing big. They've taken him away in one of the ambulances. I told them to hold the other for you." Detweiler's amazing Heineken bottle green eyes locked onto mine. "How's the baby?"

"Perfectly fine. Feel?" I put his hand on my belly. His son kicked vigorously, a reminder that he was a semi-active participant in the day's events.

"How're Lori and Leighton? Brawny? Gracie? Paolo?" I was almost afraid to ask. Was it too much to expect that the guardian angels who had protected us also safeguarded our friends and pets? Let other brides worry about the flower girls wandering off, or the best man forgetting the ring. Me, I focus on big picture issues, like, "Did anyone get killed?"

"Leighton and Lori are fine. Gracie and Paolo are back in the house. Good old Gracie took after the guy who came in here and almost caught up with him. Good thing she didn't. I think he would have...hurt her." He winced and let go of me to press a hand against his abdomen.

"You aren't used to running like that in the snow," I said. I was hanging tightly onto the sleeve of his jacket as though it was a life preserver.

"No, I'm not accustomed to running in snow. It's tiring. How about if we get the kids inside? Back-up wants to talk to all of us."

We scuttled along, clumped together like a football team in a huddle. Slowly we picked our way toward the big house. Bubble-gum lights flashed; red streamers strobed across the snow. The Webster Groves police had arrived. An ambulance also took up space in the alley. Finally, we made it to the back door. As a glommed together group, we were too wide to make it through the opening. I stepped to one side, moving away from Detweiler, to let him follow the kids inside.

My gown was covered in blood.

Detweiler's blood.

CHAPTER 8

"You've been shot! Why didn't you tell me? Anya, get help! Where's Brawny?"

My daughter dropped Erik's hand and sprinted away. I should have reacted with more restraint, because my loud cries caused my son to totally freak out. It wasn't really surprising; he'd lost both parents in an auto accident before coming to live with us. Of course he had reason to be concerned about losing another dad. In response to my shouts, Erik locked his arms around my husband's knees, effectively crippling him.

Detweiler groaned in pain.

I tried to peel the little boy away. "Erik, honey, don't cry. We need to get Daddy to the doctor, but he'll be fine."

I was lying through my teeth. I did not know if my husband would be fine or not. As a matter of fact, I've been widowed once, and I didn't want it to happen again. Especially on our wedding day.

Detweiler sagged. This was no time for me to lose control. I got my wits about me.

"It's just a scratch." He grimaced.

"Good," I said, "because I plan to kill you for not getting help before you came to check on us!"

He chuckled. "I'll be okay, sweetheart. I promise."

But as we stepped out from under the oak tree and into the sunlight, I could see the blood was rushing out of him in steady spurts. That was definitely not a good sign. It was more than a scratch. My husband was a liar. I wadded up my skirt and pressed it tightly against his gut. Glancing around, I muttered, "Where's that second ambulance?" When I spotted the second bus, I yelled out, "Help! He's been shot!"

Two EMTs ran up to Detweiler.

"He's bleeding badly. I'm putting pressure on the wound."

But one of the EMTs elbowed me out of the way, so he could see the damage. I pulled off my cape and wadded it up. "Use this."

After all, there's already a bullet hole in the hood.

"Bring a stretcher," one of the medics shouted to a man waiting by the ambulance.

In short order, the three had Detweiler flat on his back. One started an IV, while another took his vitals. After a quick consultation, they lifted the stretcher and jogged toward the waiting ambulance. I trotted after them, slipping and sliding on the icy snow, but I quickly gave up when I realized that Erik was running behind me, crying his heart out. I stopped to cuddle the little boy, although I ached to hear that my husband would be okay.

An EMT ran back to talk to me. "We're taking him to South Central Hospital. It's a gut wound. Those are—"

"Daddy!" Erik wailed as they slid the stretcher into the back of the ambulance.

"Unpredictable at best," he finished. "You might want to call the rest of the family."

For a tick, I thought I'd faint. The emergency tech took one look at me and added, "Better get yourself checked out, too. Can't be too careful. Don't drive. Is there someone who can take you?"

"Yes."

With a curt nod, he turned and ran toward the vehicle. The lights were rotating, and the siren blaring as they spun their wheels and raced away.

"Shhh." I scooped up the sobbing child who had tangled himself in my skirt. This time, I hiked his makeshift kilt up around his naked thighs so he could wrap his legs around me. The boy cried and hiccuped alternately, as I turned back toward the house. Resting his wet face against me, Erik smelled like peanut butter, his newest official favorite food.

"You Mrs. Lowenstein?" A uniformed officer came wheeling out of the kitchen door.

"Mrs. Detweiler, as of an hour ago." I stroked Erik's back.

"You sure know how to throw a wedding party." He gave me a gap-tooth grin. Like most young cops, he was buff and clean cut. Leaning close to me so Erik wouldn't hear, he asked, "You aren't bleeding are you? Detective Detweiler told the medics you are fine."

"This is his blood."

"Let's get you inside your house and cleaned up. You're bound to be freezing. My name's Harry Whooli. I work with Stan and Chad, but I'm off duty. I heard the call, and Detweiler's always been good to me, so I thought I'd see if I could lend a hand. Who's this young man?"

"Erik? Say hello to Officer Whooli."

Erik responded by screaming, "Daddy! I want my daddy!"

"Honey, it's okay. Sh, sh." I rocked the blubbering boy.

"Do you always wear a blanket, bub? Were you playing cowboy and Indians? My brother and I used to do that." Harry gave Erik a winning grin. "You are one brave dude. I heard your mama threw a pitchfork at a guy."

This caught Erik's attention. "Yes. Mama Kiki did."

"Wow. Did she really? That is seriously cool."

"I was going to hit him with a bucket."

"Way to go, pal. Got to protect our womenfolk, huh? Give me five." Harry presented his palm for a hand slap. Erik's tense little body relaxed some in my arms.

"Not trying to be overly familiar, ma'am." Harry spoke in a low voice as he wrapped an arm around me. "But you're looking a bit green around the gills."

"That's nothing compared to how I feel."

CHAPTER 9

Even with Harry's help, I stumbled a bit. Erik was heavy, and the slick snow was still icy. My knees were growing stiff as the blood scabbed over.

As we moved across the snowy yard, I noticed activity just beyond the gazebo to our right. A small knot of people were moving around a pair of legs on the ground. With a start, I realized that one of the gunmen had been felled. Was he dead? Merely hurt?

I didn't know.

As long as he was out of action, that was all that matters.

Harry caught my eye and gave me the tiniest shake of his head. Acknowledgment that the guy on the ground was dead.

"Hey, dude? Tell you what? How about if I give you a piggyback ride?" Harry offered Erik a nifty distraction.

Rather than wait for Erik's response, I offloaded the boy onto the cop's back. The strangely bunched up blanket he was wearing caused Erik to have a precarious grip. But Harry hooked his arms under Erik's thighs. Bless his heart, Harry knew the drill. He alternatively pranced and galloped while making horse-like noises. Soon Erik was fighting a smile. Leighton stepped out of the back door and rushed over to help me.

"How's Lorraine?" I asked.

"She'll be fine. It's going to be all right."

But I could tell he was worried.

"She'll be fine," he repeated, more to himself than to me.

A sudden wave of exhaustion hit me hard. All I wanted was to lie down, but I couldn't. Detweiler might need me. I had to get to the hospital, and I needed to let his parents know what was up. But how would they travel in this weather? The older Detweilers lived on a farm in Illinois. I knew from texting them this morning that many of the country lanes leading from their house to the main road were closed. On the prairie, there are few windbreaks, and blowing snow drifts easily. There's no way that the road crews can keep the streets clear.

Brawny met us at the door. "I can take her from here, Leighton. Let me help Kiki upstairs and get her changed. Erik's having a grand time in the living room with his sister."

Walking me up the stairs, she kept one arm under my elbow. "Go slowly. You've had a shock."

"Do you know what happened?"

"Two gunmen. I hit one of them with my knife. The dogs took out after the other. Detweiler and Hadcho were both shot before they gave chase, but I didn't realize that they were hurt. Both of them kept moving. Adrenaline will do that for you. So while they were chasing the man running away on foot, I checked on you and the children. Then I got Lorraine and Leighton inside the house. From there, they called nine-one-one while I was out trying to track down the second shooter. You know, of course, that he got away from me. I stopped to assist Hadcho. He was lying in the snow, bleeding. Anya says the second gunman turned up in the shed."

"Yes."

"But you dispatched him handily."

"I clipped his right shoulder with a pitchfork."

"Brave girl." She gave me a nod of approval. With her hair pulled back in its usual tidy ponytail, Brawny usually looks rather severe. But that smile always reminds me there's another side to her. I see it as she tenderly cares for the children. "Is any of this blood yours?"

"Just my hands and knees. I was crawling across the floor for the gun. Oh! Detweiler stuck it in his waistband. I wonder if they noticed it in the ambulance?"

"I'm sure it's fine. Let's get you cleaned up and changed. Harry has offered to drive you to the hospital. I need to make a statement. A detective is on the way. He'll want to talk to the kids. To Lorraine, and Leighton, too."

I pulled away to study her face. "Is Lorraine going to be okay?"

Brawny nodded. "She's had a bit of a shock, what with the tumble off the gazebo, but she'll be right as rain. It's you and your baby we need to worry about now."

Inside the master bathroom, she used a warm washcloth and gently dabbed off the worst of the mess. Once my skin was visible, we could see it was a simple matter of abrasions. As she helped me take off my wedding gown, I started crying. I'd tried to stay strong, but I couldn't contain the sadness.

"It's such a beautiful dress, and now…"

"I'll get the stains out. Don't worry yourself. It'll be good as new."

"This wasn't how I expected—"

Her gray eyes locked onto mine. "You're alive. We're all going to be fine, even the detective. Think what a story this will be to tell your grandchildren!"

That was Brawny's gentle admonition for me to "buck up," and I did. While I pulled off my slip and my stockings, she found clothes for me. As she helped me tug a stretchy blouse over my head, I flashed back to a scene from my childhood. My mother used to help us get our clothes on. She'd tug and jerk and pinch us. By comparison, Brawny's touch was tender. I appreciated her kindness. God had blessed me with wonderful friends who had come into my life in unexpected ways.

Once I was dressed, Brawny steadied me as I made my way down the same stairs I'd just climbed. The effort completely tuckered me out, but I couldn't just go and lie down on the sofa. I needed to be by Detweiler's side.

Brawny must have read my thoughts. "Let me get the children settled. The detective should be here any minute, but he can wait until I call Louis and Thelma. Then I'll meet you at the hospital, providing that Lorraine and Leighton are well enough to take over here."

"Are we sure there were just two gunmen? What if they come back?"

"I'm fairly confident there was just the two of them. But I'll talk to the Webster Groves police about that possibility. Leighton can handle a pistol, so I'll make sure he's armed if I leave the house. If the children are inside, the dogs will protect them."

"But Brawny, who were they and what did they want?"

Brawny sighed. "I wish I had an answer for ye."

Over the years I've managed to get involved in a variety of mysteries. One or two have been resolved, sending people off to jail. Was it possible that one of them had come gunning for me? Of course, Detweiler sent people away regularly as part of his job. So did Hadcho. Which one of us had so infuriated someone that they'd decided to take potshots at my family? Even more puzzling, how had they known we would be here, outside in our yard, on this snowy day?

That last question was a real puzzler, one that I turned over and over in my head as Harry drove me to the hospital.

We only decided yesterday that we'd get married this very morning. Christmas was over. Detweiler had cleared his desk, except for one ongoing investigation. He needed to get Robbie and Hadcho up to speed, but he could do that from home.

We started making calls and quickly rounded everyone up. Rabbi Sarah agreed to conduct the ceremony. Detweiler's family planned to drive over from Illinois. My sisters were going to put Mom in the car and drive across town. All my co-workers were going to be here, including Clancy Whitehead and her new boyfriend, Raoul. Sheila, my mother-in-law from my first marriage, and her husband, Police Chief Robbie Holmes were definitely planning to attend.

Such were their intentions, but in the end, the weather

changed everything. A cold front changed directions unexpectedly. Rain began late yesterday. It continued throughout the night and turned to ice that brought down branches all over town. The news stations went on and on about people trapped in their homes by broken limbs and fallen trees. Those who managed to leave the premises didn't fare much better. Many spun out on "black ice," pavement that didn't look icy but was. By nine a.m., the roads were littered with abandoned cars. Television and radio reporters encouraged people to stay home, but human nature being what it is, some took this as a challenge. For every two people who climbed in their cars and motored around town safely, another driver skidded off the roads or stalled out.

In the end, Detweiler and I called everyone back and begged them to stay home. Most of them couldn't make the short trip anyway. According to a breathless Robbie, he and Sheila were actually prisoners in her home. An old tree had fallen, blocking her driveway. I couldn't remember a tree so close to her house, but it's easy to underestimate how tall something is.

As Chief of Police, Robbie knew every detail of the conditions of the roads throughout the area, and he briskly urged us to postpone the ceremony before adding, "I've got to go."

He hung up before I could say goodbye.

I had just hung up from talking to Rabbi Sarah when Lorraine Lauber tapped me on the shoulder. "At the risk of sticking my nose in where it's not wanted, I thought I'd at least offer my services."

"Your services?" I repeated.

"Yes. I'm an ordained Unity minister. Since you have the license, and everything else is a green light, I'd be happy to marry the two of you, if you'd like. You can always have another ceremony later, but at least you'd be officially Mrs. Detweiler before the baby comes."

I glanced at Detweiler to see what he was thinking.

Wordlessly, he shrugged. After a moment of thought, he said, "That's not a half-bad idea. Given the sort of family drama that usually accompanies a big day, maybe this is for the best. We'd talked about eloping, and this is the next closest thing. We have all the privacy of a secret ceremony and none of the guilt. No one can blame us for going ahead. They know we're worried about making it legal before the baby comes."

"That's one way to look at it." I smiled. "Truth is, this storm has scared off everyone who is a non-essential. Not that we don't love them. We do. But really all we need is the kids and each other."

"Don't forget me." Hadcho wandered in from the next room. He'd fallen asleep on the sofa last night while watching a movie. "I'm here. I'm important."

Detweiler and I burst out laughing.

"Well, Hadcho. That makes you a wedding crasher, doesn't it?" I put my fists on my hips and tried to look stern. "Welcome to our very, very private affair."

Private.

Except that somehow word had been leaked to two men who had determined that this was a great day to come and use my family for target practice. Why? How? Who? And how badly had they hurt Detweiler?

This didn't make a bit of sense.

CHAPTER 10

After pulling up under the emergency awning, Harry hopped out and opened my door. But when he saw me, he hesitated. "He's a tough guy, Mrs. Detweiler. He'll come through this. You just watch."

That was the first time anyone had called me "Mrs. Detweiler," and I cried even harder. "It isn't fair."

Instantly I heard how childish that sounded.

"It's not. But you know how life goes. Nothing is fair. Nothing is totally just. But we fumble along with what we're dealt. The bad stuff forces us to appreciate our blessings."

"I've never seen Detweiler hurt. Not like this. Will it always be this way? Being a cop's wife?"

Harry grinned, but his eyes didn't smile. "I sure hope not. Otherwise, how am I going to convince a pretty young thing to marry me?"

With that, he helped me out of the car. My legs were as elastic as rubber bands. The realization that Detweiler might not make it shook me to the core. How would I carry on without him? He'd been my rock for years. And again, I found myself thinking, *It just doesn't seem fair.* Then I chided myself for being such a baby. But I wasn't feeling sorry for myself, was I? I was feeling bad for my husband and friend. All that Detweiler had ever wanted was a family, his own kids, and the same day he got his wish, someone tried to end his life?

What's with that?

As Harry and I trudged to the pneumatic glass doors, my spirits sank deeper and deeper. Was it my fault for waiting so long to say yes? If I'd agreed earlier, we could have said our vows in a nice warm church or at the temple.

Where a tag team of gunmen could have wiped out an entire congregation.

Maybe we'd inadvertently made a good choice. Maybe even a great one.

"Give me a sec," I said, standing just inside the ER. I wiped away my tears.

"You take all the time you need," said Harry. "You have to be strong for him. You can't fall apart when you see him."

"Right." I mentally steeled myself. "Let's go."

CHAPTER 11

Hospitals reek of disinfectant, alcohol, and burnt popcorn. All those pungent odors mix with the sour smell of fear. Add a splash of blood, a dash of puke, and presto, the stink was overwhelming. My sense of smell, heightened by my pregnancy hormones, set my gag reflex in motion. I forced myself to swallow hard and put one foot in front of the other. Luckily for me, Harry took the lead. He hailed a man in green scrubs, who in turn flagged down a woman wearing blue scrubs with tiny puppies prancing on the fabric. Her badge identified her as an ER nurse.

"The detective is still in surgery. Probably be there for a while."

"Hadcho?" I felt ashamed that I hadn't thought of him sooner. Poor Hadcho had no one to ask after him. All his family lived in Oklahoma on tribal lands. He'd promised me that someday he'd tell me more about his life, but that "someday" hadn't arrived yet.

With a sense of plunging dread, I realized it might never come. I wasn't fully sure that I trusted Detweiler's assertion that Hadcho had only been scratched. After all, my new husband had hidden the seriousness of his own wound. Why wouldn't he also lie about his friend?

"Detective Hadcho is out of surgery, but not awake yet. He lost a lot of blood, so we've given him a transfusion," said the nurse, before excusing herself.

"Wait until I tease Hadcho about getting his tank filled up with non-Native American blood. Man, am I going to have fun with this!" Harry's eyes were bright with amusement. But one look at me, and he immediately became more solemn. "You're not going to faint on me, are you? How about if you take a seat? I'll go get you a cola or coffee. Whichever you prefer."

"Hot tea, please. Somewhere to sit would be good. I am feeling a little woozy."

"Let's get you a chair." Harry led me into the waiting room, where we found a tall wingback chair in a cozy corner. It was probably unoccupied because it was off by itself. All the other seats were crammed with families or couples commiserating.

"You comfortable? Okay, I'll just be a minute. Tea with sugar? Yes? Milk. No? Got it."

After he'd left, I realized I'd forgotten to ask for decaf. Since becoming pregnant, I've done everything I can to assure my little passenger a healthy start in life. That has meant forgoing my beloved Diet Dr Pepper and caffeinated coffee. Oh well, one cup of strong tea wouldn't endanger my baby, and it might help my sagging spirits.

Sitting there alone, I pulled out my cell phone. Quickly I texted a message to Brawny, detailing what little we'd learned. I added a reassurance that I was fine. As I hit the send button, it hit me. I hadn't talked to Robbie and Sheila. In fact, I hadn't heard from them either. That didn't make sense. Because he's the police chief, Robbie is usually on top of everything that happens. He would have heard about the shooting, the same way that Harry had.

But Robbie hadn't called.

Why not?

CHAPTER 12

Being tucked away in the corner, I didn't feel rude when I dialed Robbie. He answered on the third ring, in a voice so terse, I thought I had the wrong number.

"I have a situation here," he said.

"So do I."

"You don't understand."

I couldn't believe what I was hearing. I yanked my hand from my head and stared at the phone as though the instrument itself was responsible for Robbie's rudeness. Anger boiled up inside me. *Excuse me? My husband is in the emergency room after being shot and I don't understand?*

"You're right. I probably don't understand," I said in a tone so flat it didn't sound like me. "Maybe that's because Detweiler is being operated on after being shot at our wedding. Or it could be because Hadcho is in recovery because he was shot too. You have a situation? Well, I'm here with two of your men who are fighting for their lives. Not that you care. You're just the chief of police! You're far too busy to worry about your underlings. Have a nice day!"

I hung up on him. As I tucked the phone away, I noticed people staring at me. The faces of other people in the ER waiting room reflected shock and awe. Had they really heard me correctly? Did I actually dress down the chief of police?

You betcha.

Of course, maybe they were staring because smoke was coming out of my ears.

I've never been so angry. Furthermore, I didn't feel one iota of remorse. Robbie had been asking for it. Lately he'd been increasingly abrupt with me—and I wasn't the one to blame. First Sheila arrived drunk at our house for Hanukkah. Then she'd gotten drunk when she was supposed to take the children to see

Santa. I'd suggested to Robbie that she had a problem with alcohol, and he'd blown his stack, so I'd backed down.

"He knows she's drinking too much," said Detweiler. "She's been kicked out of the country club and at least one restaurant."

I frowned and added, "Not to mention being picked up for driving under the influence by a cop who extended professional courtesy to Robbie by saying nothing. He has no right to be snippy to me."

But the *piece de résistance* had come on Christmas morning.

The minute Robbie and Sheila drove up, it became clear that something was wrong. He turned off the engine in his police cruiser, but they sat there in our circular driveway. They must have been fighting because all the windows fogged over. When they stepped out, there was a chill in the air between them. They gave each other looks so cold that I thought a second Ice Age was coming.

They stomped into the house without a word to each other and barely a civil greeting to our gang.

Then things got really interesting, because my sisters arrived with my mother, the Queen of Mean. Mom was in such a foul mood that the National Weather Service issued a special bulletin, "Beware of frosty glances and nasty looks."

In retrospect, I must have had a screw loose to invite my mother. My only defense sounds stupid in hindsight, but at the time I reasoned, "Hey. It's Christmas! We have kids here! It's a holly, jolly time of year! It'll be nice to have the whole family together."

In your dreams.

CHAPTER 13

Mom slapped at Catherine's hand when she tried to help her out of the car. With an indignant snarl, Mom said, "I am not a decrepit old lady!"

Taking over for the shocked Catherine, Amanda raced to Mom's side of the car. She was worried that Mom might slip on our walk, so my sister stayed glued to our mother's side. When she reached our threshold, my darling mother said to me, "If that stupid cop would have cleaned this properly, Amanda wouldn't have to hover over me."

Detweiler had sprinkled sand and salt twice that morning. Calling on the spirit of the holidays, I bit my tongue rather than say something nasty back to Mom.

After that, things went downhill faster than a bobsled team. Sheila had taken a comfy stuffed chair at one end of our living room, and Robbie had slumped into the other cushioned seat.

"They've taken all the good chairs." My mother stood in the middle of our living room and pouted.

Robbie gracefully offered his spot to Mom, who wasn't polite enough to thank him.

Anya and Erik had written a Christmas play that they wanted to perform, but Sheila snipped, "Not really in the mood. I have a splitting headache."

What she really had was a hangover. It didn't take a psychic to figure that out.

Robbie, who usually placates Sheila and dotes on my kids, added, "That makes two of us."

"I certainly am not interested in an amateur production," said my mother.

My jaw hit the floor. These were my kids' relatives, and they were acting like the backsides of horses. Worse yet, they were behaving this way in my home, under my roof, on Christmas.

Detweiler turned white with rage. Fortunately, Amanda and Catherine jumped in, declaring that they would love to see what the kids had planned.

But before Anya and Erik could get started, Mom got to her feet and toddled over to the tree. Adjusting her reading glasses, she did a slow sweep of the evergreen, moving from the top down.

"This is wrong. Totally wrong. You should have put the bigger balls on the bottom. This...this...thing is unbalanced."

"Erik likes seeing the bigger balls at eye level. He hung those, and I think he did a wonderful job." I hurried to slip an arm around the boy's shoulders.

"What does he know?" Mom gave a loud sniff.

"That's what the world needs now," said Sheila. "Bigger balls that drag on the floor."

I couldn't believe it. Detweiler turned from white to red. My sisters both blushed.

Amanda jumped in with, "Come on, Mom. What's wrong? You've been nitpicking Christmas trees all season. Criticizing the trees in the malls and in all the stores, too."

"There is nothing wrong with me. I have a trained eye for beauty," she said, "and that tree is unattractive."

"Erik?" said Catherine. "Come here, buddy. I want you to see something."

The boy with the sweet brown eyes went over next to my sister. She pulled him onto her lap as she got out her phone and flipped through the photos.

"Want to see a really, really ugly tree?" asked Catherine. "This is the one our mother decorated. See how weird it looks? Disgusting, huh? I'd take your tree over this one any day of the week. In fact next year, I think we need to put you in charge of decorating the tree at our house. Yes, at our house. Just so you know, Amanda and I pay the rent. That house really is *our* house,

Amanda's and mine. Mom is only there because we're trying to be kind to her. If we weren't such nice people, she'd be out on the streets."

"Out on the streets?" he repeated.

"Or in a tree. Maybe she could crawl up into a tree and live there." Amanda didn't even crack a smile.

I covered my mouth and tried not to laugh. This was like some strange Saturday Night Live skit, except that it was real and it was happening in my home.

"But if she's in a tree, what would the squirrels do?" he asked. "Where would they go?"

"The squirrels would probably run the other way," said Detweiler, solemnly. "They're smart like that. Now let's open presents, shall we?"

CHAPTER 14

Those memories were still fresh in my mind, as I tried to get comfortable in the ER waiting room. On a whim, I got up and turned my chair to face the corner. That took me all of fifteen minutes because I couldn't move it far or fast. Grab and grunt. That was my technique. None of the other people in the place paid any attention. Nor did any of them offer me help. Actually, that was for the best. I didn't want to strike up a conversation. I wanted to be alone. I was overwrought and more than a little bit hungry. I wondered where Harry was with my hot tea.

Once I got the chair turned around, I realized there was no way to sit down, except to crawl up and over one of the arms. A dubious physical maneuver in the best of times, but these gymnastics were complicated by my enormous belly. I couldn't see my feet.

But I was determined, and I needed to feel secure. As I debated what to do, a couple came in carrying a sobbing child. That caused me to feel more unbalanced. I wondered how Anya and Erik were doing.

I needed to block out this turmoil and get centered. Mostly I wanted a secluded place to cry. I grabbed the back of the chair, hoisted my right leg as high as it would go, and missed the mark. On my second try, I hooked my right arm under my right leg and gave myself a boost. That got my foot onto the seat. With a mighty *oomph*, I hoisted myself over the arm. Actually, I would have catapulted over the chair had I not smacked my forehead into the wall. Instead I stood on the seat, trying to get my balance. Finally, I slid down. Drawing up my legs under me, I curled up in a fetal position.

There in my solitude, I had a good cry.

I'd pretty much sobbed myself from full to empty when a woman in surgical scrubs called my name.

"Mrs. Detweiler?"

"Yes?" I peeped over the back of the chair.

"I'm Dr. Fizzio. Your husband's surgeon."

I climbed onto my knees so I could hang over the back of the chair. That allowed me to see her expression and hear her better. My weird seating position didn't faze her a bit. I got the distinct impression that she'd seen everything in her career as a caregiver.

"Detective Detweiler is doing as well as can be expected. I think we've got him patched up. The next twenty-four hours will tell the tale. We have to keep an eye out for more bleeding."

"More bleeding?" My mouth was so dry that my lips stuck to my teeth. "Will he be okay? I mean, is he going to live?"

"You mean what are his chances? I never like to give odds. Every patient is different. It's a matter of willpower, general health, and quite frankly, there's a bit of luck involved."

That's when I crawled out from behind the chair. My intention was to drop down to my knees and beg her to save my husband's life. "I have to...he needs to...please tell me..."

Her eyes drifted to my belly. "How far along are you?"

"Thirty-four weeks."

"This has to be hard." Her eyes softened with compassion.

"Today was our wedding day."

"Wow. I only had to cope with a drunken priest. Total bummer. Who's here with you?"

"I'm by myself."

That was true, because Harry had disappeared.

"I suggest you call the rest of his family. They need to be here. You shouldn't be handling this alone, and things could, um, change."

CHAPTER 15

I'd considered moving to the family waiting area outside of critical care, but I realized that when Harry came back—if he came back—he wouldn't be able to find me. So I stayed where I was.

"Sorry this took so long." Harry seemed to know I'd just been thinking of him. "Both vending machines on this floor are empty. The one upstairs is too—"

One glance at my expression and he shut up. Quietly he set the tea down on the coffee table. "What have you heard?"

I repeated what Dr. Fizzio had told me.

"Drink this. You need it. Are you hungry?"

I wasn't anymore. Actually I felt sick.

"When did you eat last?"

"At seven this morning."

"It's half-past two. Let me run back down to the cafeteria and get you a sandwich. You need to keep your energy up. Did you get checked out? Brawny just called me to say that you should be looked over. I guess you took a dive off the gazebo?"

I nodded.

I must have stood there dazed, because I didn't see him walk off. The same ER nurse wearing the prancing puppies came back with Harry. "Let's get you into a room, Mrs. Detweiler. I've heard you need to be checked out. Didn't realize you were involved in the altercation, too."

Wordlessly, I followed her. I guess she must have taken my information, but I couldn't swear to that. I was too stunned. I vaguely recall that another person asked me Detweiler's social security number, and I couldn't answer. They asked me about his medical insurance, and again I was clueless. Finally I blurted, "We've only been married a few hours."

That brought a look of surprise to the clerk's face.

By the time that Harry arrived with three different types of sandwiches: tuna salad, chicken salad, and ham salad, I was wearing the ubiquitous and embarrassing hospital gown. Sort of. It barely covered my backside because my front side was so expansive. He appeared not to notice as he handed over three different kinds of chips: salt and vinegar, barbeque, and ruffled. Finally, he passed me a bottle of water. "I thought some plain water might be good for you."

"Thanks. You're doing a great job of taking care of me. I appreciate it, and I know that Detweiler..." My throat clogged with emotion.

"My pleasure. Now you try to relax, okay? Let them check out the baby, and you, of course. I'll go and wait for you back where we were."

Two hours later, I was dressed in my street clothes and officially pronounced, "Okay." The baby seemed fine, too. I wandered over to the wingback chair in the waiting room.

"I've been keeping it warm for you." He glanced at his watch. "You could move upstairs, to be closer to Detweiler's room, but I asked and heard there are no vacant seats. This is a cozy enough spot, isn't it? Look, I'm sorry but I have to go. If you need me, just holler. I'll put my personal cell number in your phone."

I couldn't thank him enough, but I tried. As I searched for words, he gave me a parting smile. "I hope to see you again under different circumstances."

I settled into the chair and called Brawny.

CHAPTER 16

Our nanny was her usual matter-of-fact self. "I haven't been able to get the Detweilers yet. The phone lines in Illinois have been down for a while. They're saying on the telly that a tractor-trailer slid off the highway and knocked over a string of poles."

I groaned. Thelma and Louis had insisted on keeping their land line, "for emergencies." When Detweiler tried to persuade them that a cell tower could do a better job of relaying a phone call, they'd been surprisingly stubborn about the transition. Neither of them was good about answering their mobile numbers. I'd learned to phone the landline when I couldn't rouse them.

"Have you tried their cell phones?"

"Both went to voice mail. I can only assume they've run out of juice. It's possible they're off the power grid and can't recharge them. I've heard the storm did even more damage east of here. I'll keep trying. How's the detective? And Hadcho?"

After I reported what little I'd learned, she reassured me. "Detweiler is strong and young. At the peak of his life. He'll be fine. As for Hadcho, it looked to me as if it was little more than a flesh wound. I've seen much worse. Messy, but not life threatening. And how are you? Harry called me. I thought ye and the wee one should be looked at."

"Thanks for worrying over us. We're both fine."

She told me that Anya and Erik had been fretful. They'd actually gotten into an argument about what to eat for lunch. That was a rarity, a sign that both kids were feeling worried.

"All's calm now. They're in the living room, reading their Kindles. Leighton took Lorraine home, so she could get a spot of rest."

She hadn't heard from Robbie or Sheila. I told her about my brief conversation with the chief of police. I also learned that she'd called my sisters and my mother. "Catherine and Amanda send their love and prayers."

Expecting some sort of concern from my mother would be like asking the moon to change its orbit. The universe would collapse before Lucia Collins changed her ways. After all, the world revolved around her, didn't it?

After another restless half hour, my fingers shook as I hit the "favorites" button to talk to Thelma Detweiler. Surely they'd have gotten their phones charged. As a holiday gift, Detweiler and I had given his parents portable chargers. My husband had sternly lectured both of them on keeping their phones charged at all times.

At least it didn't go right to voice mail, I thought as I listened to the endless ringing. I chose to call Thelma rather than call her husband, because she's the least emotional of Detweiler's parents. Louis is much more of a softie. He tears up at old movies. Thelma seems as soft and homespun as an old flannel nightie, but under that warm and fuzzy exterior is a backbone made of steel. I've never seen her upset or flustered. She keeps her husband on an even keel.

"It's Kiki," I said, relieved when she answered.

"We tried to call you earlier! But then the landline went out. Took us a while to figure out how to use these new chargers. How'd it go? Are you my daughter-in-law in the eyes of the law? How was it? How are the kids? Did Chad cry? I want to know everything!" Thelma gushed. She barely took a breath.

I decided to give her the good news first. It might make the bad news easier to swallow.

"Yes, Chad and I are married,"

"Hurrah!" she shouted. "Louis! They did it! They tied the knot! Welcome to the family, Kiki!"

I heard him whooping in the distance.

"Thelma? I have something to tell you—"

"Let me guess," she said with a laugh. "You're pregnant."

"Thelma, I'm serious. I'm trying to tell you that there was an incident. A problem. Are you sitting down?" I hated breaking this to her over the phone.

"A problem? Let me guess! One of the kids did something silly. That happened at my sister Theresa's wedding. Or Detweiler forgot the ring. His father did the same thing. Every wedding has its story. Just remember that we'll laugh about it in years to come."

I had my doubts.

"Thelma? This is serious. Listen carefully. Your son's been shot. I'm here in the Emergency Room."

"What?" Her voice went up an octave.

"Your son. He's been shot. I'm in the hospital with him now."

I heard a loud clatter as she dropped the phone. I called out, "Thelma? Thelma, are you there?"

Whimpering and sobs drifted back to me.

Louis snatched up the phone, as he did, I heard him grumble, "What in the blue blazes is going on?"

"Louis, I have bad news for you."

"Kiki? What on earth? Where's Chad?"

"He's been shot. You need to get here. I'm at South Central Hospital."

Louis hung up on me.

CHAPTER 17

I've never felt so alone in my life. Not even when my first husband George Lowenstein died. Back then, if something had happened to me, Sheila could step in and raise Anya. That *wasn't* what I wanted. Not at all. But in my heart of hearts, I knew that Sheila was capable of taking care of my daughter. That knowledge had been strangely comforting.

A lot has changed since then.

Sheila has begun a new life as the wife of St. Louis Police Chief Robbie Holmes.

I became pregnant unexpectedly, as the result of what Detweiler laughingly called, "Equipment failure."

And to top it all off, we added five-year-old Erik and his nanny Bronwyn "Brawny" Macavity to our household.

They came to live with us after Detweiler's first wife, Gina, and her second husband, Van Lauber, died in an automobile accident. Initially, we were told that Erik was Gina and Detweiler's biological child.

However, one look at the boy quickly corrected that notion, because Erik is biracial. Gina had been having an affair with one of Detweiler's fellow police officers, an African-American, when she got pregnant. In fact, she was expecting Erik when she walked out on Detweiler without leaving a forwarding address. Detweiler never even knew of Erik's existence! Strangely enough, in the eyes of the law, Erik *is* actually Detweiler's son because he and Gina were still lawfully wedded when the boy was born.

Lorraine Lauber, Van's sister, could not raise Erik because she suffers from a debilitating form of MS. So when drafting her will, Gina left behind a letter begging Detweiler to raise the child who shares his last name.

It is a testimony to Detweiler's character that he can love a child who is proof of Gina's infidelity. As for me, well, I've been delighted to welcome Erik into our lives.

To help Erik adjust, Lorraine offered to pay Brawny's wages, so the nanny could stay with him, since she's been with Erik from birth.

And thus, our little family has grown exponentially. Whereas once I only had to worry about Anya, I now have Anya, Erik, and a baby on the way.

If Detweiler didn't make it, how would I make ends meet? Lorraine and Detweiler promised we'd sit down after the holidays and talk about finances. I suspected she would offer to pay for Erik's college. But how would I handle the day-to-day needs of three kids if my husband died? How would I meet the physical and emotional demands of three children? Especially given my obligations to the business I'm buying, Time in a Bottle, the scrapbook and crafts store once owned by the late Dodie Goldfader? Thus far I've been able to make regular payments to Dodie's widower, Horace. But would the business continue to thrive if I was distracted by raising three kids by myself?

The specter of failure loomed over my head like a big black cloud, threatening to rain down on me. My willful ignorance had brought on this stormy weather, and I cursed myself for being so stupid.

This was the same trap I'd fallen for when my first husband died. I'd thought of us as financially secure. But after his death, I learned we were maxed out on all our credit cards, and we owed other money as well. As time went on, I also realized I had no idea what the status was of his partnership, or what provisions he'd made for Anya and me.

How could I have been so stupid the second time around? Why hadn't I insisted on more information? Why had I been willing to trust Detweiler when he told me that there was nothing to worry about? Why had I agreed we could talk about all this after the baby came?

Like a swimmer pulled under by a strong current, I suddenly hungered for air. The edges of my vision darkened, and stars danced before my eyes. A powerful pressure built up in my head.

And then…the baby kicked.

Snap out of it, he seemed to be saying. Get a grip! You have to be strong! Call for help if you need to!

But who would I call?

Clancy would hop in the car and drive here from Illinois, no matter how risky the trip was. I didn't want that on my conscience. My old friend Mert Chambers and I were estranged. She blamed me for nearly getting her brother killed. Margit Eichen, who owned a minority portion of the store, was a wonderful, nurturing woman, but she is also a terrible driver even in the best of weather. I had already called Sheila and Robbie, only to be given the brush off. Jennifer Moore was out west, skiing with her children. There was only one other number on my favorites list. One other local friend who might offer me a shoulder to cry on.

Laurel Wilkins answered on the first ring. I managed to choke out what had happened, and she said, "They've finally gotten our street cleared. I'll be right there. Joe will come, too. He's pretty good at saying prayers."

That's Joe, as in "Father Joe," an Episcopal priest.

When the tough stuff happens, it helps to have God on your side.

CHAPTER 18

All things considered, I wasn't feeling very charitable when Robbie called back. I thought about ignoring his ring, but hey, life's short. That seemed to be a timely aphorism, given the events of the morning.

"Kiki Lowenstein-Detweiler," I said, determined to practice that mouthful before I went public with my new name.

"Look, I'm sorry that I cut you off earlier," said Robbie, "but I've got my hands full."

"You and me both."

He interrupted before I could tell him what had happened. "Sheila drank herself into a coma. Found her face down on the kitchen table this morning when I got up. So I lied to you about the tree blocking the drive. When you called, the EMTs were working on her. They took her to the hospital to get her stomach pumped or whatever it is that they do when your blood alcohol is point-three-zero."

"What?"

"You heard me."

"I think I did. Could you repeat that?" I was having trouble processing this.

"Your mother-in-law drank herself into oblivion. It's happened twice now that I know of. Once on Christmas Eve. That's why she was in such a bad mood on Christmas Day. Fortunately, when I found her that night, she was groggy but not unconscious. She did it again this morning. I guess she can't even wait until noon to get drunk these days. When I couldn't rouse her, I called the ambulance. I'm still here at the hospital—"

His voice sounded suspiciously near. Loud, too. I uncurled myself from the chair, stood up, and looked straight into Robbie's florid face. He's a big man, but Sheila seems to be breaking him down, inch by inch. Every time I see him, he wears his age like a wet raincoat that's dragging on the ground.

"Fancy meeting you here." I punched the button to end my call.

"You okay? False labor again? The baby all right?" He fired off these questions one right after another.

"Yes, but—"

"What a wonderful world, huh? This place was jammed packed less than an hour ago. You planning to stay like that? With your chair facing the wall?"

"Can you help me turn it around?" I figured it would be better to tell him the bad news face to face. "Is Sheila going to be all right?"

"I hope so." With a deft move, he managed to rearrange the same wingback that had taken me fifteen minutes of huffing and puffing to point in the opposite direction. As I faced the waiting room, I realized most of the crowd had cleared out.

Wearily, Robbie pulled over a chair for himself. When we faced each other, I saw how puffy his eyes were and how red his nose was. He'd been crying. Although he usually dresses neatly, his shirt was rumpled with a coffee stain on the placket. In short, he was a hot mess.

"Detweiler and Hadcho were shot. At our wedding." I paused. "I mean, my wedding to Detweiler of course. Not that I was marrying Hadcho. But you knew that. Right? Or did you?"

"You're kidding me!" It had taken him a while to process my babble. The color drained from his face. "Back up, you got married? Decided not to wait, and they're hurt? How are they? What do you know? Are the local police on top of this?"

What most people call St. Louis is actually a metro area composed of 91 different municipalities. Robbie is the Chief of Police for St. Louis County, but all the rest of these towns and villages have their own police forces. Given the varying degrees of autonomy, it wasn't entirely surprising that he hadn't heard that two of his officers had suffered gunshot wounds.

"I take it you didn't hear anything I said when I called you." I knew I shouldn't goad him, but I was still angry at how quickly he'd dismissed me on the phone earlier.

He raised an eyebrow at me. "Suffice it to say, I've had my hands full. This was supposed to be my day off. Now, what's the prognosis?"

"Hadcho's in recovery. He made it through the surgery okay, except for a loss of blood. Detweiler," and I struggled to talk over the hitch in my throat, "took a bullet to the gut."

With that, I broke down and started crying. I just couldn't hold back any longer.

Robbie gathered me into his arms and patted my back. His strength was transferred to me as he crooned, "It'll be all right. He's a tough guy with everything to live for. You'll see. Detweiler will be up and at 'em in no time."

"W-w-what if he isn't? What will I do?"

Robbie held me at arms' length and stared into my eyes. "You'll do what you always do, Kiki. You'll find a way."

CHAPTER 19

After I wet his shoulder with my tears, Robbie settled me back in the chair and went to get me more hot tea. Decaf this time. I directed him to the cafeteria, while I used the ladies' room.

We timed it right and arrived back at my special chair in tandem.

"I've got to hand it to you, Kiki, you know how to make a wedding special. Think of the stunning scrapbook page you'll be able to make. You can even use bullets as a what-do-you-call-it? Belly mint?"

"Embellishment. Sarcasm does not become you, Robbie. So you lied to me when you told me that you couldn't get out of your driveway."

He gave a tiny shrug. "I didn't see any reason to worry you. Not today, at least. I figured you might go ahead with the ceremony. You and Chad needed to make things legal for the baby's sake. If Sheila didn't have enough respect for you two to stay sober on this day above all others that was her choice. The least I could do was to try and contain the carnage."

"Didn't work that way, but I appreciate the thought." I blew on the surface of the hot beverage.

"Let me call Roscoe Gumfries and see if he has any leads. He's the Chief of the Webster Groves P. D." Robbie started pulling his cell phone out of his pocket.

"Before you do, you need to know that Brawny took out one of the gunmen. There were two of them. She threw a knife and got one. The other gunman hunted me and the kids down. I managed to fight him off with a pitchfork, but he's still out there."

"Unbelievable. He came after you and the kids? Every year, the creeps sink lower and lower on the evolution chart. What can you tell me about the guy you wounded?"

I explained about the man coming after us in the shed. "I nicked him with the pitchfork. I'm only sorry that I didn't stab him hard enough to keep him from running away. Brawny regrets that she killed the other guy because she thinks she could have gotten good information from him. Maybe he would have ratted out his partner."

"Maybe. Maybe not. You never know about these things, and it's more important that Brawny took him out. Especially since he was shooting at you." Robbie hesitated. "Any idea who was the target?"

"Me, of course."

But as soon as the words were out of my mouth, I changed my mind. "Although it could have been Detweiler. Or Hadcho. After all, they both took bullets, so the shooters must have been aiming at them."

I grabbed the back of an old magazine and took a pen from my purse. Drawing Xs and a crude oval to represent the floor of the gazebo, I said, "Here's how we were standing." Then I labelled each of the Xs.

"One bullet narrowly missed you?"

"Went through the hood of the cape I was wearing."

"What were you doing at the time? I mean, what exactly was going on? What did you hear or see? What was your initial impression?"

I must have looked confused.

"Close your eyes," said Robbie. "Think about the ceremony. You were all on the gazebo. Lorraine was pronouncing the vows."

"Erik kept bouncing up and down, trying to catch snowflakes. He was mid-air, when I grabbed at him, because I was scared he'd take a tumble off the gazebo." With that, my eyes flew open and I started laughing, hysterically. "That ought to win me the

'Mother of the Year' Award. I tackled both my kids and knocked them face first down into the snow. Almost landed on my baby bump."

With that, I started crying again. This time the tears were soft and regretful.

"You saved your kids' lives. Not once but twice. Your quick thinking got them out of harm's way. Your courage kept them safe when that creep came after all of you."

I heard him with my ears, but my heart wasn't listening. "Thanks, I guess. But what if they're in danger because the shooter was mad at me? Or at Detweiler? Over the past few years, if there was a mess on the sidewalk of life, we stepped in it."

"That's for sure. But I doubt that anyone was looking to hurt you personally. Detweiler, well, maybe. Did he tell you about the case he's working on? Keith Oberlin?"

"Keith Oberlin? You *have* to be kidding me."

CHAPTER 20

Once upon a time, there was a city named St. Louis, aka the Gateway to the West. And that fair city was so busy and prosperous that it became a Mecca for all sorts of entrepreneurs, including French fur trappers. They spent the winter up in Canada and around the Great Lakes area, setting their traps and collecting furs. In the spring, they followed the busy streams and rivers until the waters flowed into the mighty Mississippi, the super-highway of those times.

The actual site of St. Louis was chosen by Pierre Laclede. He wisely selected a bluff near the confluence of the Missouri and Mississippi Rivers, a place long occupied by indigenous peoples.

Laclede predicted that his fellow Frenchmen would flock to this newly formed trading post. Given its ideal location, he envisioned it becoming a thriving community, nourished by money from the trade in animal skins.

As a commodity, furs had the advantage of being lightweight and easy to transport. They were in high demand. Beaver felt hats were all the rage in Europe. Marten, otter, lynx and mink were also highly prized. To many young men, the lifestyle of a trapper seemed glamorous. In that role, a man could travel, live without ties or obligations, and enjoy the company of other free-spirited souls.

One such example was Francois Oberlione. He found work as a *voyageur*, which is French for "traveler." Oberlione made his living by transporting trappers from Canada to the trading outposts. His life was one of great physical hardship. He spent every day either paddling a canoe or carrying bundles of fur weighing as much as 90 lbs. each. But he relished the freedom and the camaraderie of his fellow *voyageurs*. This was a lifestyle for the brave, the curious, and the hearty. Francois would have happily remained a *voyageur*, but fate intervened when his best friend was trapped in a whirlpool and drowned. The man's cries for help echoed in Oberlione's brain, a ceaseless wail that suggested he might die next.

That spring, when Francois journeyed to St. Louis, he recognized the potential for a business selling supplies to fur traders. Since he had many friends among the *voyageurs,* he was trusted by them, and his small mercantile quickly flourished. Word of his success reached far and wide. All he needed was a wife, so he wrote letters back to his family in Canada, asking them to find someone suitable. Thus he began a stilted correspondence with a French Canadian lass, Marie de Haviland.

Arriving in St. Louis, she found a well-established business, an eager young man, and a small building with a hastily added second floor for living quarters. Marie might have expected more, but she was too stubborn to return home. Theirs was an uneasy marriage. Francois was convinced that St. Louis could only grow and prosper. Instead of buying furniture or building a house away from the dirt of the main street, he spent every coin that came his way on more land. This did not please his young bride. Before long, he had bought up most of the riverfront property and earned his wife's hatred.

Marie might have run away, if she hadn't become pregnant repeatedly. Francois, it's been said, had a dream of fathering a dynasty. To do so, he needed as many sons as Marie could give him.

Over time, Oberlione became Oberlin. Marie blessed Francois with many children. Thanks to Oberlin's wise investments, his sons went on to great riches. Following the example set by their *pater familia*, they bought up land and invested in businesses. To say the Oberlins are wealthy is like saying Ford builds cars.

The Oberlins went forth and multiplied, sometimes within the confines of marriage and sometimes on the wrong side of the blanket, so to speak, but always with their heads held high.

In St. Louis, the "old" society can usually trace its roots to those early fur trappers and beer barons. Therefore, the Oberlins not only enjoy the natural caché of being rich, they also count themselves among the blue bloods, the pedigreed few, of our city.

Young Keith Oberlin graduated from CALA, the Charles and Anne Lindbergh Academy, where my children rub shoulders with the crème de la crème of St. Louis society. For this, I have Sheila to thank. She's a donor, a diva, and a doting grandmother who wanted Anya to have the same advantages that she and her son, George, had. When Erik came along, the school balked because he's not a true "legacy," since George wasn't his father. But Sheila raised such a fuss that the administration reluctantly caved in to her wishes. I say that they did it reluctantly, but given the choice between having her change her will and accepting a smart little boy who helped them fulfill their much vaunted desire for "diversity," they made a wise choice.

Of course, Keith Oberlin is older than Anya and Erik. By thirty years.

Not that he acts like it. He's a stereotypical playboy who refuses to settle down. When our local paper boasted a society column, they ran a photo of Keith with a different woman every week. His tastes run to tall and thin, insanely beautiful, and young. Really young. Keith has been arrested for public intoxication, for driving 100 mph in a school zone, for punching out a reporter, and other crimes too numerous to mention. At the heart of his misbehavior is a drug habit. Here's the equation: money + no responsibilities + drugs = life-threatening situations.

Even so, no one expected Keith to find a sixteen-year-old girl dead in his bed.

CHAPTER 21

"Detweiler's working that case? The one involving the teenager?" I tried to keep my voice low so I didn't attract attention. While most of the other folks had cleared out of the ER, a few still warmed the seats. Robbie was sharing confidential information, the kind of scuttlebutt that people drooled over.

"I imagine that Chad didn't want to share that with you. Diya Patel wasn't much older than Anya."

"Diya Patel? She was the dead girl? They didn't release the name."

"Because she was a minor. Makes my skin crawl, and it takes a lot to bother me these days." Robbie shook his head. "Just a kid, really. Pitiful. Pretty little thing, too."

"Anya knew her!"

"But she's older," said Robbie.

I explained that Diya had been kind to my daughter, helping Anya locate her locker on the first day of Middle School, little more than a year ago. After that, Diya also made it a point to stop and chat with Anya in the halls. Of course I'd heard about a dead girl being found in Keith Oberlin's bed, but I had no clue the deceased had been Diya.

"I knew she died recently. I just didn't know how it happened. The school is planning a memorial event for her. I figured it was a car accident. With each crop of new drivers, someone dies. Usually I'm on top of the gossip at CALA, but…"

"Is Anya going to the memorial service?" Robbie raised an eyebrow.

"No. She told me she'd rather remember Diya as she was."

The loss hit me hard. Once again I was reminded how fragile life is. I couldn't help but imagine the pain of losing my own daughter, and that brought on a fresh wave of tears.

Robbie got up, grabbed a box of tissues and waved them at

me. I grabbed a handful and mopped my face, not worrying about how many I used. Fortunately, they're a staple in the Emergency Room. Robbie stared down at me and sighed. "I'm sorry. I should have realized Anya might know the girl. Detweiler has made a lot of progress on the case. He's been interviewing people, matching up their stories, tracking down details. Diya's mother has been particularly helpful."

"Maybe that's why someone took a shot at us. The public is clamoring for an arrest. The paper has been full of angry letters to the editor. Maybe someone decided Detweiler wasn't moving fast enough."

"I'll look into that, but there are only a few people in the department who know that Detweiler was assigned the case. I've made it clear that vigilante justice is not going to happen here. Not on my watch. I instructed Detweiler to go at his own pace. He's been in close contact with the mother of the deceased. According to him, we've made tremendous progress. I don't care if the hounds are baying. We want all our facts straight before we go public with our findings."

"But what if one of those hounds quit baying and decided to grab a gun? What if he and a friend dropped by my house this morning?" I stared hard at Robbie. "You counted on your people keeping their mouths shut. What if they didn't? Maybe you should have thrown those barking dogs a bone. You could have held a press conference saying you were making progress. Something, anything to give people a feeling that justice would be done!"

"Now you're telling me how to do my job?" As he sank back down into the chair he'd recently vacated, his eyes blazed with anger. "Lucky you. You've got the luxury of twenty-twenty hindsight, Kiki. It's easy from where you're sitting. But I had to make a choice. I could cave in to the creeps who said we weren't moving fast enough and ruin the lives of innocent people. Or I could trust Detweiler to do his job. Maybe I have more faith in your husband than you do!"

That felt like a blow to the gut. I had to look away from Robbie's unflinching glare. Yes, I wanted to blame him, but in my heart, I knew he was right. Was I big enough to admit as much?

"You did the right thing," I said, at last. "At least, I suppose you did. I'm being selfish. I can't expect you to coddle my husband because we're family. That's wrong of me."

"No," he said with a sigh, "that's natural. Especially given your situation." He ran a shaking hand through his hair. "And if it makes you feel any better, I've questioned my judgment on this twenty times a day."

"No one knows exactly how Diya got into Keith Oberlin's house?"

"Your husband does. At least, he's pretty sure he does." To close the topic, he slapped his thighs with his open palms. "I better order a guard for Detweiler and Hadcho's rooms until we learn more. Meanwhile, let me get back upstairs to see about your mother-in-law."

That was the topic we'd both been avoiding. As he lumbered to his feet, my heart went out to him. "I'm sorry, Robbie. I hope this will teach her a lesson. Maybe it will put a big scare into her, and she'll straighten out."

Of course, I knew better. I'd grown up with alcoholic parents. It takes more than a scare to sober up most people. Riding a wave of sympathy, I stood up and put my arms around him.

He rested his head briefly on my shoulder. "You don't know how good this hug feels. Family is all that matters, Kiki. You said I shouldn't coddle Chad, but I will. He's my son-in-law and you're my daughter-in-law. That's my grandchild you're carrying. Please remember that I'm on your side."

CHAPTER 22

As Robbie moved to leave, I spotted the surgeon in the hallway.

"Mrs. Detweiler?" Dr. Fizzio scanned the waiting room. Her surgical mask hung around her neck, as she grasped a clipboard. She looked a little lost, so I waved to her. She squinted as if trying to get her bearings. Maybe she was simply tired. I hoped it had nothing to do with Detweiler. I tried to remember what color scrubs she'd been wearing earlier. Had she changed clothes? If so, what did that mean?

Robbie looked from her to me and hesitated. His body language suggested that he would stay long enough to hear what the doctor had to say.

Dr. Fizzio came closer, consulted her notes, and slowly opened her mouth. It was like we'd been captured on film and the projector was moving super slo-mo, one frame at a time.

There are moments when you think, "After this, nothing will be the same." And it isn't, but change has already happened. There's no way back. You can only go forward. I held my breath, waiting for her to talk, thinking, "Please God, let him be okay." Then I added, "Please God, give me the strength to cope with whatever happens."

The surgeon's lips moved, and her words bounced up against me, but they didn't penetrate my brain. She said, "Your husband is awake and responding well."

But her facial expressions didn't mirror her words. An alarm bell went off inside me. Dr. Fizzio was holding information back. For some reason, she wasn't being entirely candid with me.

Robbie must have come to the same realization. He introduced himself as my father-in-law. "Detweiler's out of surgery? But you're worried about him? Doctor, could you be more specific regarding his prognosis."

That made her squirm. She hesitated, finally saying, "I think I have the bleeding stopped, but with these gut shots, you never know. I'm hopeful that he'll make a full recovery. It's just that his blood pressure isn't exactly where I'd like it to be."

"When can I see him?" Her assurance wasn't good enough. I wanted to see Detweiler with my own eyes.

"Give him another twenty minutes. He's coming around, but slowly. We're transferring him upstairs to our critical care unit." Wiping a hand across her forehead, she turned to leave.

"Doctor?" I called after her. "Thank you."

She paused, turned around, and frowned. "Thank me when he's back on his feet."

CHAPTER 23

Robbie wanted to stick around and say hello to my husband, but he was also worried about getting back to Sheila. "She might bolt on me if I don't get back soon. Or eat one of the nurses alive. Either way, it's touch and go. I'll check on Detweiler before I leave the hospital, but right now I really should look in on Hadcho."

With a sudden slap of guilt, I realized I hadn't given much thought to our friend. Hadcho always seemed so self-sufficient. But then again, lately he'd been spending a lot of time at our house. Falling asleep on the sofa had become a habit.

"Is there any way you can get them to bend the rules so I can see him, too? He doesn't have any family nearby."

"I'll see what I can do."

I realized then that I hadn't asked about Sheila. I'd been too preoccupied with Detweiler and Hadcho. "Sheila's going to be okay, isn't she? Once they get all the booze out of her system."

Robbie's shoulders drooped. "No. Not really. That's one reason I need to get back. The doctor plans to lay it on the line with her. He thinks that if she doesn't go into rehab, she'll be dead within a year."

A year?

My parents had been drinkers all of my life. Sure, my dad had died young, but Mom was still alive and kicking. According to Amanda, Mom did just fine with two glasses of wine before bedtime.

But Sheila only had a year to live?

How could that be?

"It's that bad?" I reached for his hand. He gripped mine, more tightly than ever.

"It's bad. She has a minor heart problem. A birth defect. The alcohol is making it ten times worse. We've never said anything about it because it's not worth worrying about. Or it wasn't worth worrying about until she started drinking like a drunken sailor. Between her heart, the alcohol, and her age, it's a deadly trifecta. As a binge drinker, she's really putting herself at risk. What if I hadn't found her this morning? Sheila's by herself more and more these days. Linnea only works part-time, because she's spending her afternoons with her great-grandson. I guess I could hire another housekeeper to keep an eye on my wife, but I'm not sure that would work. Not long term."

"She's always liked her drinks, but she used to have them in moderation. When did all this change?"

"I'm not sure. I think it was shortly before I moved in. She's been a binge drinker most of her life. Mutual friends would mention that she'd tied one on at this function or that. I heard about it through the grapevine, even before we got back together. But I didn't think much of it. I sort of brushed it off. Sheila is Sheila. She goes overboard on almost everything."

Pain etched his face with new lines, symbols of his concern. His voice was thick with emotion. He pulled away from me and used his hands to scrub his face. "I've loved her since we were teenagers. Now I'm supposed to stand by and lose her to booze? I don't think so. I won't give her up without a fight."

"I'll support you in any way I can. Detweiler and Anya will, too."

"That might mean a family therapy session in the future."

"Say the word and we're there."

"Thank you," he said. "You're a good kid." He ruffled my hair, turned on his heel, and walked away.

CHAPTER 24

How strange life could be. Sheila and I had once been mortal enemies. She hadn't wanted her son to marry me, and she hadn't kept her disappointment a secret. But after George died, our mutual love for Anya became the glue that bound us together. We came to respect and finally love each other.

When had she become so reliant on the pleasures of drinking? Had it happened before my eyes? A counselor once told me, "All alcoholics hit rock-bottom. Some die there." Was I destined to lose two people I loved, sooner rather than later? Would Robbie be able to convince Sheila that she had to change? Or would he eventually grow weary of fighting with her? By all accounts, he was heading for the best years of his career, so a distraction like her health was totally at odds with the strides he'd made.

Since I hadn't had caffeine in eight months, that first cup of tea had sent my mind whirling. A glance at the institutional clock told me I still had ten minutes to wait until trying to visit Detweiler. I'm not accustomed to sitting still. Not at home. Certainly not at work. The magazines looked dog-eared and gross. My skin felt like it was crawling. Just when I decided I couldn't stand it one second longer, Laurel and Joe came striding in. As they walked toward me, people did almost comical double-takes. Without a doubt, Laurel is the most beautiful woman I've ever met, inside and out. Her long blonde hair bounced along as she took long steps in her tall black boots. The fake fox collar of her quilted black jacket accented her strong jawline. At her side was Joe, also known as Father Joe, an Episcopal priest. He was wearing his clerical collar, a black leather jacket and jeans. Together they looked like a pair of other-worldly angels slumming it here on earth. All eyes followed them as they hurried my way. In a graceful move, Laurel dropped to her knees and caught me up in her arms. "It's going to be okay," she said, patting my back. "We're here. You aren't alone."

Joe reached down to stroke my hair. Under his breath, he murmured a prayer. Strange as it might sound, I could feel a shift, a change in the energy that surrounded me.

"I'm so glad to see you both," I said, between sniffles. "Thanks for coming Laurel and Joe."

It had been Joe himself who suggested we drop his religious title and simply call him "Joe." Erik was already having trouble trying to sort out all our roles. Upon being introduced to "Father" Joe, the boy's lower lip trembled. "Am I going home with you?" he asked in a tiny voice.

Kids are great observers, but poor interpreters. After calling Van Lauber "Daddy," and accepting Detweiler as his new father, meeting a third man called "Father" was too much for the child to process. The boy had a meltdown. It took Brawny two days to unravel the confusion.

"It doesn't matter what he calls me," Joe had assured us. "If I'm not more than a title, then I've failed at a larger calling. Why don't all of you call me by my first name?"

Erik's confusion eventually led to a discussion about our newly co-mingled family. Sitting the little boy down, we explained that some families are born together and others, the luckiest ones, get to choose each other. Detweiler and I emphasized that we chose to have Erik as our son.

I had hastened to add, "Van was your father, and he loved you very much. He'll watch over you from heaven."

Anya chimed in. "George Lowenstein was my first dad. Detweiler is my second father. It's cool that we have more than one, isn't it? Most kids only get one, and if he's a loser, that's tough." This explanation, plus a big sisterly hug, went a long way toward making Erik feel better. He adores Anya. Although he might not have totally understood what we were trying to say to him, he was mollified. If having two dads was okay by Anya, it was super-duper fine by Erik.

Then there was Joe, himself. His personality worked to convince Erik that all was well. With or without his clerical collar, Joe radiated a spirituality that set him apart from other people.

Clancy described it as, "A special glow. It must be where the painters came up with the idea of a halo. He has this aura. You can't quite see it, but you definitely can feel it."

Standing there in the ER waiting room, I was definitely in need of his good vibrations. As he hugged me and murmured a blessing in my ear, a sense of peace descended over me. When he let me go, Laurel wrapped her arms around me. Now I knew I could get through this. I wasn't alone anymore. My friends had arrived to help.

"Tell us everything." Laurel's nose and cheeks were pink from the cold. She and Joe led me to a clump of chairs. In fits and starts, I tried to reconstruct what had happened. Both asked questions, trying to make sense of my disjointed rendition. When I got to the part about attacking the gunman with a pitchfork, Joe and Laurel smiled at each other.

"That creep didn't know who he was tangling with." The priest nodded his head approvingly.

"Which of you is Mrs. Detweiler?" A voice interrupted. I popped to my feet as a woman in pink scrubs looked from me to her clipboard and back again. "Detective Detweiler is awake now. You can come say hello to him, but you can't stay long. Your friends can come and wait for you in the family lounge."

Laurel and Joe held onto me as I followed the nurse into an elevator. On the next floor, a jerk of the nurse's head indicated the seating area. My friends gave me a quick hug before I followed the woman down the concrete block corridor and into Room #222 at the end of a quiet hallway. My mind moved much faster than my feet. I planned to say, "Honey, you forgot to duck," which was what Ronald Reagan said to his wife Nancy after the attempt on his life. The quip would sound both cheery and upbeat.

But when the nurse left me at the door, and I got my first look at the man I loved in a hospital bed, all those cheery thoughts flew right out of my head. I wasn't prepared for seeing Detweiler in such a vulnerable state. I'd grown accustomed to depending on him. His size, his strength, and his personality had always made me feel secure. But the figure in the hospital bed appeared helpless and small. The machines and tubes attached to his body frightened me. They turned him from a man into some sort of an alien.

All of these impressions were visceral. Cognitively, I knew the tubes and machines were there to help. Detweiler was still Detweiler. He hadn't shrunk in size. Nor was he less vital than before.

Then there was my pledge. I'd promised to stand by him "for better or worse." Only a coward would turn tail and run now.

I was frozen there on the threshold, unable to make my feet move when I saw a glimmer of gold. It was his wedding band, the ring I'd slipped on his finger only hours ago. I hurried to his side. He appeared to be sleeping, but he must have sensed my presence because his eyes flickered open. He mouthed the word, "Hi." I leaned in to give him a gentle kiss on the cheek.

"How are you feeling?"

"Woozy. Hadcho?"

"He's going to be okay. Robbie is trying to get me cleared to visit him."

"Who's taking care of you?"

"Laurel and Joe. Your parents are on the way."

He nodded. "Water?"

I grabbed the plastic cup and straw. Guiding it carefully to his lip, I offered him a sip. I decided not to tell him what I'd learned about Sheila, but for his own sense of well-being, Detweiler needed to know that security precautions were being taken. "Robbie thinks that maybe our shooters are vigilantes dissatisfied with the Keith Oberlin situation."

"I'm surprised he told you. We're keeping a really tight lid on everything." His brow puckered in a frown.

"I guess he had to, didn't he? Someone was shooting at us. We have no idea who or why. So Robbie ordered a security guard to be posted between Hadcho's room and yours."

Even while lying in a hospital bed, Detweiler still thought like a cop. "We'll know more as soon as they ID the man Brawny brought down."

Very carefully, I propped myself up on the side of his bed, resting one hip on the mattress. "I think I need to take knife-throwing lessons from her. She's really something."

"Uh-huh. Are you sure the baby is all right?"

"Harry insisted that the ER docs check us out. We're both fine. In fact, this little guy is practicing his field goal kicks. I am more worried about you. What if the gunman comes back?"

"I'm not sure I'm the one they were after."

My stomach did a free fall. "W-w-what?"

The nurse stuck her head into the room. "Time's up. That's it for now. Sorry."

"Sure." I acted like I was leaving by getting off the bed and grabbing my purse. But that was a ruse because I needed to hear what Detweiler was thinking. Instead of hurrying out, I moved as slowly as I could.

He watched me with an expression of concern. "Be careful, love. Those men might have been aiming at you."

CHAPTER 25

"What?" I sounded like a broken record. But before I could get an answer, the nurse stepped between my husband and me.

"Time to go." She scowled and glanced up at the clock.

Out in the hall, I marched straight to the nurses' station. "I know that security is on the way, but in the meantime, someone needs to be protecting Detectives Detweiler and Hadcho. They are in danger."

An older woman in lavender scrubs stared up at me from a pair of bifocals. "We've been told that a uniformed officer is on the way."

"That's not good enough. These creeps came after me and my children. That means all of you are at risk, too. Don't you have security in this hospital? Someone who can sit outside their rooms as a deterrent?"

Her frown depended. The expression on her face suggested she was too tired to care. So I threw another log on the fire. "What if someone shows up here and starts shooting? You'd make easy targets. You don't want a bloodbath on your hands, do you?"

The ugly picture I'd painted shocked her into action. Picking up the phone, she talked to someone about getting a guard on the floor, temporarily. When she hung up, I said, "Thank you. I wasn't being an alarmist. I really am concerned."

"Got it." She went back to her paperwork.

Laurel guided me to a sofa in the visitors' lounge. After I staggered to a seated position, she grabbed my hand. "Joe and I will stay with you tonight. We've called the house. Brawny will switch off with us in the morning."

"How's Detweiler?" asked Joe.

"Guys, I have something to tell you," I began, hesitantly. "Detweiler thinks the gunmen were shooting at me."

Laurel and Joe exchanged long looks. Finally, he said, "Kiki, do you really think that Detweiler is in any shape to make such a judgment? Respectfully, he's pretty doped up right now. I thought that it took a ballistics expert to judge the trajectory of bullets. But he didn't get the chance to review the crime scene, did he? From what Brawny just told us on the phone, one minute you were saying your vows, and the next minute mayhem broke out. When would he have found the time to think through the angles at which the shots were fired?"

His logic was straightforward. It also made sense. I took a shuddering breath, as I agreed. "Maybe he's being overly protective."

"Mrs. Detweiler?" A uniformed county officer joined us. "I'm Luke Pinscher. Police Chief Holmes assigned me to the task of safeguarding Detectives Hadcho and Detweiler's rooms."

The nursing supervisor was staring at me.

I gave her a tiny wave.

So I'd hassled the woman for no good reason. I wanted to sink down into the sofa and bury my head under the cushions. Maybe I could find a loose quarter or two. As Officer Pinscher walked down the hall, I turned to my friends. "If Robbie Holmes is worried about Hadcho and Detweiler, then he must not think the gunmen were after me."

"When did you last eat?" Laurel stood up.

"Um, around two? What time is it?"

"Half past six. I'm going to run downstairs and grab some food for us."

"You might as well get comfortable, Kiki." Joe hailed a passing orderly and followed the man to a supply closet to bring us blankets and pillows.

I was sitting there by my lonesome when a hysterical Thelma Detweiler burst into the family lounge.

CHAPTER 26

"Calm down, calm down," I said, as she threw herself at me. Thelma's winter coat smelled of wet wool and stale perfume. Her hands were bare and snowflakes dotted her hair. Louis was a few steps behind her.

"I-I-I want to see my son!" Her face was contorted with grief, and her eyes wet with tears. Although she tried to wrestle herself away, I held on tightly.

Louis looked as if he'd aged a dozen years.

"Chad is resting. I spoke to him. We have to let him sleep. Thelma? Be strong. We have to do what's best for him!"

The urgency in my voice acted like a slap to her face. She stopped mid-sob. Her body relaxed. Louis put his arm around her shoulder. Repeating my words, she said, "Best for him."

"That's right. He's been through a lot, but he's fine now. You can talk to the nurse." I gestured toward the supervisor. To her credit, she stood and gave the Detweilers a calm smile.

"You promised me you'd hold it together." Louis chided his wife.

This was a turn-around, a reversal of their roles. I'd always seen Thelma as the calm person in the household. But it was Louis who seemed in charge of his emotions, although one glance at his shaking hands suggested he was working hard to stay in control.

A pile of blankets and pillows walked toward us. After he'd dumped them, I introduced the Detweilers to Joe Tinsley. "Actually, it's Father Joe, but that was confusing to the kids, so we simply call him Joe."

"A priest," murmured Thelma.

The Detweilers worshiped in a Methodist church not far from their home. With a pang, I realized that seeing a man in a clerical collar might be unsettling.

"Joe's a good man and a friend. He's Laurel's boyfriend. She ran down to get food for us. Have you eaten?"

"I'm not hungry." Thelma turned bleary eyes on Joe. "A priest."

I wasn't sure whether she was merely stunned or unhappy, so rather than jump to defend Joe, I kept my mouth shut.

Thelma sniffled. "I'm glad you're here, Father. I've been praying up a storm. Kiki, you certainly know how to bring people together. I swear, you have more friends than anybody I know."

The "old" Thelma returned. I gave her a quick squeeze. "They came as soon as I called. Luckily for me, their street had just been cleared. What about you? Did you have trouble getting here?"

Louis sank down into one of the overstuffed chairs. "We were lucky. By the time we got your call, they'd made one pass with the snowplow. The highways are clear. At least for now. The biggest problem is the number of cars off the side of the road."

Laurel arrived with a bag full of sandwiches and chips. After greeting the Detweilers, she reached into the paper sack. "I brought a dozen sandwiches of different types. Chips, too. How about if I go and get coffee? Or colas? What would everybody like?"

Once she had our drink orders, Laurel and Joe headed back down the hall together. Although I thought I couldn't eat a bite, the tuna fish salad on whole wheat proved irresistible. Gulping it down, I realized I was actually starving.

"Who's with the kids?" Louis picked up a turkey and cheddar sandwich on whole wheat.

"Brawny. Their Aunt Lori and Leighton are there, too."

"Are they okay? They didn't see Chad get shot, did they?" Thelma was sniffing at a ham and Gouda on sourdough bread.

Taking a deep breath, I explained about the intruder in the shed.

Thelma stared at me. "Good grief. You fought him off? The kids must be traumatized."

"Erik wet his pants. Anya's sort of weird. She recently decided she wants to be a cop like Det—Chad—and Robbie Holmes, so I think she secretly was thrilled. But I have a feeling that they're actually in shock. We'll have to deal with it later. Remember, Brawny's had all sorts of training in child psychology. Of all the people who could be there with the children, she's the best prepared to help."

Louis frowned and set down his sandwich. "But are the kids safe?"

I explained about Brawny taking out one of the creeps with her knife. "Leighton has a handgun. Gracie and Paolo are both there, and those dogs are formidable. Frankly, the kids are safer now than they were when all this went down. By the way, there's also an officer positioned between Chad and Hadcho's rooms. Really, we have every eventuality covered."

That was a little white lie. Who knew what we were dealing with? All I could hope was that we'd taken adequate precautions. There didn't seem to be any good reason for worrying the Detweilers.

A new face walked by with a clipboard. "How's my husband?" I asked.

"Are you Mrs. Chad Detweiler? I'm Elva, the night nurse. I'm going to check on him right now. If he's up to it, he can speak to family. For a very short visit."

Elva had thoughtful eyes and a sweet smile. All of us followed the nurse with our eyes as she walked away. As much as I wanted to see my husband, I knew that Thelma should visit him next. That was her baby boy in that hospital room.

"Mrs. Chad Detweiler. That has a nice ring to it." Thelma seemed to know I'd been thinking about her, as she gave me a hug.

"I didn't get to kiss the bride," said Louis, planting a respectful peck on my check.

"That's right; we're legal now," I said, grinning.

"Tell us all about it." Thelma handed her coat to Louis and snuggled beside me on the sofa. Laurel and Joe arrived with hot beverages. Tea never tasted so good to me. I'd grown accustomed to drinking it instead of coffee.

"What did you wear?" Thelma gratefully accepted a cup of coffee.

"You'll never believe it, but I had a gorgeous gown. Anya insisted that I have a white dress. As you know, everything was totally last minute. Brawny said she could whip something up, if she had material. Leighton volunteered his mother's damask tablecloths. Turns out, there was a trunk full of them in the attic. I don't know how Brawny managed to whip up a wedding dress, but she did. She even made me a hooded cape out of the same fabric."

I hesitated. I didn't want to tell everyone how close that first bullet had come. Nor did I want to explain that I'd given the EMTs the cape to staunch Detweiler's bleeding.

"So the rabbi made it after all?" Louis was happily munching on pretzels.

"No." I explained about Lorraine. "I wish all of you could have been there."

"I bet it was beautiful. Even the commons around our apartment seemed magical with the ice coating all the bushes," said Laurel.

I sighed. "It was like a fairy tale. Sparkling, quiet, and other-worldly. Then the shooting started. Maybe we're jinxed. Maybe we should have been satisfied with what we had."

Joe had been standing to one side, listening quietly. "Jinxed? You don't really believe that, do you, Kiki? You are all alive, despite the gunshots. We're here to support you. I realize you've been through the wringer today, but I see a woman who's been blessed abundantly. How about if I say a prayer? Maybe that will help you chase away those negative thoughts."

"I'd appreciate that," said Louis.

Thelma nodded, and I added, "Please."

We all bowed our heads.

"Father, protect your servant Chad Detweiler. Guide the hands of those who deliver care to him. Fill his body with strength and the will to return to health. Meanwhile, watch over his wife and his children and his family."

As we said, "Amen," Elva came racing out of Detweiler's room. Her face was creased with worry.

"What's up?" I asked, jumping to my feet.

"Something is wrong. Really wrong."

CHAPTER 27

I could only make out portions of her conversation as Elva pressed a button at her desk. "Send up an orderly. Call the surgeon. Prep the operating room. We need to get this man into surgery stat."

"What's happening?" I asked, but she didn't take time to answer.

Instead Elva went racing away, running past the officer stationed in the hall. Throwing the door open, the nurse ran into Detweiler's room. I stood there on the threshold, staring after her until an orderly shoved me out of the way. With practiced utility, Elva and the young man moved in tandem, unhooking various monitors, gathering up tubing, and making an adjustment to the bed.

"Out of the way!" She shouted at me, as they started pushing Detweiler's bed toward the door.

And then I heard him groan.

My knees turned to gelatin. His pain came from a place deep inside him. The sound he made was hollow with misery, as it signaled an almost animalistic struggle to survive.

I ran along beside them. Out of the corner of my eye, I realized that the Detweilers, Laurel, and Joe were on their feet, watching us. "What's happening?"

"I think he's bleeding internally." Elva didn't miss a step as she led the way to the elevator. Her face had closed down, her eyes were narrow with determination and her mouth had thinned out. Wordlessly, the orderly punched the down button. The light above the elevator car clicked from one floor to the next, a slow-moving countdown.

As I took Detweiler's hand, he moaned in pain. "Kiki?"

The elevator had stopped on another floor. There was nothing we could do but wait.

"I'm here, love." I leaned past the orderly to give Detweiler a quick kiss. His skin was clammy and his color gray.

"Something told me to double check. None of the monitors went off, but his color is wrong. I didn't even get the chance to speak to him, when he mentioned the pain between his shoulder blades."

"But the bullet hit him lower."

"It's what we call referred pain." Elva put two fingers on Detweiler's wrist to keep track of his pulse. "The discomfort shows up in a location other than where the trauma took place. We don't know exactly why it happens."

"But between his shoulder blades?"

The orderly nodded at me. "Could indicate that he's bleeding from the spleen." The floor indicator dinged and the doors rolled open.

"Please? Can I come with you?"

"Let us do our jobs," said Elva, as the elevator doors closed behind her

My feet were glued to the floor. I couldn't force myself to move.

I wondered if I'd ever see my husband alive again.

"Come sit down." Laurel tugged on my arm. We turned back toward the visitors' lounge. Louis held his wife, as she cried into this chest. Joe joined Laurel in getting me back to the sofa. When I felt the cushions behind my knees, my legs went out from under me. I collapsed in sobs. This had gone too far. I was going to track down that second shooter and make him pay.

CHAPTER 28

The next few hours were the longest of my life. At some point, I nodded off, only to sit bolt upright, crying out for Detweiler.

Laurel kept an arm around me as she stroked my hair. "Shh. He's still in surgery."

With her help, I got up to use the restroom. Every muscle in my body felt stiff from my fall into the snowbank, followed by crawling around on the floor of the shed.

At home, my nightly ritual included rubbing coconut butter into the stretched out skin of my belly. Without the lubricant, I felt itchy. My eyes were swollen and red. My throat hurt, and my head ached from clenching my jaws and grinding my teeth. What a mess I was.

Then I caught a glimmer of my wedding ring.

I was married to the man I loved. Finally.

However, I'd gladly give up my new status if it would put Detweiler back on his feet.

I sighed at my sad reflection. Unfortunately, turning back time wasn't an option. God doesn't make bargains with people, as much as we might wish that he would. And what if he did? We'd probably make a mess of our requests. Better that he keep his authority, and we accept his governance.

Laurel was waiting for me outside the john. She linked her arm through mine and walked me back to the sofa.

Louis and Thelma each occupied an overstuffed chair. Joe was pacing. I realized that he'd been checking on all of us during the night. Vaguely, I recalled him tucking in the blanket that covered me. The coffee table was full of half-eaten donuts, cookies, slices of cake, and cooling cups of coffee. Joe followed the direction of my eyes. "One of my parishioners works in the cafeteria. He heard I was spending the night here, so he's been sending up treats for us."

"What a kind gesture." Normally, I would have been all over those sweets. Right now, the thought of eating made me sick. "Any word on what's happening? Is Detweiler still in surgery?"

"I asked earlier," said Joe. "The bullet nicked his spleen. A wound like that is often overlooked. They're doing a splenectomy on him. The operation itself is fairly routine, Kiki. He's lost a lot of blood, but we should all be thankful they caught it when they did."

Laurel smiled at me. "An angel was watching over your husband. Elva came on duty earlier. She had no reason to go check on him when she did. Another nurse had just been into Detweiler's room, and he seemed fine to her. But Elva had this premonition, if you will. She decided to see for herself. One look at Detweiler and she knew something was wrong. When she told Dr. Fizzio on duty that there was a problem, she took her word for it. They prepped the operating theatre immediately. From what I'm told, a wound like this is very, very hard to diagnose. If things hadn't moved so fast, Detweiler's heart could have stopped."

I didn't feel particularly grateful, although I knew I should be.

I was angry they'd missed this the first time.

Angrier still that my husband wasn't beside me. That he'd been cut down in our back yard on our wedding day.

It was nearly three a.m. when the surgeon, Dr. Fizzio stepped out of the elevator with Elva at her side. Mert would have said that the doctor looked like "five miles of bad road." The woman's color was a sickly gray, her eyes were ringed with wide black circles, and her hair was matted to her head. But her eyes zoomed right in on me. "Mrs. Detweiler? I removed your husband's spleen. That should take care of the bleeding. Except for the blood loss, he's doing fine."

Biting my tongue, I nodded, but I also fumed silently. How could Dr. Fizzio have missed the wound the first time? Yes, I'd heard Joe say it was easy to overlook, but I was still angry. Two voices inside me argued. One was grateful; the other was furious. While I weighed the merits of the two opposing emotions, Laurel squeezed my shoulder. "See? He'll be up and around in no time."

Just then the elevator doors dinged. When they opened, Robbie Holmes staggered toward us. His clothes were rumpled, and his face was dark with day old stubble.

"I figured you'd still be awake," he said, speaking directly to me. "You heard about Detweiler's spleen?"

I nodded.

"He's going to be okay, Kiki." Robbie tried to send me an encouraging smile. Turning to Dr. Fizzio, the police chief added, "Thanks again, doc."

Dr. Fizzio stepped backwards, a prelude to leaving us. I couldn't find the energy to thank her. So Laurel spoke up on my behalf. "Thank you, doctor."

All I could do was bob my head.

Robbie ran a nervous hand through his hair. "Kiki? May I have a word?"

We walked a few feet away from the family lounge.

"Couple of things. Number one, you have permission from the admin staff to visit with Hadcho. Second, I made a decision last night. The addiction counselor talked to Sheila. We staged a sort of an intervention. We finally got her to agree to go to a rehab center, but she thinks that's happening sometime in the future. I've been calling around. There's a place outside of Palm Springs that'll take her ASAP. I tried to get a flight, but they're all booked. Prices for a last-minute seat are outrageous, so I'm going to run home, pack a few clothes, and drive us there."

"You what?" I couldn't believe I'd heard him right.

"I'm going to drive us to Palm Springs, California. I've already called Prescott. He's taking over the department."

Prescott Gallaway was the brother of Robbie's first wife,

Nadine. He was also the second highest ranking officer in the St. Louis County Police Department by virtue of his seniority, not because he had good sense or talent. As Sheila put it, Prescott was a "nebbish." That's Yiddish for "an idiot." I wished I knew the Yiddish word for "jerk."

"Prescott is a twit! A turkey. A creep. He hates Detweiler and Hadcho, because they're loyal to you, Robbie. He won't lift a finger to find out who shot them, and you know it. He'll say the crime falls under the jurisdiction of the Webster Groves Police Department and leave it at that."

Robbie stiffened. His eyes flashed with anger. "I am aware that Prescott is not an ideal replacement. And I regret the timing of all this, but given the circumstances, this is my only option. Hadcho and Chad are both safe. I've ordered a guard posted here twenty-four/seven. Sheila, my wife, is not safe. Her life is at risk. I've done all I can for them, and now I have to do what's best for her."

"You're leaving these men in a defenseless position with their shooter on the loose!"

"I am leaving two highly capable officers in a secure location with a guard outside their rooms. Seeing that I've given most of my life to the St. Louis County Police Department, I believe I have the right to make a choice—for once—that puts my personal concerns first. I've accrued two-years-worth of vacation. I plan to use several weeks of it, if necessary, to save my wife's life."

I started to protest, but Robbie had heard enough.

He stomped over to the elevator and stepped into the open car. Without bothering to say goodbye, he hit the down button and left me standing there with my mouth wide open.

CHAPTER 29

It all came down to Sheila.

In retrospect, I shouldn't have been surprised. Robbie had fallen in love with her when they were in high school. Back then their religious differences guaranteed they could never marry. As expected of them, they chose spouses from within their faiths. Robbie married Nadine in a Roman Catholic Church, while Sheila married Harry Lowenstein under a *chuppah*. Over the years, they would bump into each other at social events. These brief encounters would fan the flames of hidden embers, but they never acted on their feelings for each other. But they couldn't exactly keep their love a secret, either. Their attraction was too obvious.

Long before Nadine died of cancer, she'd been eaten up with bitterness, because she knew that Robbie still cared about Sheila. In fact, Nadine had poisoned their daughter Reena Marie with her suspicions, turning the young woman into a sad and twisted shell of a person. As Nadine struggled through chemo and radiation, she also enlisted the fury of her brother, Prescott, telling him that her husband had cheated on her in his heart. Meanwhile, Robbie had done everything humanly possible to help Prescott climb the promotional ladder at work.

There's a saying, "No good deed goes unpunished," and it certainly held true in Robbie's case. By boosting Prescott up the ranks, Robbie had aided and abetted his worst enemy. Not only was Prescott a mediocre policeman, he was also insecure and power-hungry. When Prescott's immediate supervisor decided to take early retirement last year, Prescott moved up another notch, into a position that gave him the ear of our mayor, Tom White.

Although he wasn't good at law enforcement and he had a horrible relationship with his direct reports, Prescott had a natural bent for fomenting unrest. Whenever possible, he spoke out against Robbie, telling the sort of stories that gave the mayor reasons to push Robbie toward early retirement. Recently, Prescott had been as busy as one of Santa's elves, running to Mayor White with imagined problems that involved Robbie.

Hadcho had told me all of this. He'd become my eyes and ears in the department, particularly after last year's departmental Fourth of July picnic. Hadcho had driven up in his antique Cutlass convertible, his personal car. The other LEOs had eyed it enviously. But it was Prescott who asked, "How about if I trade you beads and a blanket for that old car?"

It wasn't the first time that Prescott had joked about Hadcho's heritage, nor would it be the last. Hadcho recovered from the gibe brilliantly. Without missing a beat, he mussed up a portion of Prescott's comb-over.

"Hey! What do you think you're doing?" Prescott jerked away from Hadcho's fingers.

"Just checking. Lucky for you, White Man, there's not enough hair there to make a good scalp."

Everyone except Prescott had a good laugh about that.

You would have thought he would have learned a lesson, but he didn't. He has continued to make offensive comments about Hadcho's ethnicity. He's even poked fun at my pregnancy. More recently, Prescott has been called on the carpet for making lewd comments to a young female officer. But still, the man continues to open his mouth and say things he shouldn't.

I couldn't help but wonder, *Why is Prescott feeling so smug? So secure? Most people would be more careful.*

All these thoughts raced through my head, as I mulled over Robbie's announcement that he was taking time off to drive Sheila to a rehab facility way out west. His absence would give Prescott carte blanche to misbehave. There was only one reason he'd take such a drastic step: Robbie was scared spitless about Sheila's safety.

That's when it hit me that Robbie and I were both facing the loss of the person we loved. Suddenly, his actions didn't seem at all rash. Wouldn't I give up my work to save Detweiler's life? *You betcha.* If my phone hadn't been dead, I would have texted Robbie to say, "I understand, and I support your decision."

Instead, all I could do was stand there, mutely, and stare at the closed elevator doors. It was too late to offer Robbie my sympathies.

"Drink this." Joe handed me a cup of decaf tea. "I can see you're worried about Prescott taking over. Care to talk about it? Maybe it's not as bad as it seems."

I stared down at the brown sludge. My stomach turned, and bile collected in my mouth. "With all due respect, Joe, I know you're trying to help, but it's actually worse than you can imagine. If you're planning to give me a pep talk, this isn't the time, and I am not in the mood."

"There might be—" he started, but he was interrupted by a clanking sound in the hall.

In his faded green hospital gown, Hadcho came stumbling toward us, dragging his IV along behind him.

CHAPTER 30

Hadcho didn't bother with formalities. He got straight to the point. "Where's Detweiler?"

Before I could answer, Elva jumped up from where she'd been sitting at the nurse's station. "Detective Hadcho get back in your room!" She grabbed him by one elbow.

"I'm not going anywhere until I hear how Detweiler is doing."

"Is there a problem here?" The uniformed officer joined us. "Detective Hadcho? I'm under strict orders to see that you're safe. Seems to me that you're endangering yourself by wandering the hallway."

"Stuff it, Pinscher. I've got rank on you." Hadcho's normally tidy hair stuck out like porcupine quills.

Elva took one of Hadcho's arms and I tugged on the other. "Detweiler is okay, now. You should be lying down."

"What happened? You said, 'Now.' What's going on?" The gold flecks in Hadcho's brown eyes flashed with anger as he stared down at me.

I let Elva explain about Detweiler's splenectomy. As she did, I listened carefully, absorbing more information than I had earlier, because now I could actually concentrate.

"I thought I heard Robbie's voice." Hadcho dutifully crawled back into his bed, but he winced with pain.

"Yes, you heard Robbie." I told him about Sheila's problem, and Robbie's decision to drive her to a rehab facility.

"He's running off and leaving us with Prescott?" Hadcho's brown eyes widened in shock.

I helped Elva tuck Hadcho in. "Don't forget, we were in Webster Groves when the shooting took place. It's actually their problem."

"Right. You know better, Kiki. That's not how it works here

in St. Louis." He spewed a stream of coarse words, which was yet another surprise to add to my list. Usually, Hadcho acted like the perfect gentleman.

When he sputtered to a stop, he glared at me. "You realize, of course, that Prescott won't give this crime the time of day. In fact, I bet that his first action will be to call off the uniform out in the hall."

"Why?" Elva tilted her head in curiosity. "It's not surprising to have a guard posted when there's a shooter on the loose. Cops look out after each other."

"Real cops do, but Prescott is a phony. He hates Detweiler, and he hates me. Besides his personal feelings, this is a rare opportunity for him. See, he's always whining to Mayor White that Robbie wastes the department funds. Prescott keeps saying that if he was put in charge, he could slash the department budget in half. That's true, but our effectiveness would suffer as a consequence. As it is, Robbie makes do with too few officers and not enough equipment. Prescott keeps harping on Robbie's wastefulness. He's trying to convince the mayor that he could do a better job."

Elva immediately grasped the implications. "But if the armed guard is removed, how can we protect everyone on this floor? A shooter roaming the halls would endanger the entire hospital."

Hadcho used a finger to jab the air. "That's the point. Detweiler got a good look at the man we were chasing. That creep is bound to come up here and try to finish what he started."

"Oh, my..." I felt my legs going wobbly.

"Well, there's a guard here now, so we'll just have to keep our fingers crossed. Mrs. Detweiler?" Elva gestured toward me. "Time for you to go. This man needs his rest."

"First I need to—"

"Have you forgotten that you're eight months pregnant? We can't have you going into early labor. There's a recliner in

Detective Detweiler's room. You can curl up in there and try to get some sleep. You do realize, don't you, that it's the middle of the night? He should be waking up in a couple of hours. It would be good for him to know you're nearby."

"But Hadcho needs to tell me—"

"Nothing," she said firmly, as she walked over and pushed a button. "There. I just gave him another dose of painkillers. Any second and he should be—"

I followed her gaze. Hadcho had fallen sound asleep.

"You don't understand," I said, through clenched teeth. "We were shot at. I need to discover who's behind all this."

"You're wrong. I understand perfectly. For the moment, you're safe, they're safe, and if you don't see to your health, you're the problem. Not the solution." Elva's face hardened into an impenetrable mask. "Let them get their rest. You get yours. Everything can keep until later. You'll be able to think more clearly and so will they."

CHAPTER 31

Curling up in a recliner was difficult for me. My belly gets in the way. Sleeping upright can help, sometimes, because the baby is crowding my stomach and giving me heartburn. While getting comfortable took some doing, I must have conked out in Detweiler's room. I awakened when he called my name.

"Hello, sweetheart. You're okay," I said, stroking his face and kissing his forehead. "Things got a little rocky."

"What?" He tried to focus, but he looked confused.

"The bullet nicked your spleen."

As if by magic, Elva appeared at his bedside. She went into a long explanation about his emergency surgery.

"Splenectomy," he said, testing the word.

"Right."

"We're not entirely sure what the spleen does, except storing extra blood, so I doubt you'll miss it," said Elva. "Dr. Fizzio will be here to examine you a little later, Detective Detweiler. She can answer your questions. Meanwhile, you need to rest up. You've lost a lot of blood. Your body needs to start replacing your supply and start the process of healing. I can help you to the restroom, but you need to be careful. You have a lot of stitches, internally and externally. We don't want you to pull those out."

I waited while she helped him. After closing the door to give him privacy, she turned to me and said, "As long as he keeps quiet, he should be fine. Fizzio's as good as they come. She had a really, really tough night last night. Her relief surgeon drove his car into the back of a snowplow. He's here in critical care, clinging to life."

I didn't know what to say. I felt sorry for him, and for Fizzio, but my psychic energy was stretched paper thin.

"Are you still worried about a shooter?" She pitched her voice extra low. When I nodded, she continued, "I talked with the head of nursing last night. She's warned all our nurses to be careful. The head of hospital security convinced the uniformed officer to position himself next to the door at the back of the hall."

I hadn't noticed.

"That should preclude someone from gaining access through the stairway. All our visitors will now be forced to walk past the nurses' station. We aren't armed, but we do have an alarm button. It's not an ideal situation, but it's the best we can do."

I thanked her.

The bathroom door handle wiggled. Elva went to help Detweiler as he stood unsteadily beside the sink. It shocked me to see him looking so lost and helpless. But I slapped a reassuring smile on my face and chirped, "Okay, handsome, let's get you back to the business of getting well."

Together the nurse and I walked him to his bedside. She demonstrated how he should sit down before swinging his legs up, over, and onto the bed. A tiny grunt of pain told me her lessons were only partially successful.

"You'll get better at this as you go along. It's a matter of learning how best to protect your incision."

"Could he speak to his parents?" I asked. "They're really worried."

"Only if he doesn't talk for long."

I ran to the lounge and shook Thelma awake. She reached over and poked Louis. "Hon? Wake up. Come on. We can talk to Chad now. Louis?"

I followed them into the room, hanging back to give them a little privacy.

They both made a fuss over their son, while at the same time congratulating Detweiler for his good taste in brides. Despite her brave act, fat tears ran down Thelma's face. Louis gripped the metal bar around the hospital bed until his knuckles turned white.

"Okay, folks, that's enough for now. Let's get Detective

Detweiler back to the Land of Nod." Elva clapped her hands the way a schoolteacher does to get attention.

On his way out of his son's room, Louis made a sharp right turn toward the men's restroom. I had a hunch that in the privacy of a stall, he'd allow himself the luxury of a good cry. Thelma watched him as he disappeared. She turned sad eyes on me, but she seemed to have calmed down a little. I gave her a hug, promised her that everything would be all right, and went back to the recliner.

CHAPTER 32

The next morning the sun peeped through the blinds and crept softly across the white surfaces of the hospital room. Detweiler's breathing was slow and regular. His cheeks were pinker than they'd been the night before. Rather than disturb him, I slipped out into the hall. The Detweilers were sprawled on the sofa. Joe and Laurel were gone. A new face had taken Elva's place at the nurses' station. I introduced myself to the nurse on duty and headed for the ladies' room. As I splashed water on my face, I felt a heavy hand on my shoulder. I blinked up, recognizing the scent of citrus. "Brawny?"

"*Aye,* 'tis me. They told me about Detweiler and his spleen. 'Twas a near thing. If that nurse hadn't realized that he was bleeding, things could have gone pear-shaped." Holding a finger close to her thumb, she illustrated her next point. "We came that close to losing him, you know."

"Tell me about it. How are the kids?"

"Fine. Laurel and Joe are there with them. She's a fine young woman, and Joe's a good man. The kids were looking forward having fun with them."

"Lorraine and Leighton?"

"Also fine. She's a bit under the weather. The excitement takes it out of her, don't you know?"

Lorraine's MS is aggravated by stress. One night, sitting in front of a fireplace of embers, Lori and I had talked about her death. She has a very sanguine attitude. "I plan to live until I die. I want to have the fullest life possible. In that way, my illness is a gift. Most people wait. They put off what could bring them joy. I don't procrastinate on life's pleasures."

Brawny handed over a fabric tote bag. The action brought me back to the here and now.

"Have you checked on Hadcho?" I looked inside the bag and

discovered clothes, my notebook computer and power cord, plus an assortment of craft supplies to keep me busy.

"*Aye.* He's fine. Already had his breakfast. Been barking at the poor wee nurse about their miserable excuse for salsa. I gather he's rather a foodie, eh?"

"Uh-huh. So he told you about Robbie leaving?"

"I talked to the police chief myself. Caught up with him after he'd gone back to his house to pick up a few things. He's worried about Detweiler and Hadcho, but more concerned about saving his wife's life. The choices are tearing him apart, but he trusts that the authorities here can handle the shooting incident, whereas there's no one who can put Sheila into a rehab facility. No one except for him."

I hadn't seen it that way, but now I did. Who but Robbie could take Sheila on a road trip and survive the journey? Who else had the power to sign her into a rehab center? And none of us could testify to her alcohol abuse like Robbie could.

I realized that Robbie had done the right thing.

But that still left me feeling frightened and alone. Especially since he'd turned over his job to Prescott.

"Let's get you downstairs for breakfast." Brawny motioned toward the elevator. In short order, I was staring at a plate of scrambled eggs, whole wheat toast, and hash browns. Brawny also brought two steaming cups of tea to the table. Mine, of course, was decaf.

"Okay, I understand that Robbie has to do, what Robbie has to do. I get that. But I'm not confident that locals can handle this. Not if it's connected to the Keith Oberlin case. There have been lots of complaints that no arrests have been made. It's entirely possible that a vigilante group of citizens has decided that Detweiler is dragging his feet. Maybe they fired those shots as a warning to speed things up."

"Our shooters weren't local."

"What?"

"I went through the pockets of the man I brought down with my knife. His driver's license is from Alabama. There's more," she said, holding up her fingers, so she could tick off the points. "They acted like professional hit men. They were properly armed for the task. They had a stolen car parked in the alley, ready for their get-away. They were carrying cash."

"They were carrying cash?" I rubbed my eyes and poured sugar into my decaf tea.

"The man I neutralized had wodges of paper money in his pockets. Also, he was from Walker County, Alabama. It was on his driver's license."

"So?"

"Walker County happens to be the best place in the US to find a hit man. I called a few friends and shared his name. He definitely was a pro. That means his partner probably is a professional, too."

"You have to be kidding me. There's, like, a place in the US where you can hire hit men?"

"Aye."

"That doesn't preclude Keith Oberlin from having hired them. Maybe Detweiler was planning to arrest Keith. The Oberlins have a ton of money. I'm sure they have connections we can't even imagine. I bet it isn't hard to hire an assassin if you've got the money."

"That's true." A tiny smile played on her face. Her graying ponytail was, as always, neatly pulled back with an elastic band. Very little about Brawny ever varied. She was wearing her usual kilt and blouse. Once when Anya asked her why she wore the same thing, day after day, she had smiled and answered, "It frees my mind to think about more important tasks, such as caring for you and your family."

She continued, "My associates are doing their best to find out more about the man I killed. After all, his partner is still out there. Even though you clipped him with that pitchfork, he might still be dangerous. Our best option is to find out the person behind hit men. Then I will neutralize the money man."

Neutralize? You'd have thought she was talking about pouring Round-Up on weeds. Her voice was that casual. I shivered.

"I'm convinced this has to do with Keith Oberlin. Robbie told me that Detweiler had been talking to the dead girl's mother. CALA is holding a candle lighting service this evening in memory of Diya Patel. Since you're here, I can take the Highlander and drive over to the school. I have a good reason for going. Anya knew Diya and liked her a lot. My presence shouldn't arouse any suspicions. If need be, I'll come right out and ask Diya's mother where Detweiler was with his investigation."

"Hadcho doesn't know what Detweiler was on about?"

"Not entirely. As I understand it, they were working together, but Detweiler had a break-through, putting the pieces together while doing his interviews. He'd planned to talk to Hadcho and Robbie at the same time, getting them up to speed on what he'd learned. They were actually walking into the conference room, when an emergency came up. Robbie had to leave. He later text-messaged Detweiler and Hadcho to say he was taking a few personal days off. Detweiler thought the discussion could wait, so it did."

With a start, it dawned on me what sort of emergency that might have been, some crisis involving Sheila.

"*Aye,* and Detweiler expected to see Robbie at your ceremony, despite the bad weather. That story about the fallen tree was a farce."

"Right." I frowned. "I'm sure Detweiler was playing his cards close to the vest because the Oberlins have a lot of clout. Detweiler knew he was dealing with an incendiary issue, what with the death of a minor. Not to mention, the power of the Oberlin name. The reputation of the department. The pressure from CALA."

"CALA would have weighed in?" Lately Brawny had been dropping the kids off in the morning. She was becoming a fixture in the mothers' carpool lane, but she was still a newcomer to the community. She didn't entirely understand the dynamics. Sometimes, I didn't either.

"Absolutely. Anything that happens to a CALA student reflects on the school. At least, that's the way they see it at CALA. Detweiler told me that he was working a case where he couldn't afford a misstep. I just didn't know how close to home it was."

"What time is the candle-lighting service?"

"Six p.m.," I said with a yawn.

"Good. That will give you time to take a nap. If Detective Detweiler wakes up and is clear-headed, perhaps he can tell you what he knows and save you a trip."

"Here's hoping."

CHAPTER 33

Detweiler stirred in his bed. "Kiki?"

"I'm here, love." I raced over to kiss his brow. While I was there, I hit the nurse's button for good measure.

A dark-skinned woman scurried in. "I'm Leezie," she said, offering me a rough hand before quickly turning her attention to my husband. "How are you doing, sweetheart? You need to get up and use the john?"

Leezie pushed a button to raise the head of the bed. Then she helped Detweiler roll to one side and push himself into a seated position. Turning to me, she said, "When he's home, remind him to sit still for a minute before he stands up. Otherwise the blood will drain from his head too fast, and he might faint."

"Gotcha."

She helped him to his feet and into the bathroom. Once he was stable, she closed the door.

"I've been looking in on him. Checking his vitals. You've slept through most of my visits. He's doing pretty well, especially considering."

"When can he come home?"

"You'll have to discuss that with Dr. Fizzio."

I decided to step out of the room to check on Detweiler's parents. Thelma was watching Good Morning America. Louis had disappeared. Brawny sat in a chair at the other side of the sofa, reading a book on British history.

"How are you?" I asked my mother-in-law.

She smiled at me. "Now that my son is out of danger, I'm fantastic. How are you?"

"Much better. Tired, but I'll live."

"Louis ran downstairs to get some food. He's bringing it up. We didn't want to take off at the same time." She patted the empty space on the sofa, signaling me to come and sit down.

"Brawny didn't want anything," Thelma added.

Brawny winked at us.

"Oomph." I plopped down on the sofa. I'd lost all hope of elegance. Between my monstrous belly and being tired, I felt like I was behind the wheel of a big tour bus. And unfortunately, I didn't have a license to drive an oversized vehicle.

"Did you get any rest?" Thelma asked.

"A little. My skin itches all the time. I find myself digging at it. I'm really running out of apartment space." I patted my belly. "Sitting up is actually better than lying down, but even so. This little guy keeps shoving his foot under my ribs. When I press back, he switches feet and pokes me on the other side."

She laughed.

The local weatherman took over the screen. "More freezing rain and snow is scheduled to begin late this afternoon. The state highway patrol is asking that all non-essential traffic stay off the major arteries, especially those east-west corridors."

"That would be us," said Thelma, shaking her head. "Of course, the weatherman might be wrong, but I'd better talk it over with Louis. We'll probably head for home in an hour or two."

"Did Ginny and Jeff manage to get out?" Detweiler's sister and brother-in-law had planned to leave on a cruise ship out of Miami. I knew that Detweiler's parents had agreed to watch their granddaughter Emily.

"They took off late on Christmas Day. Emily is over at a friend's house right now. We need to go and get her, but we wanted to make sure Chad was out of the woods."

"I have a hunch that your son won't have much to say. They've got him pretty doped up. I don't blame you for going back home—and I'd feel better knowing you two are safe."

I purposely didn't tell her that I had plans for later that evening. There was no reason to worry Thelma by explaining that I was going to play amateur sleuth, talking to Sarita Patel and getting up to speed on a case that Detweiler had been working before he was shot. Better for my in-laws to drive across the river, pick up their granddaughter, and sit tight.

"I hate to admit it," Thelma said with a sigh, "but you're probably right. I doubt that Chad will be feeling chatty. You're here. He's safe. We promised Ginny and Jeff to watch our granddaughter, and we can't impose on Emily's friend's parents much longer. All the barn cats will need to be fed, as will the cows and pigs. Louis could ask a neighbor to help out, but I hate to do that. Most of our neighbors are our age. It's getting harder and harder for them to do chores. Seems like we're the last of a generation of farm families. The young folks have seen how hard we work, and they don't want any part of it. I can't blame them."

"Are you worried about what will happen to the farm?" I was surprised. She'd never shared this with me before.

"Yes, I am. It's been in the Detweiler family for more than a century. I'd hate for us to have to sell out, but equally, I hate seeing Louis work so hard. Once in a while, I'd like to be the ones going on a cruise, you know? I'd love to see a Broadway play in New York City. But we can't do that. Not with the daily responsibilities we have. Of course, it's not my place to tell Louis what to do with his land." With that she gave a tiny shrug.

If the farm had belonged to her side of the family, she might have felt more comfortable sharing her opinions. As it stood, she had to tread carefully.

The elevator door rumbled open, and her husband stepped out with a tray of food. "Kiki! How are you? How's my boy?"

"I think the crisis is over. There's a nurse in there with him now. He's groggy, but his color is better."

"Saints be praised. Come sit down and eat with us. I bought enough food to feed an army. Brawny? I got something for you, too. I know you said you'd already had a sandwich but I thought maybe you'd like a little fruit salad."

She looked up from her book and smiled. "Thank you."

"You girls need to keep your strength up," said Louis. "Running around after the kids and tending to that big house like you do. Taking those stairs ten times a day has to be a real workout."

He was right. Since moving into the big house, my butt muscles often ached at night. I'd noticed a definite lift to my derrière. As for Brawny, I wondered if Louis had any idea how tough she really was. Most mornings, she went running with Detweiler, who had told me that she could easily out-run and out-last him, if she chose to. After putting in their distance, they went downstairs and lifted weights, spotting each other. Detweiler had been delighted to find a new work-out partner. "We've got a bet going to see who can bench press the most weight. She's a great coach. Keeps me sharp."

Interesting.

To Louis, Brawny was our sweet Scot nanny, a wonderful woman who watched the children, helped around the house, and knit sweaters.

To Detweiler, she was Arnold Schwarzenegger.

To the kids, she was Mary Poppins.

To me, she was Wonder Woman in a kilt.

I couldn't help but laugh.

CHAPTER 34

The Detweilers spent ten minutes with their son. Thelma came out wiping her eyes, but wearing a tremulous smile. Louis was stoic, as he jingled change in his pockets. After giving me a big hug, they hit the road, heading back to Illinois. The rest of the day dragged on. I spent a lot of time in the recliner at my husband's side, but he was too doped up to talk coherently. To keep myself busy, I rummaged around in my tote bag. Brawny had thoughtfully included tissue paper, a glue stick, and a notebook. She knew that I'd been working on an idea for a new class, turning tissue paper and scrapbook embellishments into nifty decorative bowls.

When I tired of that, I opened my computer and Skyped Erik and Anya. The conversation was short, as the kids were too busy to waste time on Dear Old Mom. Erik was over-the-moon thrilled because Joe had shown him how to make paper boats that they sailed in the bathtub. Anya had practiced putting on makeup with Laurel. In fact, they'd been in the midst of working on their up-dos when I'd called, so I got a glimpse of my daughter with her hair in a stylish chignon.

"They're fine. We're fine," said Laurel. "Don't worry about us. Joe and I are having a blast with the kids. How's Detweiler?"

I told her the latest, which wasn't much. "He's weak and tired. Not making much sense. However, his color is good and the surgeon is pleased."

"We're happy to stick around as long as you want," said Laurel. "Leighton and Lorraine are making dinner for us. I guess she can cook a mean standing rib roast."

"If you need to take off, let me know. I'll send Brawny home. Right now, there's a uniformed officer guarding Hadcho and Detweiler's rooms, but I'm not sure that Prescott will let the guard stay on duty. He's sort of a jerk. I can't guess what he'll do when he realizes the department is paying the guard's hourly wages."

The tiny Laurel on my computer screen bobbed her head in agreement. "I hear what you're saying, but that's what friends are for, Kiki. To help out. Anyway, try not to worry about keeping someone there on duty. It'll work out. That reminds me, I talked to Margit. She opened the store for a couple of hours. A few customers wandered in. Not enough to make the cash register ring. I guess Mona Goodman came in and wanted to return everything her husband bought for her."

"What?" That was nearly two-hundred-dollars-worth of scrapbook supplies. Darvin Goodman had asked me to fix them up in a nice basket. The process had taken a chunk out of a day when I could ill afford to step away from the sales floor.

"I have no idea what's going on, but Margit said Mona was adamant about returning all that stuff. Get this, she hadn't even opened the cellophane to see what was in the basket."

"Then she doesn't even know what she's bringing back!" I reminded myself to take a long deep breath and release it slowly. Like all merchants, I despise taking returns. They represent a lost sale and a lost opportunity. But this turn of events had me puzzled. Darvin Goodman had spared no expense in choosing a bountiful amount of materials for his wife. This was her favorite hobby. So why was she so determined to bring it all back?

"Since it's a return totaling more than fifty bucks, Margit explained she'd need your approval. That'll buy you time. Maybe you can figure out what the deal is, and why Mona doesn't want all that stuff. It is really odd. She goes through scrapbooking supplies like I go through hairspray. Oh, and Margit's planning to send out an e-blast telling all our customers that we're closing early because of the incoming bad weather. I doubt that there's any point to us opening up tomorrow. Not with the ice and snow they're predicting. I guess they're now saying it will start early tomorrow morning. They keep going back and forth, changing their prediction on the timing. All the meteorologists know for sure is that it's going to happen, and it will be nasty."

It was good that the Detweilers had already left.

"Closing the store is the smart thing to do. Have you heard anything from Clancy?"

"I had told her what happened. She pointed out that most people have a reception after their ceremony rather than a confab with a crime squad. I've been keeping her updated, because she doesn't want to bother you. I explained that Margit has the store covered, and she said, thank goodness, because the snow plow left a mountain ten feet tall in front of her driveway. Raoul is with her, so she's snug and happy. I hope you don't mind, but I took the liberty of telling her to stay put."

"I agree. It's better for all of you to stay safe. Our customers can wait. The Detweilers left a few minutes ago. Thelma messaged me from the highway to say it is snowing over in Illinois already. The real mess will start with icy rain. That'll hit us after midnight, if the forecasts are correct."

Secure in the knowledge that all my responsibilities were covered, I fell back to sleep in the recliner. The past few weeks, in the run-up to Christmas, I hadn't gotten much rest. Between working at the store, moving into Leighton's big house, and buying gifts, I'd been run ragged. Now I had every reason to sleep, knowing that Detweiler was on his way to recovery. But before I closed my eyes, I set the alarm on my phone for seven p.m. That would give me an hour to get to CALA for the candle-lighting service.

Unfortunately, my little passenger refused to cooperate. The baby poked me under the ribs. I couldn't get comfortable in the recliner. When I finally drifted off, I dreamed of Anya waking up in a strange bed and crying out, "Mama! Mama!" It didn't take a psychology degree to decipher the meaning of that nightmare. Diya Patel had been only two years older than Anya.

Why had she crawled into a stranger's bed and died?

What had Sarita Patel told Detweiler?

Why wasn't Detweiler in more of a hurry to share his findings?

Who was really responsible for Diya's death?

I couldn't get back to sleep. Detweiler's color had improved. His breathing was deep and even. The big black and white institutional clock on the wall suggested that I should get up and get dressed.

Taking my fabric tote bag into the bathroom, I tidied myself up and changed. A glance out the windows confirmed I'd have to scrape ice off the Highlander, my least favorite job of all. In preparation, I dressed as warmly as I could. After one last look at Detweiler, I headed for the hallway, knowing I'd soon be out in the cold at the mercy of the elements.

CHAPTER 35

I was leaving Detweiler's room, when Brawny waved me over so we could talk quietly. The only other people lingering in the halls were hospital staff, but given the circumstances, being secretive still seemed prudent. "Hadcho's awake. I told him what you're planning, and he wants to talk with you."

"If he's going to try and stop me, he has another think coming."

"No." She waved away my concern. "That's not the impression I got. He's all for you talking to Sarita Patel, but he figures the more you know about the circumstances, the better shot you'll have at getting a straight answer."

I'd been geared up to brave the weather and clean my car, a task I hated with a passion, and this diversion would only delay the inevitable. On the other hand, if Hadcho had important information, it was worth my while to stick around and chat.

Giving a nod to the uniformed officer on duty, I tapped on the door to Room 224. After Hadcho grunted a greeting, I went inside and pulled up a chair by his bed.

I wasn't prepared for how frail he looked. His normally ruddy skin tone had taken on a grayish undertone. Somehow I'd convinced myself that Hadcho was okay, having only been lightly grazed by a bullet. One look told me that I'd underestimated how badly hurt he was. He seemed so helpless there in the bed. With a pang, I remembered that Hadcho was alone, whereas Detweiler had his family to bolster his spirits.

I gave our friend a quick peck on the forehead. "Hey, buddy. Glad to see you awake. How are you feeling?"

"Fine." His response came as a grumble. "You going to see Sarita Patel?"

"Uh-huh. In fact, I've got to head out soon, or I won't make it to the candle-lighting ceremony on time." I dragged over a plastic chair.

"Don't worry. I'll get you up to speed quickly. It's not like I know a lot about the case, but at least you won't be totally clueless." According to Hadcho, Diya was supposed to be spending the night at the home of another CALA student, her best friend, Isabella Franklin. Around eleven, the two friends snuck out of the Franklins' house. They walked a distance of approximately six blocks to the home of one Mark Jackson, a senior, whose parents were out of town. One of Mark's classmates brought over a case of beer, and Diya downed a couple. Isabella admitted that was "unusual" for her friend. Thanks to the miracle of social media, word got around quickly that Mark Jackson was "having a party."

Hadcho snickered. "I guess to this generation, it's acceptable to open your home to perfect strangers. As you might imagine, in no time at all, things were totally out of control. Not surprisingly, Isabella lost track of her friend."

A sudden pain caught him up short, and Hadcho gasped for air.

I jumped up from my chair, ready to ring for the nurse. "Can I get you anything?"

"Water, please?"

I filled a cup for him, and he continued the story. "Keith Oberlin's house is nearly a mile away from the Jacksons'. That night, Oberlin had gone to bed early. Shortly after one a.m., Oberlin was awakened by his dogs raising a ruckus. Someone was banging on the front door. Oberlin discovered a shivering Diya Patel on his doorstep."

"According to Oberlin, she had booze on her breath. Diya was disoriented and shivering, so he let her in… and this was where the story gets fuzzy."

"Fuzzy?"

"Doesn't make much sense, does it?" Hadcho frowned at me. "Why would a sixteen-year-old girl who's never been in any trouble go to a drinking party? And why wander off in the cold?"

"Hormones. Don't forget I live with a thirteen-year-old girl. Anya's emotions are riding a perpetual roller coaster. At that age, kids don't think through the consequences of their decisions. I bet the party sounded like fun at first. And then it got scary when things got out of hand. So Diya probably decided to head back to the Franklins' house. Only she wasn't sober enough to find her way in the dark. She got lost and wound up on Keith Oberlin's doorstep."

"Kiki, it was freezing cold that night. Who wanders around in the dark and the cold?"

"A teenager. Trust me on this, Hadcho. They are incapable of fearing for their lives. They think they are invincible. Look, Anya shares stories with me about stunts her classmates have pulled. It's horrifying! We can give our kids everything, but experience is something they have to accumulate for themselves. And usually, there's a cost involved."

He shook his head. "I hear you, but it just doesn't make sense. If the party was out of control, why didn't Diya call her parents and ask them to pick her up? Wouldn't you gladly go and get Anya if she needed a ride?"

"Of course I would, but that's not the point. Think it through, Hadcho. Diya couldn't call her parents because if she did, she'd get Isabella in trouble. Diya probably figured she could get herself back to the Franklins' house, and no one would be the wiser. Instead, she got turned around. It was a twist of fate that landed her on Keith Oberlin's doorstep."

"I don't believe in coincidences." Hadcho's mouth pressed into a sour line. "Or fate. Even when it's twisted like a pretzel."

"Okay, I get what you're saying, but you and I are approaching all this information logically. Kids that age aren't good at predicting the consequences of their actions. Add booze to the mix, and there's even less rational thought going on." I said my piece, and then shut up. My argument had reminded me of Sheila and her self-destructive behavior. Alcohol was a thief that robbed sentient people of their ability to foresee consequences. On the other hand, maybe that was part of the appeal.

"Maybe." He sounded mollified but not convinced.

"What's Oberlin's address?"

Hadcho rattled it off.

"It's a big house, isn't it? Tudor? I've seen it. He doesn't live far from Sheila and Robbie live. Can anyone corroborate Oberlin's story?"

"One of Oberlin's neighbors remembers hearing dogs barking around midnight."

"Look, I need to get going. Can you tell me what happened next? And make it fast?" My cell phone told me I needed to get a move on if I wanted to make it to the memorial service.

"Oberlin let her in. Diya was obviously drunk, and her clothes were soaking wet. She complained of a headache. He gave her a couple of Tylenol and agreed to let her spend the night in one of his guest bedrooms."

"He didn't call her parents?"

Hadcho shrugged. "I guess not."

That made me raise my eyebrows. "Really? You're kidding! What kind of idiot lets an underage girl he's never met stay overnight in his house?"

"Keith Oberlin isn't exactly known for being a paragon of good judgment." Hadcho's voice had an ironic edge to it.

"What did Diya have on when she was found dead? I mean, if you suspect foul play, isn't that significant?"

"When her body was found, she was wearing a pair of Keith's flannel drawstring pants and a Rams sweatshirt. Plus a pair of his socks. According to Oberlin, Diya's clothes were soaked. The techs found them in the dryer. They hadn't been washed, only dried. See, that doesn't make sense either. Who dries the clothes of a girl he plans to molest?" Hadcho scratched his head and continued with his story.

"The next morning around ten, Keith figures his guest has slept long enough. He knocks on the bedroom door, but she doesn't answer. Because he has a cup of coffee in one hand, he walks away and comes right back. He knocks again. Still no response. Now he starts to get worried. He calls out to her, but Diya doesn't respond. In a total panic, Oberlin breaks down the bedroom door."

I thought that through. "The door must have been locked from the inside."

"Right, and Kiki? We're not talking about those el-cheapo, flimsy hollow-core doors. We're talking six-panel solid wood. Oberlin's so shook up that he actually kicks the door until it pops off the hinges. Once inside, he finds her cold and unresponsive. Calls 911 immediately. When they arrive, the coffee was still warm on the kitchen table, but she isn't. Her body is cold as ice. She's dead. Long gone. And he's inconsolable."

"Horrible. Just awful," I said, shaking my head.

"You're telling me. Remember the splash it made in the papers? Sure, they didn't release her name, but the rest of the details were front and center. When you've got a rich playboy like Oberlin and a dead underage girl, you've got industrial strength fireworks. People have been phoning the police station, practically howling for this Oberlin guy's skin. That's why Robbie instructed Detweiler to work the case and keep everything quiet until he had all the facts. Sure, I've done some of the footwork, checking out details and such, but you know Detweiler. He's calm, cool, and collected."

"But he had come to a conclusion?"

"Yes. Right before Christmas, he said he had everything we needed. He wanted to walk us through the case, and let us— Robbie and me—poke holes in his reasoning. That way we'd be sure to have everything air-tight and buttoned-down."

"But he didn't get to talk to you two because Robbie had a personal crisis."

Hadcho's laugh was mirthless. "A personal crisis named Sheila. Detweiler hated that our meeting was postponed. He told me that he couldn't wait to put this case behind us. I can't blame him. The fact that Diya Patel was close to Anya's age, well, it really got to him."

CHAPTER 36

Hadcho's description of the case weighed on me. So did the time. I had just twenty minutes until the memorial service, but I couldn't leave without checking on Detweiler one more time. The light slatted through the vinyl blinds, blinking across his bedclothes. He seemed to be fine. But how many secrets did he keep from me for my own protection? What pains ailed him that I'd never know? How did his job weigh on him, press on his heart?

Tearing myself away from him seemed almost impossible. Brawny appeared in Detweiler's doorway. Some sixth sense had told her I was reluctant to leave.

"You better get going." She handed over the keys. "I cleaned the car off."

"Right. Thank you. You know how I hate that job." I started to wrap a red scarf around my throat.

Tugging the red scarf out of my hands, she replaced it with hers, a navy knit. When I looked askance, she said, "Mine is less conspicuous. Let me remind you to be careful. Look around before you get out of your car. Park as close to the entrance as you can. Stay with groups of people as much as possible. Don't be a straggler."

"Really?"

"We can't be sure who it was that the shooters were targeting. Look around you. Stay aware of the exits. If you hear anything suspicious, duck. You can always pretend to be tying a shoelace or some other nonsense," and she paused, "I am rightly worried."

The lights indicated the elevator car was one floor away. I was eager to be out of here, on my way, and being productive. "I'll be careful."

"Do you still have that pepper spray I gave you? It will drift down, so aim high. Do not extend your arm fully, because a straight arm makes it easier for an assailant to grab your hand and pull you toward him. Carry the spray with you, but make sure you have it pointed in the right direction. Don't squirt yourself accidentally. Remember what I've taught you."

At the start of the school year, Brawny had held a quickie self-defense class at our house. Originally the session was for Anya and her best friend Nicci Moore, but the girls had been so impressed that they insisted Brawny repeat it for us moms, Jennifer Moore and me. Our nanny drilled it into our heads that vigilance is paramount if you want to stay safe.

"That's not the same as being fearful," she'd said. "I'm not advocating that you run around like scared fluffy bunnies. Be aware of your surroundings at all times. That's the key."

As the elevator door dinged and creaked open, I said, "Don't forget, I'm headed for CALA. There will be security guards all over the campus. That's the way the school operates."

"But what if our gunman is disguised as a security guard?"

My heart did a flutter-step.

She was right.

I could be walking right into a trap.

CHAPTER 37

The cold hit me like a slap to the face, but the Highlander is good in bad weather. We hummed along, the car and I. All roads leading to the hospital had been cleared. I zipped right onto 40, which is what the locals call Interstate 64/Highway 40, the main east-west corridor.

There weren't any other cars around, so I took the opportunity to call my kids and see how they were doing.

Laurel answered the phone with a giggle. "We were making snow candy. Erik has sugar all over. Here, I'll put him on."

"Mama Kiki!" he shouted into the phone. "I made candy! It melted the snow. It's so good. Bye, got to go, love you!"

The phone clattered to the floor, but Anya snatched it up quickly, "Hey Mom, how's Detweiler? And Hadcho?"

I filled her in on the men's progress.

"But they're okay, now? Good. Meemaw and Pop-pop were there?" she asked, calling the Detweilers by the nicknames their granddaughter Emily had chosen for them.

"Yes, sweetie, but it was a short visit. They would have stopped by to see you, but they had to get back to Illinois to pick up Emily. Her parents are out of town, remember?"

"Yeah, I understand, it's just that I miss them, you know? And I miss Gran and Robbie, too. Where are they? I've been calling Gran all day."

"Anya, you'll have to be strong. I have bad news for you."

"Did someone shoot them?"

"Oh, no, honey!" Her response told me exactly what was on her mind. She'd come to believe her whole family was in danger. "Nothing like that."

"Well, what is it?" she sounded peevish.

"You know that Gran has been drinking too much. Well, she had a couple of black-outs. That's what happens when you consume too much alcohol in too short of a period. Robbie has decided that she needs professional help. He's taking her to a rehab clinic."

"About time."

"Anya!" I was shocked to hear her blasé response.

"It's true, Mom. I didn't want to worry you, but twice when I've been with her, she's gotten really, really drunk. So embarrassing. Once she couldn't even stand up. I had to get the doorman at the country club to help me with her. He called a cab for us. I guess Robbie went back and got her car later."

"Why didn't you tell me about this?"

"There was nothing you could do but worry. Robbie knew. I could tell he was upset. He's the one who had to figure out what to do next. We even talked about it."

"You did?" This irritated me. So Robbie was discussing Sheila's alcoholism with my thirteen-year-old daughter. What right did he have to involve Anya in such a discussion? Given all the changes in our lives, she didn't need the additional pressure of helping him decide how to treat Sheila's addiction.

"Mom, calm down," said Anya, reading my thoughts. "It wasn't like that. I told him that I was worried. We learned about alcoholism in my health class. Gran fits all the descriptors. I told Robbie I was worried about her. He sort of laughed it off, and then the next day, she and I went together to that mother-daughter tea at the club, remember? You were working at the store? So she and I went?"

"Yeah, but they didn't serve alcohol at the tea!"

"No, they didn't," said Anya, "but Gran brought her own booze. She has this silver flask, and she poured the booze right into her iced tea. I saw her. By the time they served dessert, she was slurring her words."

"Honey, I am so sorry that you had to see that."

"Why?" she asked. "It was Gran's problem. Not yours."

CHAPTER 38

Thanks to the clear streets and the empty highway, I actually arrived at CALA early. Only ten cars were in the parking lot. Finding a spot near the doors of the auditorium was easy, but the scattered mounds of snow and ice blocked a three-sixty view of my surroundings. Despite my brave assertion that the place would be crawling with security guards, only one uniformed man stood at the mouth of the building. His was a familiar face; I'd seen him at school events before.

The entry to the auditorium had been decorated with black bunting. Visitors walked past a table covered with a black damask cloth. Photos of Diya Patel were on display. She'd been a lovely young woman, dark-haired with luminous eyes that seemed wise beyond her years.

"Kiki?" I turned to see my friend, Jennifer Moore, Nicci's mother.

"Jennifer!" I gave her a hug. "I thought you were still in Aspen!"

"We got back late last night."

When we first met, I had been dismissive of Jennifer. I saw her as one of the Ladue Ladies of Leisure, women who live for their next nail appointment or their daily visits to the gym. Since then, I've come to reconsider my prejudices. As the CEO of her family business, Jennifer juggles a lot of responsibilities, and yet she's always willing to help me when I come to her with questions about my own small retail concern. Not only that, she's a terrific mother to Nicci and Stevie, and she's proven herself to be a wonderful friend.

"Guess what?" I told her excitedly. "We got married! I'm officially Mrs. Detweiler!"

"Woo-hoo!" she cheered, and then glanced around to see if anyone heard. "Oops, I guess that whoop was inappropriate given the occasion."

Looking around, I agreed. "Yeah, I guess. But wait until you hear what happened at my wedding."

I told her about the gunfire.

"You have to be kidding? Is Detweiler okay? And his friend?" She took both my hands into hers.

"They will be. It was touch and go for a while for Detweiler. They had to remove his spleen. I'm a nervous wreck. Someone's trying to kill him, Jennifer. I'm here to find out who it is."

She shook her head. "Wait a minute. Why would you come here to find someone who took a shot at Detweiler? What does poor Diya Patel have to do with all this?"

In a hushed voice, I explained that my husband had been looking into her death. "So you see, I need to know what he learned."

"Isn't that Robbie's job?"

I told her about Sheila going to rehab.

"Whoa. Your family sure knows how to cram a lot into a holiday season. Marriage, shooting, rehab. Gee. But I'm not surprised to hear about Sheila. I didn't want to worry you, not with the holidays coming and the baby on its way, but Anya called me one night when she was spending the night at her grandmother's house. She asked me to come over and help her put Sheila to bed because she'd been drinking."

"I can't believe that my daughter has been covering this up!"

"She hasn't been. We discussed it, and she planned to talk to you after the baby came. Come on, Kiki, can you blame Anya? This is like that old saying, 'How do you boil a frog? You put it in cold water and turn up the heat gradually.' See, Sheila's gotten slowly worse. Thank goodness Robbie has the guts to do something about it. You can't. Anya can't. But he can."

I shook my head in disgust—and agreement. Anya had been protecting me. I got that. But had she also been trying to take on too much responsibility? As a kid growing up in an alcoholic home, I'd often thought I could make my father quit drinking. On TV, parents would see how their addiction hurt their children and vow to never imbibe again. But in real life, that wasn't how it happened. Or if it did happen, it was a rarity.

Jennifer threw an arm around my shoulders. "Look, you've got enough to worry about without taking on Sheila. How was your holiday season at the store?"

We walked together into the auditorium. More parents were arriving. Fortunately, they left us to our private conversation.

"I only have the preliminary figures, but it sure looks like we went over our target number. Considering that I don't have my usual energy, I think we did well. That assumes, of course, that all the sales stick."

"Why wouldn't they?"

As we took two chairs in the back row, I told her about Mona Goodman's big return. "Restocking all those supplies will be a mess. I'll have to take a loss on some of them. Handling paper ruins it. The edges get tattered. I took a few of the tools out of their packaging so they'd look cute inside the basket. So they can't be sold either. Next year, I'll institute a non-return policy on custom gift baskets."

"You know why she's doing this, don't you?" Jennifer asked in a whisper.

"Not a clue."

"Because Darvin cheated on her. He's been trying to make it up to her by buying her all sorts of gifts."

"You're kidding!"

Jennifer was über-connected to the school grapevine. Because she lived in Ladue, the same town where CALA was located, she regularly bumped into other parents at the grocery store or post office.

"Would I kid you about something like that?" she asked. "Darvin has been shagging everything with two legs—and maybe a couple of creatures with four legs as well."

I frowned as she continued, "He's always been that way. Why Mona thought she could change him, I'll never know. She's turned a blind eye for years. Maybe it's gotten to the point that she can't ignore his cheating heart anymore."

"Welcome to the club," I muttered. Jennifer nodded. Her husband was a philanderer, and my late husband had been, too, so we both understood the intricate mechanism of denial. You admit to yourself only as much as you can tolerate. When the pain becomes unbearable, the seams unravel and the marriage comes apart.

"Wow," I said.

One of the school administrators walked over to the microphone, tapped it, and announced, "We're going to start in five minutes. Everyone? Please take your seats."

CHAPTER 39

Because CALA's headmaster was on family vacation in Switzerland, Karen Myers, Dean of the Upper School, took his place. Karen is a no-nonsense sort of woman, and her approach to the ceremony was completely in keeping with her reputation. Promptly at the appointed hour, she approached the podium. After welcoming us, she quickly stepped aside to let others take over.

Thank goodness Jennifer had two packages of tissues in her purse, because we were both quickly reduced to tears. Mrs. Amore, Diya's advisor, spoke of a compassionate young scholar who would be sorely missed.

Mr. Punicello, a world religions teacher, explained that Diya had a keen interest in all religions, as well as a desire to teach her fellow students about her own Hindu beliefs. Toward that end, she had brought in statues of the various gods and goddesses, as well as samples of food. "She opened a new world to her friends."

Mrs. Atwell, an English teacher, spoke of Diya's love for literature. "That child read more than any student I've ever had, and she was eager to discuss each new book with me. I learned to gobble down my lunch on Wednesdays, because Diya would arrive early for class with a book in hand that she just had to talk about."

All the speakers described a young woman who left an indelible impression on those whose lives she'd touched. Their comments moved all of us to tears. But what use was it to cry? We couldn't bring the girl back. And yet, I tried to imagine that we were watering the flowers around Diya's grave.

With trembling hands, Isabella Franklin unfolded a sheet of lined notebook paper. She tried to read her thoughts about Diya, but the poor child broke down and had to be rescued by her father. Mr. Franklin finished his daughter's thoughts, explaining, "Diya was like a second daughter to us. We will miss her terribly."

Finally, Sanjay Patel took the podium. He gripped the lectern with both hands to steady himself. "Diya means 'light,' and we have lost the light of our lives. Now it is up to each of you to bring that light back into the world."

Ushers first passed out unlit candles, and then returned to share their flames. The overhead lights were dimmed. The air in the auditorium thickened with the pungent smell of wax.

"We would like to close by sharing our daughter's favorite music," said Sanjay. "The constant tone you hear in Indian music is called a drone. Some say it is the home to which all wanderers return. I prefer to think of it as the pulse of creation, the force that holds the material world together—which seems only fitting since our world has fallen apart."

When the sitar note faded away, we snuffed out our candles, one by one.

A fitting reminder of a life cut short.

As we got to our feet, Jennifer turned to me. "Wow. I haven't cried that hard in a long time. Look at you. You're all red-eyed, too. I bet your hormones are on high alert."

"You've got that right."

"Let me introduce you to Sarita. She and I have served together on a couple of school committees." Jennifer and I joined a line of people waiting to offer their condolences. As other parents mumbled words of sympathy, I had the chance to study Diya's parents. I knew that Sanjay was a researcher at Washington University. As I recalled, he was heavily involved in studies about the human genome. The man looked like a scientist. Several times during the ceremony, he had adjusted his wire-rimmed glasses, as he fought to control his grief. Everything about him seemed precise and measured. Sarita was similarly restrained in her movements. Her long dark hair was twisted back so tightly, the knot at her neck looked painful.

A memory book had been set up on a second table near the one with the large photo of Diya. Parents and students paused there to write notes of comfort to the family. An easel propped up an enlarged version of an essay Diya had written. Photocopies were available, so I grabbed one to read while Jennifer and I waited our turn.

<< >>

A Life Well Lived
By Diya Patel

My grandfather died last week at the age of eighty-two. He had seven children, including my father, who was the youngest. Because he lived in Goa, India, I didn't get the chance to spend a lot of time with him, but when I did, Grandfather tried to want to pack my head full of wisdom. Here are some of the things he taught me:

* *When you ride the back of the crocodile, you can expect to get bitten.* Grandfather said that if you indulge in dangerous activities, you'll get hurt. Even if you think you're safe, you probably aren't. He warned me to be especially careful when everyone is telling me that there's no problem. There probably is!

**Divinity lives in all creatures, not only in humanity.* These are the words of a famous Indian dancer, but Grandfather repeated them all the time. To hurt any living creature is an affront to all creatures. This is why I don't eat meat.

* *A nation's art and monuments reflect the soul of its culture.* When I visited Washington, DC, it made me sad to see how many monuments were built to honor soldiers. This is not to say that I don't believe they made the ultimate sacrifice. However, I think we, as a nation, put too much emphasis on war and not enough on those who have striven for peace, such as Martin

Luther King.

   * *Self-criticism is a virtue.* By examining ourselves and our actions on a daily basis, we can improve. Although it is difficult to look at our mistakes, they can teach us lessons so we can correct ourselves and grow.

   There are many more lessons that I have learned from my Grandfather. I think that all young people should spend time with their elders, as they will benefit from the wisdom of older family members.

   << >>

   "What a smart young lady." I sighed, thinking about the potential that had been lost.

   "Yes, but notice when that was written. See the date? Diya would have been thirteen at the time. When she turned fourteen, she changed. Sarita was beside herself with worry. Or maybe it was just a mother's intuition."

   "Hormones?"

   "Hmmm." Jennifer tapped her lips with the tip of an index finger. "Possibly. I think it was more than that. The change came shortly after Diya had her appendix out. She went from sunny to sullen. Sarita and Sanjay were at their wits' end. Sarita joked that their daughter needed an appendix transplant. To hear her tell it, that missing organ was the key. She knew better, of course, but Diya was giving her fits."

   I had to choose my words carefully so I didn't give away what I'd learned from Hadcho. "Hmmm. Anya always talked about how straight-laced Diya was. What you're telling me is so confusing. Especially since I heard that she died after going to a party. And she'd been drinking."

   "Uh-huh. That was evidently her first and last experience as a party animal. No, she changed before that. At home. Diya started giving her parents a big dose of attitude. For example, she refused to accompany them to family events, like her brothers' piano recitals. She became angry. Withdrawn. Sarita was very worried."

It sounded to me like Hadcho and Detweiler had only gotten a partial picture of Diya Patel. Her parents had wanted to protect their daughter's memory. I couldn't blame them; that was all they had left of her.

CHAPTER 40

Sarita and Sanjay stood ramrod straight, their nearness suggesting that they were drawing strength from each other. He was a handsome man, with hair as black as the wings of a crow. Behind his spectacles, his eyes glowed with intensity and intelligence.

Sarita's oval face framed limpid brown eyes, perfectly shaped brows and a noble nose. She attempted a smile of gratitude as guests offered condolences.

When our turn came, Jennifer introduced me as, "Kiki Lowenstein," and then caught herself. "But now she's Kiki Lowenstein-Detweiler. She and Detective Chad Detweiler got married just this weekend."

The Patels' expressions changed from politely interested to surprised.

"You are married to Detective Detweiler? Of the St. Louis County Police?" Sanjay asked.

"Yes. Look, I know that my husband and his partner Detective Stan Hadcho would have wanted to be here today. But unfortunately, they are both in the hospital."

"Oh, no," Sarita moaned. "Was it a car accident? The roads are still slick."

"A shooting." I kept my voice as even as I could, because I wanted to see their reactions.

"Are you kidding?" Sanjay stepped closer to me. Anger flared in his brown eyes. "A vigilante?"

"We don't know."

Sarita spoke breathlessly, "But they'll be all right?"

"I hope so."

"Thank goodness." She touched a tissue to her eyes. "Detective Detweiler warned us. We saw the letters to the editor. We realized there might be danger, but even so..."

Feet shuffled behind me. The line was growing, and I was holding it up.

"Please accept my condolences and their sympathies as well," I said. "Anya is my daughter, and she was also saddened to hear about Diya."

I leaned in to give Sarita a quick hug and whispered in her ear, "I need to talk to you." Her skin was fragrant with an exotic blend of patchouli and roses.

"Afterward," she whispered back. "Promise you will stay!"

"Of course. If I can."

But the crowd didn't cooperate. I waited for fifteen minutes, checking my cell phone frequently. Finally, I told Jennifer that I couldn't wait any longer. I was nervous about how Detweiler was doing. Outside the sky had grown dark with clouds as pregnant as I was.

"Oh, boy. Looks like more wet stuff on the way." I pointed at the windows and elbowed Jennifer. "I really need to get back to the hospital."

"Look, I've got to get going, too. I'm parked on the other side of the building. Give me a hug and push your way to the front of the crowd."

I hated being rude, but I didn't have a choice. I murmured, "Excuse me," over and over until I could reach out and grasp Sarita by the hand. Pressing my face next to her, I whispered, "Is my husband in any danger? I need to know."

"No. Not from anyone that we know of. And I would tell you if I knew differently. Your husband has been very kind to me." Dropping her voice to a whisper she added, "Tomorrow, okay?"

I gave her hand one last squeeze and said goodbye.

As I turned to walk away, I felt Sanjay's eyes drilling holes in my back.

CHAPTER 41

Sure enough, the weather forecasters had it wrong. The precipitation scheduled for after midnight began at half past nine. Out in the CALA parking lot, sleet smacked me in the face, tiny stinging blows. The predicted rain had frozen into tiny spitballs of ice. I tried to heed Brawny's warning to look around and pay attention to my surroundings, but I couldn't because my eyes were watering so badly.

When I got to the car, the door didn't want to open. I cursed my luck. I'd managed to park so that the driver's side was taking the brunt of the oncoming sleet. If I had parked facing the other way, I would have been fine.

As it was, I tugged and tugged on the door. Bracing one foot against the frame, I grabbed the handle with both hands. The wind whipped around me, blowing Brawny's scarf into my open mouth. She would have had a cow, watching me, there in middle of the parking lot, totally exposed. It was an epic match: Kiki versus the car. I glanced up to see the security guard trotting toward me.

"Frozen?" he asked.

"I think so." My teeth started chattering.

He gave it a mighty yank and it popped open.

The baby kicked me twice, as if to say he was fine.

"Thanks," I said, sliding past him to climb in. Now the door mechanism refused to lock, so there I sat, a perfect target—except that no one could see into the car because the windows were iced over. There was nothing to do but turn over the engine and hope the Highlander heated up quickly. I reminded myself that Toyotas are known for their great heaters. Sure enough, the vents dumped hot air on me in minutes. The tiny ice balls in my hair melted so fast, I was dripping cold water. The only remedy was to shake myself the way a dog does. Yes, I was wet, but I was also sitting in a sauna, thanks to the over-active heating system.

An old Mercedes drove past. I tried to hide by slumping down, as far as my burgeoning belly would let me. After watching the clock on my cell phone tick off two minutes, I cautiously poked my head up and looked around. My heart was racing.

All clear.

Cracks had formed in the ice on the windshield. I opened my door and stepped out with an ice-scraper in my hands. My leather gloves gave my fingers scant protection as I chipped away at the glassy sheet. Slivers of ice slid down into my sleeves. My feet were freezing, but I managed to clean off small patches. There wasn't enough clarity to drive, but at least the thawing could now start in earnest.

I got back behind the wheel and shivered. A vehicle pulled in at the far side of the lot. It was a big white SUV, and it was pointed right at me. Could this be an attempt to ram my car?

"No, no, no," I whimpered.

To my great relief, the SUV swung wide, circled, and drove back out.

A tear leaked down my face. "I can't live like this." I spoke to no one in particular, and to the Universe in general. But hearing the words gave me a renewed sense of purpose. Somehow, some way, I would track down that second gunman. I had to.

Otherwise I was going to be a nervous wreck.

Thirty minutes later, I pulled out of the CALA lot. I couldn't tell if anyone was following me. Between the sleet and the dark, I could barely find the edges of the pavement. Things were a little better on the highway, but not much.

As I entered the hospital parking lot, a salt truck passed by, spewing its gritty mix. With added traction under foot, I hustled my way into the building. But I quickly walked past the grit and back into icy slush. Sleet was blowing right into my face. The needle-like shards of ice made it impossible to keep my eyes open.

Walking blindly, I tucked my head down and hurled myself at the hospital entrance. Diya's memorial service had drained me emotionally. Fighting the ice had tired me physically. I could barely put one foot in front of the other, but I had no choice in the matter. If I wanted to rest and be safe, I had to keep moving.

Lifting my gaze, I measured the distance to the entrance and said out loud, "Buck up, babe. You can do this." The pavement changed to concrete. The awning overhead offered a bit of shelter. When the sensor detected me, the sliding glass doors opened. A rush of warm air greeted me. I moved forward, blinking blurrily—and ramming right into Prescott Gallaway.

CHAPTER 42

"Well, if it isn't Kiki Lowenstein, ace detective." Prescott's comb-over looked as if it had been laboriously glued to his scalp. His skinny upper lip was lifted in a sneer. Both eyes were crusted with eye-winkies. In short, there was nothing attractive about this man.

"Actually, it isn't Kiki Lowenstein."

The soles of my shoes had picked up ice as I'd trudged through the parking lot. My feet were so slick that I could have been wearing roller skates. Rather than fall over, I grabbed at a nearby stanchion to recover my balance.

"You okay?" An orderly noticed my struggle and raced over to help. He walked me to an indoor-outdoor floor mat. I thanked the helper and turned my attention back to Prescott, who hadn't moved an inch to offer me assistance.

"For the record, my name is now Kiki Lowenstein-Detweiler," I said. "Detective Chad Detweiler and I have gotten married."

Prescott covered his mouth and snickered. "Right. A real shotgun wedding, wasn't it? And not a moment too soon. At least this baby will have his father's name."

I hate Prescott. He's mean, nasty, and ugly. Not necessarily in that order. You have to see him to believe him. If Ichabod Crane came to life, you'd be staring at Prescott. The man's built like a bamboo skewer, except for a huge, hook-like nose that juts out of a chin-less face. Of course, I'm not being entirely fair to Ichabod. He was a teacher, a learned man, and Prescott is a dope, a real ignorant twit. Why Robbie ever helped him get promoted is beyond me, because Prescott doesn't deserve to be a member of the county law enforcement team.

His snide comment that my child would have Detweiler's name is the sort of remark that Prescott makes all too often.

Ironic, really, because I've seen photos of Nadine Gallaway, Robbie's first wife, and I find it hard to believe that Prescott and Nadine had the same set of parents. In fact, I once mentioned as much to Sheila, and she smirked. "Who says they did? I don't believe that for a minute, do you? Nadine looks like her father, but Prescott looks exactly like Presley Gallitano, who was the alderman for that district. I've seen the photos. And then there's the matter of his name, Prescott-Presley, see?"

Yes, I did see.

But unlike Prescott, I don't stoop to innuendo, so I bit my lip rather than sink to his level.

"Good thing I ran into you, Mrs. Detweiler. Now I can inform you personally that I'm calling off the guard outside your husband's room."

"You can't leave them without protection. Come on, Prescott."

"That's Lieutenant Captain Gallaway to you." He pursed his lips in a prissy way.

In my heart of hearts, I had hoped that Prescott would put department morale above his petty quarrels with Detweiler and Hadcho. Police look out after their own. They have to. Otherwise, how could their families handle the stress and heartache? How could they put their lives on the line, day after day? But Prescott had an agenda. Fairness wasn't in his playbook.

"The shooting in Webster Groves was obviously a family matter," he said, lifting his upper lip like a dog does to snarl. "It's not a department concern, and we don't have the budget for shenanigans like this."

"Family matter?" I heard myself screech. "You don't have any proof that this is a family matter. Shouldn't you at least wait until there's been an investigation?"

"There won't be one," he said, with a feigned yawn of boredom. "I talked to the Webster Groves police chief. As you know, we often assist the smaller municipalities with their crime lab reports. I personally looked at the bullet trajectories, and being the expert I am, I can tell you that there was only one shooter. That weird babysitter of yours brought him down with her knife. There will be an investigation, but it looks like self-defense."

Prescott? An expert? I stifled the urge to roll my eyes. "You might have looked at the trajectories, but you've got bad information. I was there, remember? A second man attacked me in the shed."

"That's your story, and we all know you're an attention-seeker."

"Talk to Detweiler! To Hadcho!"

"Unfortunately, both of them are indisposed right now."

"Lorraine Lauber and Leighton Haversham saw the second gunman, too. He came into the shed and threatened me and the kids. He had a gun!"

"I don't doubt that. There are all sorts of reasons for someone to want to shoot you, Mrs. Lowenstein-Detweiler. I personally can come up with at least a dozen. None of those are my concern. You're obviously a cop-wannabe with an inflated sense of self-importance."

His cool demeanor had me rattled. Prescott seemed incapable of taking into account any information that didn't mesh with his agenda. I tried another tactic. I appealed to his sense of importance by begging.

"Please don't do this. It isn't about me. It's about your men. Detweiler almost didn't make it. Hadcho was wounded. What if the gunman who attacked me comes back? He might finish what he started."

"There's ample security here at the hospital. Besides, you love playing cops and robbers, don't you? As I recall, you shot a man in cold blood. So if your honey in there is in danger, then you better get your big backside in gear and protect him, right?"

CHAPTER 43

"I hate that man," I said, as I threw my purse down next to Brawny. She was sitting outside of Hadcho and Detweiler's rooms, taking over for the guard who had been stationed there previously. I continued to kvetch, "Prescott Gallaway is worse than useless. He's a menace. How on earth Robbie could have helped him get promoted is beyond me! He sits behind a desk and sends other people to do dangerous work, but does he care about their safety? Not one bit!"

"Don't worry. I have it covered." Brawny's hands were tightened into fists.

"What do you mean? Are you planning to stay here around the clock? I hope not because we need to figure out who's really behind all this. You said so yourself."

"Hadcho and I discussed the matter. He's given me a list of officers he thinks would be willing to come and guard Detective Detweiler."

"But who will pay them?" I felt like I was falling apart. All the emotion I'd suppressed during the service for Diya, all the disappointment that Sarita couldn't talk to me, all the frustration of dealing with the bad weather, and all the anger I felt at Prescott was taking me down.

Brawny shrugged. "I'm betting they'll work for free, but if not, Lorraine will handle the bill."

I groaned. "She can't keep whipping out her checkbook every time I have a problem."

"Sure she can." Brawny smiled at me. "Kiki, she's richer than you can imagine, and she doesn't have anything to spend her money on, so why not? It makes her happy to help. Lieutenant Captain Gallaway was up here, acting all humpy. I heard him telling the man on duty to go on home. Taking liberties, I asked what he was doing, and he explained that the department budget didn't include personal bodyguards."

"That man is an idiot." I stomped my foot.

"*Aye,* he is. Just as soon as he stepped into the lift, I phoned Lorraine. She didn't hesitate. Believe me, the money doesn't mean anything to her. She'd be more than happy to die with empty pockets. Remember, she was there, too. One of those bullets could have hit her. She certainly understands the gravity of the situation, even if Prescott Gallaway doesn't. Come on. Let's sit down. You look all knackered."

I like that word: *knackered.* It's British slang, not a Scot's term, but it sounds exactly like what it means to convey. I was, indeed, knackered. Tired beyond all reason.

Sure, I could whine and carry on about Lorraine's open checkbook policy, but in my heart, I knew that Brawny was right. A few inches to the left, and Lorraine would have taken a bullet to the chest.

If Leighton hadn't reacted quickly by grabbing her and tossing her off the gazebo, she might be the person in one of those hospital rooms.

"You don't think the shooters were after Lorraine, do you?" The thought horrified me. I sank down next to Brawny on the tired family lounge sofa. The cushions sagged from the weight of so many people fearing the worst.

"I am keeping an open mind. I don't have enough information to make a properly informed judgment." Brawny sounded thoughtful. "In times like this, I've found it useful to keep putting one brogue in front of another. To deal with problems as they come up, all the while keeping an eye on the goal."

"I hate it that Lorraine is involved."

"*Aye,* but she was involved even before the shot rang out. She considers herself part of your family, or hadn't you noticed? Remember," said Brawny, squeezing my arm. "There's Erik to think about, too."

Erik was as close to a son or grandson as Lorraine would ever get. She adored the boy. If he hadn't been hopping up and down, he could have been hit. And of course, if anything happened to Detweiler, the child would be devastated.

"I guess it's her money to do with as she pleases," I said. "I will need to thank her. At this rate, I owe her about a zillion thank-you notes. Or a million loaves of that banana nut bread she likes so much."

To that, Brawny smiled. "You've already done plenty for her. You've welcomed her into your lives."

CHAPTER 44

After I looked in on Detweiler, I returned to the family lounge. Its poverty had begun to wear on me. All the seat cushions had been pressed flat by legions of buttocks. The coffee table's surface bubbled with memories of hot drinks. The magazines were old. Their dog-eared corners I could take, but the missing pages really irked me.

I wanted to go home. I wanted to begin my life as Chad Detweiler's bride.

"We're on our own here," I said to Brawny. "Prescott isn't going to help us figure out who did this. The Webster Groves police may or may not give the case a high priority. Robbie isn't here to put this on the top of the department's must-solve list. But that doesn't mean we can let it go. There's too much at risk."

Brawny nodded, making her ponytail bob up and down. "I know. Hadcho and I spoke for a minute. His assessment agrees with yours. We can't let this slide. For all we know, the gunman might have infiltrated the staff here."

I hadn't thought of that—and I wished she hadn't mentioned it. Now I was scared. *Really* scared.

"Could someone have been aiming at Lorraine?" All this talk about her wealth had gotten me thinking. "Are there people who would benefit from her death?"

Brawny's jaw tightened. "I'm not at liberty to discuss her finances. However, I can tell you she's made a variety of provisions that will benefit certain organizations. Other than Detweiler's investigation into the death of that young girl, has he stirred up any other hornets' nests?"

"Hadcho might know."

"He told me he couldn't think of anything. Of course, they've worked together to put away a number of miscreants, and any of those might be out for revenge. In the morning, he'll call around to see if any have been let out of jail recently."

I slipped off my boots and put my stocking feet up on the sofa. From down the hall came the smell of popcorn. That wasn't surprising. I'd spent enough time in hospitals to know that the nursing staff practically lived on popcorn. "Okay, let's think in broad terms. Here's an idea: There's always the possibility that this has to do with Erik's biological father. He was investigating his fellow officers in Illinois when he was killed. I don't know anything more than that about the situation, but I suppose it's possible."

She nodded. "Someone on the police force in Illinois might think that Gina left information about the investigation in her will."

"But that doesn't make sense. Why now? Erik has been living with us since August. Besides, why would Gina leave information like that in her will? If she really had concerns, she could have talked to the Illinois authorities before this."

"You're right," said Brawny.

"It could also be a case from Hadcho's past. He grew up in Oklahoma. I don't know if he worked on the police force there. He's been in and out of Detweiler's life. First he and Detweiler were partners, then they were reassigned to other officers, and now they're back working together. We don't have access to everything that Hadcho has investigated."

"Or that you stumbled into," said Brawny. "Margit and Laurel are always talking about the way you've helped your customers. You have a knack for solving crimes and zeroing in on culprits. Maybe someone blames you for something that didn't go right?"

I couldn't think of anyone in particular. As I turned names and faces over in my mind, I had a thought, one that had been bugging me since the shooting occurred. "Brawny, who would have known we'd be out in the yard that morning? Think about it.

From when I decided to have the ceremony to the actual event, we spent about forty-eight hours, right? So who could have known we'd be out there in the open and distracted enough to be easy targets?"

She pondered this. "Who did you invite?"

"My staff, of course. Clancy, Laurel, Joe, Margit, Rebekkah Goldfader, and her father, Horace. Then there's Rabbi Sarah, my sisters, and mother. Detweiler's parents. His whole family."

"Any one of those people might have spoken to someone else," she said.

That made sense, although it didn't make me happy. "What other avenues do we need to pursue? Prescott isn't convinced that second shooter even exists, but we know better. I saw him. The kids saw him. Detweiler and Hadcho were chasing him. Did you see him?"

"*Aye,* but I didn't get a good look at his face. I was pre-occupied while aiming at the first shooter, the man I neutralized."

"How about Leighton and Lorraine?"

"They wouldn't have seen him. Lorraine was fumbling with the prayer book and her walker. Leighton was helping her."

Outside, a car spun its wheels, trying to get traction on the frozen sleet. The sound typified futility. We were like those tires, making endless circles, going nowhere fast. Instead of narrowing down the list of suspects, we'd broadened it considerably.

"It's bad outside." Brawny craned her neck to see out the window. "The weatherman predicted more of this overnight. But it's supposed to warm up tomorrow afternoon. Enough that the ice and snow should melt. I plan to go back to the house and do a search of the grounds. Perhaps there's something the crime scene people missed."

"But Hadcho and Detweiler…?" I started to whine about their safety.

"Officer Whooli will be here tomorrow morning. He'll take a shift. He volunteered to organize other men and women for me.

How did your memorial service go?"

I summarized the event for Brawny. "Jennifer Moore told me that Diya's personality changed after having her appendix removed. Odd, isn't it? I wish I could have talked privately with Sarita Patel."

"You did your best. You look all done-in. Why not get a little sleep?"

It didn't take much coaxing from her; I could barely keep my eyes open.

Grabbing a fresh cotton blanket from the supply closet, I headed to the recliner in Detweiler's room. Shaking out the worn coverlet, I climbed into the chair and tipped it back. In that position, I stared up at the ceiling—and smiled.

Someone had glued florescent stars to the hospital room ceiling. They spelled out a simple message: *God Bless You.*

CHAPTER 45

The next morning, I woke up before Detweiler did, took a quick shower in his bathroom, and stepped out fully dressed.

"Hello, love," he said.

I nearly squealed with joy. "You must be feeling better."

"Not really. I'm not as groggy. I sort of feel worse because some of the pain meds have worn off."

"Consider that a message from your body. The solid yellow caution flag is being flown. No hopping up and running around." I leaned over and kissed him just as a new nurse appeared. She helped him out of bed and into the john. At first, he was a bit wobbly, but Belinda reminded him that he'd lost a lot of blood, and that standing up caused everything to flow away from his brain.

After he was back in bed, he asked, "How're the kids and Hadcho?"

I told him that I'd Skyped the children, and that they were having a blast with Laurel and Joe.

"In fact, your detective friend hopes to be discharged this afternoon," the nurse told us. "It's a little quick, if you ask me, but he's insistent."

"Probably can't stand this ugly hospital attire," said Detweiler, plucking at his own gown.

I grinned because my husband was back to his old self.

After the nurse left, I told Detweiler what I'd learned about Sheila and Robbie.

"I had a feeling she was getting worse. Robbie wouldn't talk about her. Not even mention her in passing. He'd change the subject straight away. That got me thinking that something was up."

I took his hand. "I talked to Jennifer Moore. She told me that

Anya had called her some time ago and asked for help with getting Sheila to bed. Did Anya tell you about that, because I had no idea?"

"No, but it doesn't surprise me. Anya's at the age where she wants to feel capable. She probably didn't want to worry you, especially with the baby coming, so she tried to act like an adult. We're lucky that she feels close enough to Jennifer that she could pick up the phone and call for help."

From there, I eased into the subject of his safety. "Brawny and I can't figure out who's out there gunning for us. She's tracked the dead guy down to Alabama. A hired assassin. Prescott refuses to believe we're at risk. He suggested I was making it up about there being a second shooter.

"Of course there were two shooters. That's a given. Prescott is trying to punish Hadcho and me because we won't play his games."

"Even so, that puts us all at risk, doesn't it?" I perched on the edge of his mattress. "Brawny and I have been trying to figure out who paid the shooter. Could have any connection with Diya Patel's death?"

"No." His answer was terse.

"Are you sure?"

"I said no, and I meant it." His tone surprised me. I bit the inside of my cheek rather than burst into tears. Detweiler is never abrupt with me. We'd only been married, what? Two and a half days? And he'd changed?

Taking his hand from mine, he rubbed his temples. "Look, my head is pounding. Could you call the nurse?"

I did. We waited for her.

A cart rattled in the hall, and I smelled food. Specifically, the smoky scent of bacon caused my mouth to water.

"Maybe your head is hurting because you're hungry. I am."

Belinda the Nurse walked in. Like every care practitioner, she looked harried but alert.

Detweiler waved me away. "I'm fine. You go eat."

That caused me to gasp. Never has he spoken like that. The nurse looked from him to me and back to him. "On a scale of one to ten, how's your pain?"

Detweiler mumbled, "Eight."

"Going without pain meds isn't going to speed the healing process. But it will help you run off everyone who loves you. Starting with that very pregnant lady over there."

Detweiler couldn't meet my gaze. "I don't want to get addicted to pain meds."

"You won't. But suffering isn't the answer." With that, Belinda fiddled with the button on his IV. "Don't try to tough this out. Pain is a stressor."

Seeing that he was in good hands, I said, "I'm going down to get breakfast. Brawny is out there in the hall, if you need her. Knowing her, she's already eaten. Harry Whooli is on his way."

"I'll be fine." He waved me away. But he followed that with a soft, "Sorry, Kiki. I know I'm being a grouch."

"It's okay." I hurried away before my emotions got the better of me. On my way out, I passed a volunteer delivering Detweiler's breakfast.

"How is he?" Brawny met me in the hall.

"Much better. Lucid. Talkative. Irritable. Having his breakfast."

"Whooli has been diverted by Prescott." Her eyes were hooded with concern. "Even though it's his day off, he was called in. What a lot of baloney. But Whooli's sending other officers. Prescott might have stopped Whooli from appearing in person, but he can't stop the entire department from helping out."

"It never ends, does it? Have you eaten?"

She nodded yes. "You should go get your breakfast while the detective eats. I saw them take the tray into his room. By the way, I talked to Laurel earlier. The kids are fine. They watched movies last night. Ate popcorn and had a grand time."

"That's great. Be right back." I went downstairs to the cafeteria, where I had a quick bowl of cereal and a cup of coffee. After grabbing an apple for later, I took the elevator back upstairs.

"I just checked. The detective has fallen asleep," said Brawny. *"Aye,* and that's good news because his body needs all the rest it can get. He's weak as a day-old kitten."

The *ding* of the elevator door interrupted her. We turned and watched as its passenger stepped out.

Her head was wrapped in a pashmina shawl so that only her reddened eyes showed, but I knew her instantly. It was Sarita Patel.

"Mrs. Detweiler," she said quietly, lowering the aqua fabric so I could see her long dark hair. In a pair of tailored black slacks and a matching cashmere turtleneck, she managed to be both stylish and appropriately grieving. As she pulled off leather gloves, she asked, "Is this a good time for us to talk?"

"Sure." After introducing her to Brawny, I gestured toward the chairs and sofa. "There's no one in the family lounge. Let's go sit down."

"How is the detective?"

As we headed for the lounge, the uniformed officer passed us on his way to the men's room. I didn't recognize him, but I appreciated his presence.

"Stop!" Brawny yelled.

I thought she was shouting to the cop. Maybe warning him not to leave his post.

"Freeze!"

Sarita and I turned around to see what was happening.

A man was standing in the middle of the hall. He wore a long coat and a black fedora pulled down low. My heart raced as I realized that he had come up via the stairway at the end of the hall. There the intruder stood, less than ten feet from Detweiler's door, with his back to us.

"Put your hands in the air!" Brawny snarled.

Out of the corner of my eyes, I saw that the uniformed guard had cancelled his visit to restroom. Cautiously, he drew his service pistol. With the gun in two hands, he advanced on the intruder. "Hands up! Do it now!"

Slowly, the visitor raised a pair of black leather gloves.

"No, please," whimpered Sarita.

"Do you know him?" I asked her, as Brawny shoved the intruder into a wall and jerked one of his arms up behind his back.

Sarita grabbed at me. "Please don't hurt him!"

Was this an armed assassin?

My mind reeled in confusion.

Why was Sarita so worried for his safety? I couldn't see the man's eyes, so I couldn't tell if he was defiant, surprised, or afraid. The tableau was frightening. A drawn gun, an intruder in black, and my helpless husband. Not to mention that Hadcho was also unprepared for another attack.

The intruder shoved one of his hands deep into his coat pocket.

"Brawny! Stop him!" I screamed. "He's going for a gun!"

With a quick sweep of her leg, she brought the interloper down, face first. He hit the tile floor with a loud smack. The young police officer raced over to help, while fumbling with his handcuffs. In short order, he snapped them around the man's wrists.

"Ow," yelled the man in black. "Get off me! Stop it!"

His hat popped off his head and rolled away, like a wheel broken off a kid's Radio Flyer wagon.

"No, no, no," moaned Sarita. "I warned him!"

With one hand, Brawny hauled the cuffed visitor to his feet. His face was bloated, his eyes were red, and his complexion was pale.

Sarita ran to his side. "Keith? Are you okay?"

CHAPTER 46

"Keith?" I repeated. I was trying to wrap my head around what had just happened, but I couldn't. Not quite. "Keith Oberlin?"

"That's me. I was trying to show you my ID. I've got my driver's license in my pocket if anyone cares to see it."

While the cop frisked the visitor, Brawny fished around in his coat and brought out a wallet. Flipping through, she flashed us a laminated Missouri driver's license. "He is who he says he is."

The young officer said, "No weapon. But better safe than sorry."

"Keith? This is Mrs. Detweiler." Sarita pointed at me.

"I'd shake your hand, but..." He gave a mirthless laugh and displayed the handcuffs.

I took a deep breath. "I thought you were going for a gun."

"No, just a pack of gum."

"My bad. I'm jumpy. I apologize. I'm Kiki Lowenstein-Detweiler." I stuck out my hand, right as the young officer unsnapped Oberlin's handcuffs.

"It's been that kind of week." Keith Oberlin must have been a handsome man, years ago, but right now he looked horrible. His eyes were puffy. The tip of his nose was raw, as though it had been wiped repeatedly. He needed a shave. Obviously he'd hit a rough patch that had aged him emotionally.

"Why are you here?" Now that the crisis was over, I felt bold—and angry. How long would my husband be at risk? Would I always feel so frightened?

"I came because Sarita asked me to. She told me about Detective Detweiler getting shot. My lawyer called down to the police station to get details. He found out that Robbie Holmes has left town. That idiot Prescott Gallaway knows nothing about..." and he paused. To my shock, his voice broke and he sniffed back tears. "Knows nothing about anything. So Sarita called Jennifer Moore. To get the straight scoop. Because you two showed up last night. Together."

"Let's go sit down."

In the family lounge, Sarita sat ramrod straight on the edge of a chair, while Keith huddled as though he hoped to disappear. She began by saying, "I know Jennifer, so I thought it best to start with her. She explained that you were worried that the shooting might be connected to my daughter's death. I talked it over with Keith. We felt that we owed it to Detective Detweiler to clear this up."

Brawny and I exchanged looks. I was totally confused. So was she.

"This is our friend Bronwyn Macavity. She has a background in law enforcement."

That was true enough, and I sure wasn't about to introduce her as my nanny.

Brawny shook everyone's hands and took orders for hot drinks, as we arranged ourselves around the coffee table. Keith rubbed his wrists.

"Are you okay?" asked Sarita.

He gave her a weak smile. "I'm getting used to the way handcuffs feel."

"Oh." She shook her head sadly. "How is the detective?"

"Better, but very weak. We almost lost him." For the next few minutes, she and I exchanged small talk, mainly about CALA. Keith didn't say a word. Brawny brought back two coffees and two teas. After producing creamer and sweeteners from her sporran, she raised a questioning eyebrow toward me. I signaled her to take a seat as I set about explaining our concerns.

"Detective Detweiler and I got married two days ago. We decided on an outside wedding in the gazebo on our property. Two gunmen appeared out of nowhere. Detective Stan Hadcho was shot, as was Detweiler. One of the shooters was brought down by Brawny. She's had extensive training in personal protection."

That was the understatement of the year, but it served our purposes, so I continued my explanation.

"Since Robbie is out of town, and the incident happened in Webster Groves, I'm concerned about the authorities finding out who did it. I'm not sure whether they have the full story or the resources. Or the will to follow up. While brainstorming possible motives, I learned that Detweiler was working up a report on the death of Diya Patel. That led me to wonder if someone out there was enacting vigilante justice. As you are well aware, there are members of the public who think Detweiler is taking too long to investigate. We also wondered if there was some other connection. Some other reason someone decided to use us for target practice. One that you might be aware of."

I shut up. I'd said my piece.

Keith reached across the table and took Sarita's hand. He was sitting at right angles to her, so the gesture was out in the open, unhidden. She lifted sad eyes to him and nodded. "You tell them. I can't bear it."

He took a shuddering breath. "Diya was my daughter."

CHAPTER 47

I felt my mouth fall open. I nearly did a cartoonish double-take.

Brawny's face was inscrutable, but Sarita looked at Keith with great tenderness. That's when I realized I'd heard him right.

"Keith and I fell in love in high school. As you might imagine, our parents were not pleased with our relationship," said Sarita.

"My parents were livid," said Keith. "They called Sarita every racist name in the book and even held back their yearly gift to CALA, suggesting that it was the school's fault for allowing 'non-whites'—and those were their exact words—to attend."

"My mother and father are old-school Indian. They had already chosen a husband for me, someone with a similar background. Sanjay Patel. I met Sanjay and liked him. I couldn't see any future for us, Keith and me, so I did as my parents wanted," explained Sarita.

"The week before the wedding, we met for one last time," Keith said.

Sarita nodded, sending Keith a sad smile. "I didn't know it but I was pregnant when I married Sanjay. I thought I was vomiting because of nerves."

"We went on with our lives. I honored her marriage, although I've never met another woman like Sarita," said Keith. "Sure, the press calls me a playboy. Everyone thinks I'm having a terrific time as a single guy. But the reality is that I can't have the only woman I'll ever love."

"Sanjay has been a wonderful father to Diya. We have two other children at home and a good marriage. Sanjay and I share so much! We think alike. We were both raised Hindu. Our families mesh well together. It would never have worked out for Keith and me. I knew that from the beginning." With a shake of her head, she concluded, "I will always love Keith, but if I'd agreed to marry him, I would have ruined both of our lives."

Keith picked up her hand and kissed it. "No one would have ever known that I'm Diya's biological father. We certainly didn't. When Diya had her appendix removed, everything came unraveled."

Sarita took over. "Sanjay was out of town at a research conference when Diya was rushed to the hospital for an emergency operation. While she was there, she saw her blood type and realized Sanjay could not possible be her biological father. Fortunately, I had been honest with him from the beginning. But I didn't know I was pregnant when I married him! So I didn't realize what Diya had found out. It never even occurred to me! And Diya didn't tell me what she knew. Instead, she became angry and rebellious. I couldn't figure out what was wrong. Then one day, she confronted me, calling me all sorts of names. Once I got her calmed down, I told her about Keith. I also explained that I hadn't kept anything from her father. Thank goodness for that."

Keith never took his eyes off of Sarita. His expression was one of such longing that I could almost feel my own heart breaking. "Sarita is so wonderful. She has always been totally honest about everything."

"What did Sanjay do?" I asked.

Sarita sighed. "He was upset. But he was more worried about our family than he was angry about the past. You see, Diya insisted on meeting her natural father. In part, she wanted to confirm what I'd told her. And of course, she was curious. Sanjay and I weren't sure what to do. I phoned Keith. In the end, the three of us decided to get professional help. I made an appointment with a psychologist, a specialist in adolescent issues."

"Dr. Westin suggested that we all meet in his office, Diya,

Sarita, Sanjay, and me," said Keith. "I was cool with that. If it made things better for Diya, that was fine by me. I have to admit I was totally shocked to hear I had a daughter. I wanted to know everything about her. Sarita told me how good Diya was in school, that she loved horses, and then she sent me a picture. I couldn't get over how beautiful Diya was. She looks—looked—exactly like her mother."

"We had a difficult time scheduling the meeting because of the holidays," said Sarita. "I told Diya about our appointment. She didn't believe me. She thought I was procrastinating. We quarreled. I thought we'd made up, and that she had come to realize I was telling her the truth. Then she asked if she could stay at Isabella Franklin's house for an overnight. The girls spent lots of evenings at one house or the other, so of course, I said yes. It never occurred to me that Diya was planning anything."

"Isabella told Diya about the party. A couple boys they liked were going to go. Diya must have looked up the address and realized it was close to my house. So the two girls snuck out and walked to a party in my neighborhood," said Keith. Shaking his head, he added, "Only a couple of kids would walk around in that kind of weather. But I guess Diya was determined. After she had a couple of drinks, for Dutch courage I guess, she slipped out of the party and walked to my house. When I opened the door, I knew immediately who she was and why she had come. She was already feeling the booze and had a headache. I called Sarita. We decided it was best to put her to bed and tackle the conversation in the morning with fresh heads."

"Keith didn't know Diya had been having bad cramps. I'd given her Midol, and she'd also taken Tylenol Extra-Strength at Isabella's house."

"She'd been drinking. She complained about her head hurting, so I gave her a couple Tylenol. She asked for two more, and—" his voice cracked, "God forgive me, I had no idea it wasn't safe. I've never raised a kid. They talk about Tylenol for children all the time on TV. It's my fault that she overdosed. I killed my own daughter!"

CHAPTER 48

Keith broke down into noisy sobs, not holding anything back. He keened with misery, pulling on his hair, beating his fists against his thighs.

"Sarita, I am so sorry. I'm such a waste," he told her. "No wonder your parents didn't want us together. They were right. I'm a total loser. I've done nothing with my life since I lost you—except to bring you pain."

"No, Keith, no." She grabbed at his hands to stop him from hurting himself. "This wasn't your fault. It was an accident. You didn't know what she'd taken. You didn't know it wasn't safe."

"But I gave those pills to her! I killed her!" and his head rolled back on his neck as he howled, a sound so animalistic it had to have come from his gut.

The duty nurse came running. Brawny hopped up and intercepted her. "It's under control. This is a man who just lost his daughter."

"Do I need to call a doctor?" The nurse surveyed Keith with calculating eyes. "Someone to prescribe a sedative? Who's his family care provider?"

Sarita put an arm around Keith and patted his shoulder. "He'll be all right."

"If you say so." The nurse shot us a dubious look before turning toward her desk.

"We were honest with Detective Detweiler." Sarita sounded defiant as she tried to sooth Keith Oberlin. "We told your husband everything. He's a good man. He was fair to us. First he needed to check out our stories. Of course, there was the lab report. The comments from the emergency technicians. He took statements from some of the other kids who were at the party, and of course, from Isabella. There was no way to keep it out of the news. Those reporters watch Keith like vultures. Someone leaked that an underage girl died at his house. The media just doesn't have any respect for other people's lives!"

As Sarita talked, I marveled at her strength. Perhaps my astonishment showed up on my face, because she dropped her gaze and sighed. "It's been a nightmare. The only reason I'm not falling apart is that I can't. Not when I have two other children at home. They need me. So does Sanjay. He's devastated and embarrassed."

Keith wiped his eyes with the sleeve of his coat. "People make money spying on me. I'm used to it by now. With a name like Oberlin, everything I do makes news. Now I've got bricks being thrown through my windows, eggs smashed against my car, and all sorts of pranks happening around the clock. I don't care. They can do all they want. It's nothing compared to how I blame myself. Nothing can bring back Diya. I have to live with knowing I killed my own daughter."

Sarita nodded. "We thought about going public with the full story, but Sanjay worries it will hurt our younger children. And of course, our families. Our parents would never understand. Nor would our extended families. We both have brothers and sisters who live nearby, and they would be horrified."

She reached into her pants pocket and brought out an iPhone. With one hand, she scrolled through the camera roll. Once she found the photo she wanted, she pushed the iPhone across the table so Brawny and I could see the family picture of Diya and her two siblings, a boy and a girl. They were younger but not by much. In fact, I remembered that the boy was right behind Anya in school. I'd seen him at a class play.

"It's been tough enough on them," said Sarita. "They loved Diya. They didn't understand why she was so angry."

"I don't want to hurt the other kids." Keith's mouth trembled. "That's the last thing I want. I've done enough harm. If that means taking a certain amount of harassment, fine. I'm a big boy.

Sanjay has been wonderful about all of this. I respect him. He wants to protect his family, and I'll do anything I can to help. He's a good man."

"Meanwhile, the vigilantes are braying for blood," I said, more to myself than to them. "But did two of them come after my husband?"

Brawny had been listening quietly. Her fingers traced a pattern on her kilt. "Kiki, you have to remember that after one went down, the other still came after you and the children. That suggests they weren't gunning for Detweiler."

"But maybe that's just because they're whack-jobs," said Keith. "These vigilantes don't seem to be organized. Or even logical. The things they're saying are ridiculous. It's more like they're mad at me for being rich than really being concerned about a young girl's death."

Sarita frowned. "A man came after you? And your children?"

"We were hiding in a shed. I heaped straw over the kids so they couldn't be seen, but the creep heard my son crying. He threatened us. It was awful."

"Eight and a half months pregnant, and she still has the heart of a lioness." Brawny gave me a nod of approval. "He had a gun, but Kiki went after him with a pitchfork."

"You fought off an armed gunman with a pitchfork?" Keith shook his head in amazement.

Sarita gave me a knowing look. "Never underestimate what a mother will do to protect her children."

CHAPTER 49

After Keith and Sarita left, I went back in to see if Detweiler had gotten any pain relief. To my surprise, he was sitting up and watching television, an activity he never does at home. At first I worried he would snap at me again, so I entered softly and stayed by the door, hoping to observe whether he was more like his usual self.

"Come here, you," he said, when he noticed me. "You don't have to cower. I'm sorry I was such a jerk. I hate feeling helpless, so I hadn't taken any of the pain meds."

"You can hate it all you want, but pretending you aren't in pain won't help." I stood at the side of his bed, looking down on him.

He took my hand. "I know, I know. I was one hundred percent in the wrong. Please don't be angry or hurt."

I resisted at first, but when he pulled me in for a kiss, I gave up. I tried to think through what had happened. Detweiler had once told me that he went into law enforcement to protect the people he loved. But here he was, laid up and helpless, while a gunman threatened his family.

"Look, you're still a cop. You're still able to help us. Okay, so you can't get up and run around."

He gave me a mirthless laugh. "I'm like that character in the Jeffrey Deaver books."

"No, love, you are not a paraplegic like Lincoln Rhyme. But you are wicked smart, so instead of feeling sorry for yourself, how about if you help me figure out what was behind that attack on us?"

Detweiler's green eyes twinkled with mirth. "Boy, you are one tough lady, Kiki Lowenstein."

"That's Mrs. Detweiler to you." I kissed him, and launched into a narrative about my meeting with Keith and Sarita. He shook his head at the image of Keith getting tackled and handcuffed in the hall.

"It's not really funny," Detweiler said, rubbing his chin. He's fastidious about shaving, so seeing him with a two-day beard was unusual. "Given all the trouble he's had recently. Keith's actually not a bad guy. If he could have married Sarita, his whole life would have turned out differently. Funny, isn't it? His parents thought they were forcing him into a good decision, but maybe they didn't know what was best for him. Sarita has a stabilizing influence on him, doesn't she? Makes me worry about the mistakes that we'll make as parents."

"There will be plenty," I said, pulling myself up on the edge of his bed so I could sit next to him. "And like the Oberlins, we'll make them out of love and from our desire to do what's best for our children. In their experience, a mixed marriage wouldn't have worked. That's all we parents have to draw on, our own experiences, and since the world doesn't stand still, what we've done and heard and seen is always ten paces behind the new reality."

"Now that you know what really happened, you can see why I took my time releasing the results of the investigation. It won't go down well with folks who think of Keith as a ne'er-do-well playboy. And I'd like to spare the Patel family as much scrutiny as possible. Diya *was* a minor, and Isabella is still one, and she has her whole life ahead of her. Isabella felt like she was to blame. After lying to her parents, she didn't keep an eye on her friend. Her guilt alone should be reason enough to keep the proceedings private. I've asked the court to seal the documents. That's why everything is moving so slowly."

"Do you think that a vigilante took a shot at you? Because of Diya's death?"

"No, I don't. If anything, the vigilantes think I'm the answer to their problem. Shooting me would only slow down the justice they think Keith Oberlin has coming."

I explained to him what Brawny and I concluded. "Seems logical that I should close the store for a few days. No one should be out and about in this weather. I don't want to put Margit or Clancy or any of my customers at risk."

"But there's no reason for anyone to take a shot at you," said Detweiler. "Or is there?"

I put my hands on my hips, which must have looked pretty silly since I was sitting on the bed and my belly took up all my frontal real estate. "What a sneaky way of asking me if I've been snooping around. I haven't. Between Christmas and our wedding, I've had my hands full."

"I figured as much. Although Brawny has a good point. The remaining gunman went searching for you, even though we were hot on his tail. So maybe you were the target all along. I've been thinking. What happened to that woman who missed out on the adoption? The one who blamed you? Bernice Stottlemeyer, right?"

"Not a problem. Not for me at least. She's now angry with Bonnie Gossage, her *former* adoption attorney. See, Bonnie finally told the Stottlemeyers that she couldn't help them, not ethically, because she considers Bernice mentally unstable."

"I bet that went over like a balloon full of concrete."

"Don't you know it? Bernice was furious. I guess she threw herself at Bonnie and tried to strangle her right there in the law office. Her husband had to pull her away. Proof positive that Bonnie was right on the money. So like I said, Bernice has a new best enemy, and I'm not it."

"Other than that, any disgruntled folks who might have decided to take you out?" Detweiler squeezed my fingers. "Think hard."

"I'm trying, but I have hormone brain. Now that there's been a bit of a thaw, Brawny plans to do a canvass of our lawn. Maybe the crime techs missed something that can help us direct our search."

"Your search? There is no 'your search,' babe. You need to stay safe and keep out of this. Let the Webster Groves police take care of the investigation."

"Of course," I said, as I kissed his forehead. "I hear your nurse rattling her clipboard outside the door. Time for me to go."

Right.

I'd stay out of this.

Not hardly.

Sure, he meant well, but how on earth could I sit idly by while a gunman was targeting my family?

CHAPTER 50

On the way back to the sofa, I looked out the window. Yes, some of the snow had melted, but an icy rain had started to fall. As the sun dipped lower in the sky and the temperature went down, we'd get another freeze, a new layer of ice. I needed to call Margit and tell her to close the store.

She didn't answer. My calls went straight to voice mail. I gave it five minutes and tried again. After the third time, I started to freak out. Margit is a model of German precision. She can be incredibly rigid in her beliefs. For example, she goes absolutely crazy if the phone isn't answered by the second ring. I've actually seen her jump over a box of paper to get to a ringing telephone. That's pretty amazing considering she's pushing seventy-five years old.

So why wasn't she picking up?

Brawny watched me dial and redial.

"No answer?"

I shook my head.

"That doesn't sound like Margit. She's keen on answering the phone."

I swallowed hard. "Seems like all I do anymore is worry. First I was panicked about the safety of everyone at the wedding. Now I'm frightened about Margit."

"Did you try calling her at home? Perhaps she's already closed up shop." Brawny's knitting needles began to click rapidly.

I went to my favorites and dialed Margit's land line. No luck. I also tried her cell phone. She didn't answer. Then I tried the store phone again, and struck out.

"This doesn't make sense," I muttered. Margit's aging mother is in a care facility, so she's very, very careful about answering her cell phone and staying in touch with care providers.

"I'm going to see if her mother is all right. If there's a problem, it might explain why Margit's not available." Going to Google, I punched in the number for the assisted living facility. I explained who I was and why I was calling.

"We haven't seen Mrs. Eichen today, but her mother is fine," said the receptionist.

So where was she? Could she have taken a tumble in her home? Or at the store?

There was no way around it; I had to check on my friend. Brawny watched me, waiting for me to decide what to do. "I need to see what's happened to Margit. You'll have to wait here while I take the car, because someone needs to keep watch over Detweiler and Hadcho. I'll try to get back quickly so there's still enough light for you to do a search of the grounds around the house."

"Over my dead body," said a deep voice.

Hadcho stood at the edge of the lounge. He was dressed in a starched white shirt, a navy jacket, and pants with a crease so sharp it could part your hair.

"Wow, look at you." I was amazed by his dapper appearance. My clothes looked like they'd been slept in, because they had. "Where'd you get the clothes?"

He gave me a level gaze, as if the question was beneath him. "Where do you think? I had my dry cleaner drop them off. I do a lot of business with him."

I imagined he did. I sniffed the air appreciatively. "Toilet articles, too?"

"Like I said, I do a lot of business with him. He's got a key to my house so he can drop off my things."

"Ah. Let me guess. In return, you fix parking tickets."

Hadcho glowered at me. "That's a low blow. Even coming from you."

"Sorry."

The half-smile on his face told me I was forgiven. But he still sounded gruff when he said, "Look, ain't no way that you're going gallivanting around by yourself. I'm riding with you."

CHAPTER 51

"While you were busy flapping your gums, a new officer showed up to take a turn at guard duty," said Hadcho, with a jerk of his chin toward the hall. "I know him. He's good people. Your new husband is safe. For the time being."

I straightened my shoulders. "Good. But now I have a new problem. Margit isn't answering her phone. I need to drive over to the store and make sure she's okay."

"I can take a taxi back to the house, check on the kids, do the search, and pick up the BMW. That way we would have two cars here at the hospital," said Brawny.

"Okay," I said reluctantly. I really wished that I could be the one going home. But this made more sense. "Come on Hadcho. Let's get bundled up."

Once we made it to the parking lot, he insisted on driving. But we didn't even make it out onto the street, before he realized his mistake. Turning the steering wheel caused him to groan with pain. The up-and-around motion put a lot of stress on his stitches.

"Listen, tough guy," I said, "wouldn't it be smarter for me to drive? After all, you're the person with the gun."

We swapped places.

"What are you planning to do about your old BMW when the bambino comes along?"

"Tie the papoose to the top of the car," I said, backing out carefully.

"Ha, ha, ha."

"Hey," I said, "I know you don't feel good. Come on; let's make the best of this. You don't need to pick on me. You know how sensitive I am about that car."

That old BMW was the only material possession that had survived my first marriage. I hadn't sold it because it had no Blue Book value. Something about the cheerful red of the car always lifted my spirits. But admittedly, it was not a good car for this climate or my lifestyle.

My mind had wandered while Hadcho was talking. "Feel good? I don't care about feeling good, Kiki. I care about the fact that whenever Robbie isn't around, my life and my career are left in the hands of a total nincompoop. Prescott is a menace. I intend to talk to Robbie when he gets back. In fact, I plan to do more than that. I'm going to file a formal grievance. The fact that he'd cancel protection for two LEOs makes me sick, and I have a hunch that my brothers and sisters in blue are going to be as angry as I am."

That made sense to me. "I'll do whatever I can to help you make your point," I said. "As the wife of a Law Enforcement Official, I find it incredibly shabby that he'd leave you two high and dry in the hospital. If he'd done an investigation and determined that you were safe, I'd feel differently, but this is Prescott being malicious, and we all know it."

"Amen to that."

In short order, we pulled into the parking lot of my store. Margit's Subaru sat in the far spot. My heart sank a little at the thought of her walking across the icy pavement. Although Margit's as spry as they come, a broken bone could be disastrous at her age.

Hadcho jumped out to get my door.

"Cool it with the manners," I said. "I'm perfectly capable, and you shouldn't overtax yourself."

"You don't have to ask me twice," he said.

We were halfway across the lot when a red pickup truck pulled in. I recognized the vehicle immediately. It belonged to Mert Chambers.

My former best friend.

CHAPTER 52

Mert always dresses to "show off the merchandise." Even though it was freezing outside, she had on a tight pair of jeans, a low-cut top, and a thin leather jacket that buttoned under her bust. Multiple earrings dangled on each side of her face.

I hadn't seen her in nearly a year, and she had aged a decade in that time. Despite the makeup she'd carefully (and thickly) applied, Mert looked old. A deep crease lined her forehead and parentheses framed her mouth.

The Mert I'd known was confident to the point of being cocky, but this woman approached us hesitantly. Her eyes sought mine as a way of asking, "Am I welcome?"

"Your move," said Hadcho. He knew that Mert blamed me after brother Johnny had gotten shot while trying to help me out. I still blamed myself. A little.

To make matters worse, Johnny told his sister that he had fallen in love with me. Of course, I had had fond feelings for Johnny. I mean, who doesn't love a bad boy? With his penchant for flirtation and his love of living on the edge, most women find Johnny irresistible. But I had fallen deeply and irrevocably in love with Detweiler, so that was that.

Mert was convinced that I'd given her baby brother the brush-off. She retaliated by cutting me out of her life entirely.

I missed her terribly.

But I also learned an important lesson. You can't force people to love you. Either they will or they won't, and you have to accept what they choose. As time passed, I began to wonder if we'd ever really been friends. I'd always known that Mert was quick to anger and slow to forgive, but I thought I'd proven myself to her.

Our estrangement hurt. A lot.

Now here she stood—and I wasn't sure what to do next.

"Hi," she said. Her earrings twinkled at me in the light.

"Hi."

"Heard about the shooting." Her smile was crooked.

"Yeah. My second shotgun wedding, and this time someone actually brought a firearm. Go figure." I tried a little laugh, but it sounded weak.

She grinned. "Yeah, I heard. Congratulations for tying the knot. Laurel called me from your house. She says Erik is as cute as all get out."

"He is."

"She says he's a busy little guy. Anya is growing up."

"Laurel is like a big sister to both of them. I don't know what I'd do without her and Joe. The kids love having them around."

Laurel is Mert's daughter, the product of rape that happened while she was in foster care. It had taken years for them to meet and find a way to build a relationship. Actually, I was surprised to hear that they'd been talking with each other. It wasn't that Laurel didn't forgive Mert for adopting her out. She did. Mert never had the chance to keep Laurel. She'd been tricked by her foster family into giving her baby up. And Laurel didn't hold that against Mert.

No, Laurel had another reason for holding back. Her adoptive mother had terminal cancer. Watching one mother die made it doubly-hard to welcome a second mother into her life. Laurel didn't have the emotional energy to deal with both women at once.

"I figured that Margit might be here alone. I thought I'd come and help out." Mert frowned, as if waiting for me to tell her that she wasn't welcome.

"That's really kind of you."

"Ladies? I'm freezing my keister off. Could we take this reunion inside?" Hadcho jerked his head toward the store.

"Sure," I said. "Why not?"

CHAPTER 53

"Margit?" I called out to her from the back room. "Hello?"

She's gotten a bit hard of hearing. I kept calling as I moved from the stock room onto the sales floor. There I found my friend with her head bowed over a pair of socks. She was knitting on a circular needle.

"*Mein Gott*!" she shouted, as I put a hand on her shoulder.

"Sorry. Didn't mean to scare you. I called out, but you didn't hear me."

"It is this pattern. *Ach*. The devil himself must have designed it. Such a problem. I wish I'd never started this mess," she said, setting aside the blue and green argyle needlework.

She rose and gave me a hug. She smelled of moth balls and lavender. Our embrace knocked her cat-eye glasses askew.

"So now you are Frau Detweiler," she said, her eyes shining with tears. "Good. This is good. For you, for him, and the children."

"We plan to have a second ceremony, one that everyone can enjoy, but time was running out." I patted my belly.

"*Ja*, customers have been asking all day if you weren't here because you were having your baby."

"Well, as you heard, our wedding ceremony ended with a bang."

Then I realized what I'd said and we both busted out laughing.

"*Ach*, that is good," she said, wiping her eyes. "How is he?"

"Detweiler will be okay," I said, "but I'm concerned for your safety while you're here at the store."

Briefly, I explained what we had concluded about the shooter's goals. I wrapped it up with, "Sure, this is all speculation, but under the circumstances, I think it's best that we go ahead and close the store. We can say it's for inventory, but really, it's to give the assassin one less place to visit."

She adjusted her glasses. "It has been slow this afternoon, but come and look at what happened this morning."

I followed Margit out of the small room dedicated to our needle arts materials and into the back room. After saying hello to Hadcho and Mert, she clasped her hands together formally. "This morning when I opened the store, there were four cars waiting for me in the parking lot. Six more came later. Five more came after that."

Stepping to one side, she opened the refrigerator door. Every shelf was filled with food.

There were casseroles, roasts, salads, desserts, and side dishes. I'd never seen so much homemade chow. Before I could speak, Margit opened the freezer compartment. It was packed with frozen meals. "Word got around about the shooting. Everyone wants to help. They cooked their best recipes and brought them in, so you wouldn't have to worry about making food while running to the hospital."

Through tears, I stared at evidence of something I've said over and over: Scrapbookers and crafters are the kindest, most generous people in the world. They believe in giving of themselves to others. Our handmade wares are but one example of how we keep our hands busy while our hearts are breaking. Sure, I've helped out over the years when I've heard that a friend or a customer is facing tough times, but I've never expected anything in return. I gave out of gratitude because I've been blessed with enough to share.

"That is a ton of food," said Hadcho. "I bet there's good stuff in there."

I was so stunned by their largess that I didn't know what to say.

"That's not all," Margit continued. She walked over to her desk and pulled out a mesh bag bulging at the seams. "These are all cards addressed to you and your family. Most are homemade, but some are not. There are even a few handwritten notes. Plus this."

From under her desk, she pulled out another bag. Inside were wrapped packages for Anya and Erik and Baby Boy.

"You've touched a lot of lives," said Mert. "Done a lot of good."

Coming from Mert that was a big compliment.

CHAPTER 54

I helped Margit close Time in a Bottle. We emptied out the cash register, dumped the small trash into a larger bin, rounded up everything that could be recycled, changed the signs, and finally dialed down the thermostat. After I loaded a lot of the food into mesh carrier bags, I instructed Mert and Margit to take whatever they wanted.

"You, too, Hadcho," I said. "There's so much here. We won't be able to eat it all."

He chose a salad. He's very picky about what he eats.

"I can write up an email blast from my notebook computer," I said. "Margit? Could you put a sign in the front door?"

While I'd been busy, Mert had cleaned the bathroom for us, which was a really nice touch. A clean john is one of life's joys, in my humble opinion. Call me weird, but I love the smell of cleansers, as long as they aren't perfume-y. Putting away the Formula 409, Mert said, "I can also clean your house for you. Laurel has her hands full. I guess that nanny of yours hasn't been around much."

"That's right," I said, feeling a little irked at the smug way she hinted that Brawny was slacking off. "Brawny brought down one of the gunmen with her knife. Since then, she's been standing guard over Detweiler. I think that's a wee bit more important right now than cleaning the house."

Mert looked appropriately chagrined. "S-s-she used a knife?"

"Uh-huh," I said. "She used to be a member of Special Reconnaissance Regiment. She's been trained for all sorts of combat situations."

"Good thing," said Hadcho. We'd parked him at the table and served him a cup of coffee. "Brawny was faster with that knife than I was with my gun. Cold doesn't seem to bother her. And run? Deer can't move faster than that woman does. She practically flies! There I stood, dripping blood, gripping my shoulder, and watching her race through the snow. If you recall, it was two feet deep in some places, but she plowed through as though it was nothing. The woman is positively fearless."

I nodded. "She told me once that her family motto is *Tutum te robore reddam*, which means *I shall render you safe by my strength* and she means every word of it."

"Where in Sam Hill did you find her?" Mert rinsed out the coffee pot.

"I didn't find her. She came with Erik. Been with him since birth. Van Lauber, Erik's adopted father, hired Brawny. Van was incredibly wealthy, so he wanted to be able to travel with Gina when the whim struck him. He also needed to be sure that no one would kidnap Erik and hold him for ransom. I guess when you have that kind of money, it's always a worry."

Hadcho agreed. "I'm surprised more of the parents at CALA haven't hired some sort of security for their own kids."

He had a good point. Many of the wealthiest families in St. Louis sent their children to CALA. Jennifer and I had once talked about how easy it would be to have a child kidnapped from the school. With its sprawling grounds, many buildings, and open campus, a kid could easily be grabbed and spirited away.

"The only answer I can come up with is that those families probably don't even know someone like Brawny exists." I crossed my arms over my chest and leaned against the counter. Mimicking the way my darling husband liked to stand. It felt oddly reassuring. "In addition to Brawny's military training, she's a graduate of a school in England that turns out professional nannies. Believe me; you'd have to bring in an entire army to get between her and the kids. Speaking of CALA, the first week she was here, she sat down with the head of security at CALA and made a few suggestions. Too bad the man barely gave her the time of day."

"*Ach*," said Margit, "and she can knit, too. She comes every

Wednesday to help out with our knitters. Very, very patient."

Margit's words pleased me greatly. She and Brawny had had their differences. I was happy for every little sign that they'd put them in the past.

"Sounds like you found a perfect mother's helper," said Mert, but her voice didn't agree with her words. I could tell she was feeling jealous because all these accolades were being thrown at Brawny. My life had moved on without Mert. I'd forgotten how easily she could get her tail feathers in a twist.

"No," I said, "she's not perfect, but we are really lucky to have her. Van did his homework when he hired Brawny, and we're reaping the benefit of his diligence. She's at the house right now, going over the grounds."

"Actually," said Hadcho, "she's walking the grounds in a grid. The other officers searched the place earlier, but now that the snow has melted, there might be an entirely different set of clues. Things we missed when they were covered in white."

I held up my crossed fingers. "Here's hoping. Otherwise, I have no idea how we're going to chase down that missing gunman."

CHAPTER 55

After loading the cars with food, I gave Margit a hug and thanked her for watching Time in a Bottle while I was at the hospital.

"It's nothing," she said. "You tell Detective Detweiler that *Rom ist auch nicht an einem Tag erbaut worden.*"

"Translation, please!"

"Rome wasn't built in a day. He needs to take time and heal. I am sure he is eager to be on his feet. Too eager, in fact. Your new husband is a restless man."

I sighed and hugged her again. "You are right about that. Earlier today, he refused his pain meds, trying to tough it out."

Margit shook a finger at me. "Tell him that I expect him to follow the doctor's orders and get well. Or I will come and box his ears."

"I will." I've always wondered exactly what it means to box someone's ears. It certainly sounds like a punishment worth avoiding.

The Highlander fit snugly into our garage. It took me a while to wiggle my way between the cars, thanks to my big belly. When I turned around, Hadcho was struggling to get out of the passenger seat.

"Here." I offered him my hand. As he stood up, his jacket and coat fell open. A bright red stain spread slowly across his white shirt.

He let loose a string of curses. "This is a bespoke shirt that I had made in London."

Brawny had heard my car pull in. She stuck her head into the garage to greet us. But her words died in her throat when she noticed the blood on Hadcho's shirt.

"You're bleeding," she said. "That's not good. Not good at all."

"I'll be okay," he sputtered.

"No, you won't," I said. "Quit trying to play the tough guy. You need to go back to the hospital. Get in bed and stay there."

"Huh-uh," he said, vehemently. "I'm sticking close to Kiki. Brawny, you want to play detective? Go right ahead. We've got Detweiler covered—but what about the children? This house is huge. Do you think Father Joe and Laurel could handle an intruder if someone broke in? Think again!"

He was right.

Standing there in the garage, I studied the house, seeing it from his point of view. There were multiple entrances. Tons of windows on the ground floor. Sure, Brawny had heard us pull into the garage, but that's because she was expecting us. The kids and the other adults hadn't come to greet us. Gracie wasn't barking. That meant an intruder could have entered the garage and walked right in. Everyone inside could have been killed by now.

I buried my face in my gloves. What were we going to do? How could I safeguard my children and track down an assassin at the same time? Should I hire more off-duty police to watch my home?

And my business?

Where would it end?

Climbing slowly out of her truck, Mert walked over to where I stood. She waved her cell phone at us. "I have a solution to this here problem of yours. I put a call in to my brother Johnny."

CHAPTER 56

"Whoa, Nellie!" I snapped back to life. "First you quit speaking to me for months because your brother gets involved in my life and takes a bullet. Now you're volunteering his help? I don't think so!"

She glared at me and then gave a short hoot of laughter. "I cain't win. He's been on my back all this time, telling me over and over that I've been unfair to you. I musta heard him whine about it a million times."

"He has?"

"Of course, he has. Pestering me day and night." She shook her head and her earrings danced merrily. "According to him, you done saved his life that day at the slough, and I'm an ungrateful piece of dog doo-doo."

"Yes, and I'd do it all over again if I had to," I said and clamped my mouth shut, because I wanted to add that Johnny had been right. I'd made one of the toughest decisions of my life that day. I'd taken a man's life. Shot him right in the head. I'd done it because otherwise he would have killed both Sheila and Johnny on the spot. I'd made a hard choice, a decision I'll have to live with. To top it all off, my best friend quit talking to me!

Mert stood there with a hurt look in her eyes.

I had mixed feelings. Did I really want to go through this again? We would never have the same relationship we'd had before the shooting. When we first met, I had been dependent on her. She was the grown-up, and I was the dithering child. But since then, I'd learned to rely on my own judgment. I'd discovered I was more capable and more resilient than I would have ever guessed.

Everything we have will be taken from us…eventually. If we want to live happy lives, we need to be gladder for what we've had, instead of sadder for what we've lost.

I didn't have the time or the patience to wait for Mert's approval. I had new problems that demanded my full attention. "If Johnny wants to help, I could sure use it, but it's up to him. Thanks for making the call."

"You're welcome."

I started toward the house. I wanted to see my kids. I badly needed a hug from them.

Mert stood there in the middle of the driveway, waiting for an invitation. We'd lost that easy familiarity that best friends have in each other's homes. Part of me wanted to let her freeze to death. The other part reminded me to be the bigger person.

I motioned toward the door. "Let's get inside. Hadcho? How about if you stay here with Erik and Anya? Laurel and Joe will take care of them, but you'll provide extra security. You can rest up and protect the kids at the same time. If I need to go back out, I'll ask Brawny and Johnny for help."

He frowned. "I don't suppose I could talk you into staying home and leaving this to the police, could I?"

"Not likely. Prescott won't lift a finger to help. You know that."

"That's what I thought you'd say."

When they heard my voice, the kids came bounding into the kitchen, as eager as a pair of puppies. They were full of energy and chatter. Gracie, our Great Dane, ran along beside the children, prancing with excitement.

"Mama Kiki!" Erik rushed me, throwing his arms around my waist. A lump swelled up in my throat as I hugged him. He'd bonded with Detweiler almost immediately when they had met in California, but it had taken him longer to accept me. I understood why. He'd been close to Gina, his mother, and he didn't want to replace her. While he'd loved Van, and Van had been good to the boy, Van had never spent a lot of time around young children, so his relationship with Erik had been somewhat stilted.

I leaned down as best I could and planted kisses in Erik's soft curls.

"How's our baby?" he asked, running his hands over my belly.

It tickled me how the boy had taken ownership of my unborn child.

"Just fine. How's his big brother?"

But I didn't get an answer because Anya demanded a hug. With my belly bump in the way, we managed an awkward embrace that served to fill up my heart. Meanwhile, Gracie pawed at me, demanding that I give her some loving, too. I reached down to rub her velvety ears.

"Detweiler?" Anya asked, her eyes moist and her voice unsteady.

"Fine. He'll be fine," I said. "The bullet nicked his spleen. I guess it's hard for them to detect that. He came out of surgery, and then they hustled him into the OR again. The second time they took out his spleen."

"Do you even need your spleen?" My daughter screwed up

her face in derision.

"They aren't really sure, so I guess that the short answer is no."

"I want to see Daddy!" Erik wrapped his arms around me tighter.

"I know you do. And he wants to see you. He'll be home soon."

"Not soon. Now," said Erik, his eyes filling up with tears.

"Hey, honey," I said, stooping to his level. "You want Daddy to get better, right? He's in the hospital so they can make him better. Then he can come home. But if you're a good boy, Daddy can Skype you tonight. Would you like that?"

Erik nodded eagerly.

"Good," I said. "Erik? Brawny? This is my friend, Mert. Oh, and how about a hug for Hadcho?"

Erik gave Mert a shy wave as he and Anya turned their attention to Hadcho. "Be extra gentle. Remember? Uncle Hadcho was hurt, too."

"Yuck. You're bleeding!" Anya noticed the spreading stain on his shirt.

"Anya? Go get him one of your father's shirts, please. Erik? Could you grab the First Aid kit? Remember where we keep it? Good boy." I hoped that giving them both a job would make things more normal.

"Don't you got a hug for me before you run off?" Mert demanded of Anya.

Tentatively, my daughter put her arms around our old friend. I watched as the tension in Mert's body slackened.

"I missed you," Anya told her.

"Me, too." That was the best that Mert could do.

During all this, Brawny eyed my friend carefully, sizing her up.

Mert let go of Anya and stared at Erik in wonder. "Ain't you just the cutest thing? Give me a high five, partner."

As the mother of a nineteen-year-old boy, Mert surely must miss short guy energy in her life. Her eyes were bright as she offered him her palm for a hand slap.

"Okay, shirt and First Aid kit." Anya beckoned her little brother upstairs.

In the midst of this, Laurel and Joe had joined us. But they hung back, watching all the activity. I appreciated their sensitivity. The intensity of the past few days had been overwhelming.

"Hey," Laurel said to Mert. She came over hugged us both, as did Joe.

"Could you help Hadcho?" I asked. "He's bleeding. He might have ripped one of his stitches."

"No problem." Laurel waved to him. "Come on into the bathroom. I'll clean you up in a jiffy. Joe? Will you run upstairs and check on the kids? Erik might have trouble reaching the shelf with the supplies on it."

Mert stood there, looking uncomfortable. I gave her a job, too. "Could you grab the stain remover? It's in the laundry room."

Finally, Brawny and I could talk in private.

"Here's what I found." She handed me something small. It was a matchbook with the name of a men's club printed on the cover.

CHAPTER 58

The matchbook was white with a curvaceous woman's silhouette printed in black. Red lettering announced that it was a souvenir from the Badda Bing Gentleman's Club.

I turned it over and over in my hand. "Where'd you find this?"

"In the shed on the floor under a bit of straw," she said. "I've asked Leighton if it's his, and he's never seen it before. Besides, he doesn't smoke. Think hard, Kiki, was the man who attacked you a smoker?"

Sinking down onto a kitchen chair, I closed my eyes. I heard the front door open and slam shut. Mert was talking to someone. I ignored the voices and focused on my memories. Bit by bit, I reconstructed those terrifying moments in the shed. I remembered the smell of the woolen blanket I'd wrapped around Erik. I sniffed the damp straw and the rich leathery scent of Monroe's hide. Anya's strawberry shampoo came to mind, as I recalled pulling her close to me. Then the images jumped forward. My hands tensed, imagining the feel of the wooden pitchfork handle. The heft of it. The sound of the man's feet as he ran into the shed. Taking my time, I forced myself to be in the moment, and then—

"Yes! Cigars! He smokes cigars!"

Brawny smiled. "Good. Then we've got two clues, actually. I looked up the club—"

"Got a hug for an old friend?" Johnny stepped into my kitchen.

"I'll go check on the children," said Brawny, excusing herself.

"I always have hugs for you," I said. His black leather jacket crackled with the cold as he pulled me close and kissed my hair.

Mert wandered in behind him. "I got to go. Things to do at home."

"When all this is over, why don't we go out for lunch?" I asked.

"I'd like that." With a tiny wave of her fingers, she was gone.

"I heard you got hitched," Johnny said, after his sister left. "That Detweiler is a lucky, lucky son-of-a-gun, and he better never forget it."

My words tumbled out in a rush. "It was some wedding. We were attacked by two gunmen! One of the shooters nearly killed Detweiler. Hadcho got shot, too. I was so scared. One of them came after me and the kids. We were hiding in the shed, so I stabbed him with a pitchfork, and then I thought we were okay, but Detweiler was bleeding so much. And they overlooked the damage to his spleen. That happened to you, too? Didn't it? What's wrong with these doctors? Can't they do their jobs? What if I'd lost him?"

"But you didn't lose him. He's not going anywhere. He's going to be fine, girl." Then Johnny noticed the matchbook in my hand and laughed. "Since when did you start hanging out in men's clubs?"

"This? You know this place?"

"Don't hold it against me," he said, with a rakish grin.

"I won't." Between hiccups, I explained to him how Brawny had found the matchbook. "I remember that the man who came after us smelled of cigars. This has to belong to him."

Johnny flipped back the cover. "There are matches missing so your shooter is definitely a smoker. Some folks collect matchbooks, but I think you can forget about that."

"Where is this place? This club?"

"Up by the airport." He gave me that smile that broke hearts. When it comes to sex appeal, Johnny has been blessed in abundance. "I guess the owners figure that men who fly into town on business will get lonely and visit the club for a little fun."

"What's the best time for visiting a strip club like that?"

Johnny's smile was rakish. "Long after your bedtime, little girl."

CHAPTER 59

I felt bad about not returning to the hospital, but I knew what I had to do, so I phoned Detweiler. He sounded surprisingly chipper.

"Have you heard from your parents?" I asked.

"Yes, they sent a balloon bouquet." He dropped his voice to a whisper, "There's even a teddy bear in it. Can you believe? My mother must have conveniently forgotten I'm a grown man."

That made me laugh. "To Thelma you'll always be her little boy. I'll probably feel the same about my little guys."

"How's Hadcho?"

I didn't tell him that his friend had torn one of his stitches. "He's in the living room sound asleep on our sofa."

"How's Gracie?"

"Why don't you ask her yourself?" I called my dog. The big Great Dane trotted over obediently from the other side of the kitchen. I put the phone up to her ear, and she listened intently. After two words from Detweiler, she threw back her head and howled. "Um, I guess that's her way of saying she's worried about you."

He laughed. "Tell her I'm on the mend."

"Look, if you don't mind, I think I'll spend the night here at the house. The kids are acting really needy. Laurel and Joe both need a break." For good measure, I added, "I had promised them that we could do crafts together, and we haven't gotten around to it. Not yet."

"Anya's probably missing you a lot, especially with Sheila being gone. Erik, too. Besides, you need a good night's sleep. I know you've had a hard time getting comfortable in the recliner."

He sounded so reasonable that I felt even worse because I wasn't being entirely honest. "I'll miss you," I said.

After telling me that he loved me, Detweiler said goodbye. I didn't want him to know that I had big plans for the evening. Johnny had promised to take Brawny and me to the Badda Bing Gentleman's Club.

"I know most of the dancers," he'd explained. "They'll talk to me. If they've seen anyone like the creep who came after you, we'll find out."

"I've never been to a strip club." I refilled my water glass.

While Brawny defrosted a casserole for dinner, Johnny counseled the two of us. Among other tidbits, we learned that the girls prefer to be called "dancers" not "strippers." I also learned that a gentleman's club is considered more of a high-class establishment than a strip joint. Different clubs had different rules. In certain states, there was a no touching law, but that wasn't the way things worked here in Missouri.

"Here it depends on what the owner wants." Johnny shrugged.

I was simultaneously grossed out and fascinated. I wondered if Detweiler had ever been to a men's club, but I decided not to call him back and ask. No reason to upset him unduly. My husband needed to concentrate on resting and getting better.

I could do neither until I knew my family was safe.

CHAPTER 60

First I took a nice long nap. Then I played Candyland with Erik and Anya. After we had a snack, I helped the kids cut old sweaters into wool embellishments.

"Mama Kiki? This used to be a sleebe. See? It's different now." Erik proudly showed me a piece of felt.

"I spent a whole twenty bucks at the thrift shop on bag day and bought ten wool sweaters," Laurel said. "We washed them in hot water and dried them last night."

"Mom, isn't it cool? I'm going to make a scarf out of felt." Anya was on the verge of a crafting frenzy. I recognized the signs, having been there many times myself.

"I think this is fabulous!" I couldn't wait to concentrate on our project and get my mind off my problems.

For the next two hours, we had fun pinning patterns onto fabric and cutting out various designs. The children stayed up until nearly ten. After Brawny gave Erik his bath, I read to him but he couldn't keep his eyes open for long. Anya was happily texting her friend Nicci when I tapped on her door.

"Nicci thinks that scarf I made is really cool." Putting down her cell phone, Anya modeled her creation for me.

"Yes, it sure is."

"Mom? Are we safe? I know you're worried about that guy with the gun coming back."

Although I wanted to lie to her, that wasn't the way I parented. Instead, I told her, "I'm doing everything possible to keep you safe. Leighton and Lorraine are on their way over. He's got a gun. Paolo has been trained as a guard dog. Between her and Gracie, I don't think anyone could break in. Hadcho is on the sofa. Of course, he's not feeling up to much, but we both know he'd rally in a pinch. All that aside, it's a good idea to be watchful. Why don't you plug in your cell phone and keep it next to your bed?"

"I'm not scared." Her blue eyes crackled with energy.

"Good. You shouldn't be. But that's not to say that you shouldn't be prepared, right?"

She nodded. "Could I grab my sleeping bag and sleep on the floor in Erik's room?"

Whether she was asking for her sake or his didn't matter. If being next to her little brother made Anya feel better, I had no problem with her decision. "Of course you can."

At eleven o'clock, Johnny decided we should head out for the Badda Bing Club. Brawny excused herself to change clothes.

Leighton and Lorraine walked over from across the yard. A light snow dusted their hair. I introduced Lorraine to Johnny, and then explained what our plans were. Paolo greeted Gracie with an enthusiastic sniffing. Lorraine wanted to know how Detweiler was doing. I assured her that he was fine.

Standing there in my cozy kitchen, surrounded by people I love, I couldn't help but feel a little more cheerful. "Thanks for coming, Leighton and Lorraine. Hadcho has his gun with him, but he's asleep out there on the sofa. I think he's more tired than he realized. His stitches were bleeding earlier. I know he would help out if things got dicey, but I feel better knowing you're here and armed, too."

"It's my father's army pistol," Leighton patted his holster. "Never thought I'd need it, but he always insisted that I keep it oiled and ready to go."

"Paolo will be a big help." Lorraine reached down to stroke her dog. "If I'd realized what was happening at the wedding, I would have given him the command to take down the shooters. It just all happened so fast!"

"He was trained to alert on someone threatening Lorraine," explained Leighton. "Those two men kept their distance."

Lorraine sighed. "Really, it's my fault. I took Paolo home too early. He hasn't been totally trained. We were supposed to take classes together, but I haven't had time. I feel so stupid! The breeder tried to dissuade me from rushing things. Paolo is so wonderful overall that I had a false sense of confidence."

"I should have yelled when I saw someone coming around the corner," said Leighton. "It never dawned on me that those guys planned to harm us. I figured they were friends of Detweiler's. They looked like tough guys to me. And they were. I just didn't think fast enough."

"We need to stop this blaming ourselves, right now," I said. "We can all find a million reasons to feel regretful. I wonder why I thought a wedding outside on a snowy day was a brilliant idea! But who could guess we'd be targeted by a pair of gun slingers? It's no use beating ourselves up. Let's just hope that we'll learn something useful tonight."

I smiled, trying to look more confident than I felt. "Johnny, is it time yet? We're off to visit the Badda Bing Club, huh? Am I dressed appropriately?"

I'd gone upstairs, showered, dried my hair, and put on makeup. I didn't have much in the way of fancy maternity clothes, so I settled for an embroidered peasant blouse and a pair of dark maternity jeans.

"You look just fine," said Johnny.

"No one will be looking at me, except to wonder if I've lost my mind. I'm more in tune with a PTA meeting than a visit to a strip club. Where's Brawny?"

She came around the corner wearing a pair of black pants, a black turtleneck, and a black jacket. I'd never seen her outfitted like that, and I guess my expression showed my surprise.

"In case I need to go outside," she explained. "No one will see me in the dark dressed like this."

"But are you packing?" According to the rules of his parole, Johnny couldn't carry a gun.

"I am well-prepared for any eventuality." Her tone didn't

invite more questions. I decided to adopt a "don't ask/don't tell" policy.

After a few more last minute instructions for Leighton and Lorraine, we walked out of the house and into the cold. It had started snowing again. But that was fine because we were taking Johnny's truck, a black Ford F-150. Brawny had suggested it because we didn't want to draw attention to ourselves. As I walked around the back to get in, I noticed the big Badda Bing bumper sticker. Brawny did, too, and she nodded in satisfaction. I got in first and scooted to the middle. I was grateful to be sandwiched between her and Johnny. It was bitterly cold outside, and the leather bench seat was frigid.

"Nice bumper sticker, buddy. You really weren't kidding when you said you were familiar with the place," I said, as Johnny turned over the engine.

"Uh-huh." He pulled forward in the circular drive. After Brawny signaled the all clear, he drove into the street. "I've been dating a girl who works there off and on. She goes by the name 'Sassy.' I think she'll be dancing tonight. Great gal. Got a cute little boy."

"She's a mom?" I stared at him.

"Most of the girls you'll meet tonight either want to have kids or already are mothers," said Johnny. "A couple are going to college. One's pre-med at Wash U."

"You have to be kidding!"

"Nope. Everyone has a stereotype of what these girls are like. I've found that most of the generalizations are way off-base. There are those who've had hard luck, of course. A few of them got into this line of work because they like to dance. One thing led to another, and they realized they could pull down a six-figure income working at a club."

"Six figures? You have to be kidding."

"I'm not kidding. These women are well-paid. Sure they have

to hustle for lap dances, but a couple of them make as much money as a doctor or a lawyer would."

Brawny said nothing. It was her habit to listen carefully and soak everything in. Johnny pointed his truck north. When we crossed 40, she turned to me. "Kiki, we need a plan. It's not smart to walk in there without discussing what you hope to achieve."

"She's right," said Johnny. "Waving around that matchbook won't work neither."

"I was thinking about this when I was in the shower. See, I managed to clip this guy in the shoulder with the pitchfork. It tore open his jacket. He was bleeding. I figure he's got a shoulder injury. At the very least. We can ask if anyone has seen a cigar-smoker with a bum shoulder."

Johnny started laughing. "You really think they'll point out a customer to you? Not likely. Let's try again."

"What do you mean?" I felt irritated. I was tired and scared, and I hate being laughed at.

"Look, no one in this club wants trouble. They value their jobs too highly. That means that nobody is going to finger a customer," he said. "You need a better strategy if you want to locate your attacker. Sure, we can ask Sassy if she's seen him, but what if she hasn't?"

"How big is the club?" asked Brawny.

"Five thousand square feet."

"Wow," I said. "That's a lot of space to cover."

"Yes, ma'am, it is. The bar runs along one wall on the right. There's a big horseshoe-shaped stage that juts out into the seating area where the tables are. Dressing rooms and bathrooms in the back, behind a door. Private booths are all along the left side of the show floor across from the bar. There are also private luxury boxes on the mezzanine floor. You have to go up a short flight of stairs. In the middle are all the tables."

"What I really need to do is get up on that stage," I said. "From there I should be able to spot the guy who attacked us."

"Good luck with that," said Johnny.

CHAPTER 61

Johnny popped in a CD, and we headed north, while listening to Taylor Swift.

"I liked her best before she quit being country," he groused.

The farther north you go on Highway 40, the rougher the neighborhoods get. I could almost feel a change in the atmosphere. Brawny must have felt it, too, because her coiled energy set my nerves on edge.

More and more neon signs punctuated the winter darkness. They advertised all sorts of vices: liquor, adult entertainment, and sexy lingerie. With every mile, my nervousness grew. I felt totally out of sync with this brassy, sensual world.

I'm a soccer mom! A crafter who makes scrapbooks! I whined inwardly. *And hello? Could I just add that I'm pregnant?*

Johnny noticed. He reached over and took my hand. "Don't look so scared. I have friends at the Badda Bing. Ladies who'll take care of you."

Ladies? I mulled that word over in my head.

I'm doing this for Detweiler, I told myself. But then, what other choice did I have but to see where the matchbook led us? It wasn't like the authorities were all over this investigation. In fact, the more I thought about it, the more I did a slow burn realizing that Brawny had found something that the crime scene investigators had missed. Shouldn't they have found the matchbook?

We weren't far from Lambert International. A jet roared overhead, flying so low that I could see the lights of the passenger windows. The smell of diesel seeped into the cab of the truck. As I watched, the blinking red lights of the plane faded into the velvet night sky. Idly, I wondered where its passengers were going. Were they running away from St. Louis? Traveling to some place warm? Too bad I couldn't go with them. I made a mental note to schedule a vacation down in Florida with my friend, Cara Mia Delgatto. Of all the women I knew, Cara Mia could best understand my plight. Things were definitely not going the way I'd planned.

I had hoped to spend last weeks of my pregnancy sitting at home with my feet up and learning to knit baby booties. Instead here I was, staying up past my bedtime and visiting a strip joint.

Cara's grandmother used to tell her, "Man plans and God laughs." I bet He was ROFL (Rolling On the Floor Laughing) at my life. Looking up into the darkness, I considered shaking my fists.

But then, Brawny shifted her weight, her shoulder braced up against mine, while Johnny turned to give me an encouraging smile. Just that fast, I was reminded how blessed I was. Instead of making this trip alone, I had two friends along with me. Brawny and Johnny were warriors who had already demonstrated they'd put their lives on the line for me and mine.

Maybe God wasn't laughing. Maybe He was watching over me tenderly.

I was thinking all these deep thoughts as Johnny took an exit off Lindbergh. A poorly lit side road led us into a parking lot, jam-packed with vehicles of all shapes and sizes. Johnny prowled the lanes slowly.

We passed cars displaying the unfurled wings of a Bentley, the leaping figure of a Jaguar, the Mercedes Benz peace symbol, and the shield associated with Porsche. I'd expected the patrons to be working class men, so these symbols of affluence shocked me. Yet, there they were, parked side-by-side with Hondas, Toyotas, and other much more affordable rides. All I could conclude was that men are men, no matter how expensive their wheels.

Brawny's head swiveled this way and that, keeping a close eye on our surroundings. Her hypervigilance was palpable.

"We still need a plan." She frowned at me.

I wondered if the plan should be: *Turn around and go home.*

But instead, I said, "Maybe we can come up with something after we get inside."

Johnny pulled into a space under an orange-yellow sodium lamp. He turned off the motor in front of a sign that read: Parking for Expectant Mothers ONLY.

"Expectant mothers only?" I repeated. "Do they get a lot of pregnant women here? Is this someone's idea of a joke?"

Johnny laughed. "You'd be surprised about who frequents this place. Couples looking to spice up their lives. Single women who want a change of pace. More ministers and preachers than you can shake a hymnal at."

"You have to be kidding!"

"Nope. These religious characters will tell you that they are here to rescue these poor straying lambs. They make it sound like they're shepherds bringing lost sheep back into the fold."

Brawny gave a loud harrumph of derision as Johnny continued, "Truth is, they come to leer. Just like the rest of us. Only, they can't bring themselves to be honest about their intentions."

"Wow."

"Let me text Sassy and tell her we're here." With a few quick keystrokes, he did exactly that. After he put his phone away, Johnny ran around to open the passenger side for Brawny and me. Before she climbed out of her seat, she instructed me, "Stick close to Johnny. Let me bring up the rear."

He slid a protective arm around my shoulders. A big jet flew over our heads, the roar of its engines splitting the cold night air. My friend bent low and mumbled in my ear, "To infinity and beyond!"

CHAPTER 62

As we waited our turn to get in, I was able to observe the bouncers seated on bar stools on each side of the front door. The two men could have been reverse images of each other. One was big and black, the other big and white. Both had shaved heads. They wore identical Badda Bing tee-shirts stretched tightly over well-developed muscles. On their feet were huge Doc Martens.

The admittance process was time-consuming because so many of the patrons handed over cash. As a consequence, change had to be counted out. I didn't mind the wait because the vestibule was warm, and I needed to stretch my legs. The slow pace gave me the chance to get acclimated. Standing on tiptoes, I tried to look into the club proper. My view was partially blocked by a fluttering curtain made of heavy plastic strips.

Bit by bit, I was able to see the club floor. It seemed cavernous, like a giant warehouse, and as far as I could tell it was populated only by tables and chairs.

Suddenly, a flashing light lit up the interior. It reminded me of the old "Blue Light Specials" made famous by Kmart. Johnny explained the strobe was a signal that Happy Hour was over. The main show would start soon. Someone cranked up the volume of the piped-in music. The line in front of us thinned out, allowing me to see more of the club's main room. The Badda Bing was a lot like any other restaurant, except for a narrow U-shaped stage that protruded into the center of the floor. The décor was black with touches of purple, green, and gold, with garish touches of silver and more gold. Not surprising at all, since St. Louis boasts a Mardi Gras second only to New Orleans.

The air was thick with perfume…and hormones. The atmosphere was charged with sexuality. I felt really uncomfortable and out of place.

Finally we made it to the front of the line. "This is my friend,

Kiki," Johnny said, as he gave me a slight push forward. "And her pal, Brawny."

Both of the bouncers shook my hand gravely. "Hello, Sugar," said the black guy. "I'm Peevey, and he's Lucerne. We've heard a lot about you."

"You have?" I thought he was shining me on.

"Sure thing," said Lucerne, who smelled strongly of spicy cologne. "Johnny told us how you saved his life. When's the bambino due?"

"January fifteenth."

"My lady and I are having our third baby the end of March," Lucerne said with some pride. His smile radiated happiness.

"Congratulations!" I said. "Good for you! This is our third child, too."

"Kiki has a problem." Johnny leaned in and lowered his voice. "Some creep decided to use her husband and his friend for target practice. With real guns."

"Seriously not cool," said Peevey. "How's your man doing?"

"Better," I said, "but Detweiler had to have his spleen removed."

"Detweiler? Chad Detweiler? I know Detective Detweiler," said Lucerne. "He worked a case that brought him here. Righteous dude. Treated us with respect, didn't he, Peeve?"

"That he did. I'll never forget it. He's good people."

"Thank you," I said. My nervousness made me extra-chatty. "His friend Detective Stan Hadcho was shot, too. Can you believe they were shot at our wedding? We'd just been pronounced 'man and wife' when the first bullet whizzed past me."

"Some folks have no sense of decorum," said Peevey, shaking his head. "What brings you here, pretty lady? A night out so you can forget your troubles?"

Brawny pushed forward to show them the matchbook.

"Actually, we found this on the floor of the shed where the scumbag tried to attack Kiki and the children."

"Who tries to hurt a mama-to-be?" Peevey growled. "And her little ones? That is seriously evil. What's the matter with people these days?"

Lucerne took the matchbook, frowned at it, and returned it to Brawny. "Definitely one of ours."

"Putting kiddos in danger is totally unacceptable." Lucerne shook his head with disgust. His arms were covered with tattoos. When he noticed that I noticed his ink, he pointed each image in turn. "This one is for Fabiana, my lady. This is for Juliana, my oldest. This is for Steven, the middle one, and I'm planning on getting one up here on my bicep when the baby comes. I'd do anything for my babies and my lady. Anything."

"So would Kiki. To protect her children, she stabbed one of the shooters with a pitchfork." Brawny took back the matchbook and tucked it into a pocket of her pants.

"You did what? A tiny thing like you? And pregnant, too? Way to go, girlfriend." Lucerne reached over and gave Peevey a friendly punch. "So we got your replacement here, Peev, next time you go on vacation."

I shook my head. "No way! I'm sticking to my scrapbooking."

"My wife loves scrapbooking," said Peevey.

"Here." I reached into my purse. "These are coupons for discounts and a free class."

Both men thanked me profusely.

After waiting politely until they finished, Brawny explained, "Kiki got a close look at this creep's face. We're thinking he might be one of your customers."

"We also know that he smokes cigars. There's a good chance he's from Alabama. Does that sound like anyone you've seen? He was about five-ten, medium build, and his right arm would be bandaged up. Because that's where I got him with the pitchfork."

Lucerne scowled. "I'm thinking there was a guy like that here last night. I remember because his drawl was so thick, he was hard to understand. Do you recall him, Peeve?"

"No," said Peevey, "but I was handling a situation. Some mook got frisky with one of the dancers."

"Right, right, right," said Lucerne, shaking his head and clapping his palms against his thighs. "That dude isn't here now, but who knows? He might show up later. How about if we get you a table in the back? You could see our guests as they come in."

"Not optimal," said Peevey, with a frown. "She could get a better look from the stage."

"Right," agreed Lucerne. "Getting her on the stage would work best, but tonight no can do. We've got a problem."

"A problem?" Johnny echoed. "What sort of problem?"

Peevey spread his hands wide in a placating move. "Little Chuckie is scheduled to be in the house."

CHAPTER 63

Johnny's groan of disgust was audible. "Tonight? He has to show up tonight?"

"Who or what is a Little Chuckie?" I wondered out loud.

"Sweetheart, you don't want to know," said Lucerne, laying a ham-sized hand on my shoulder gently.

"But we have to explain this to her," argued Peevey. "Otherwise, she won't understand."

Lucerne sighed. "I guess. Johnny? You want to do the honors?"

"Little Chuckie is Charles Esterhaus. He's the assistant manager, and he got the job because he's related by marriage to the owner. The guy's a real twit. He makes your pal Prescott look like a boy genius."

"Oh boy." I felt my heart sinking. What was it with nepotism? Why was incompetence so highly rewarded? Okay, family is everything, but can you let it totally bring down a business? Or a police department? Don't you have to draw the line somewhere?

Peevy shrugged. "Little Chuckie is a short guy with a big, big ego. I think they call it a Napoleon complex."

"Nobody likes him. He can't get along with anyone. Not for two seconds," said Lucerne.

"He and I have had our moments," said Johnny, rubbing the back of his neck. "He's been a real jerk to Sassy. Why did he have to be working tonight? Geez Louise. I was hoping that Kiki could go through the dressing room and have a peek through the curtains. If our creep is here, she'd see him. This would have been over and done with in no time!"

"How were you planning to take him down?" asked Lucerne. "You know we don't allow firearms in here."

Johnny gave the bouncer a half-smile. "Meet our secret

weapon, Brawny. She was in the military in the UK. Believe me, she doesn't need a firearm to be lethal."

Color me surprised. I hadn't realized that Johnny had kept up with my life and the new additions to it. Then I realized that despite the fact that Mert had shut me out, Laurel and I had become much closer. She must have told her uncle about Brawny's background. Apparently, my support network was as close-knit as a pair of cotton socks. I quickly recovered from the surprise and tried to act unfazed.

"Really? You've had that sort of training?" Lucerne looked at my nanny with a whole new respect.

"*Aye.*" The tone of her voice quelled any doubt.

"Back to the problem at hand, you're telling us that if Kiki could point out this creep," said Peevey, "then Brawny here could remove him with a minimum of muss and fuss, is that right? We don't like disturbances."

Giving him what I hoped was my most winning smile, I said, "I totally appreciate that. I'm not up for a hassle either."

"Worries me." Lucerne shook his head. "Peevey, are you down with this?"

But before Peevey could answer, Brawny stepped forward. "I assure you that I shall do my best to bring the man down with a minimum of disturbance. In any event, you don't want him in here, do you? He's a hired assassin. Surely that would be horrible for business. Wouldn't you prefer that we handle him? Of course, we could always call the authorities and let them come and arrest this man."

She was in top form.

Peevey and Lucerne exchanged thoughtful looks. Peevey nodded. "Good point. The big boss, Little Chuckie's uncle, he's given us strict orders that we need to keep the riffraff out. Cop cars in the parking lot are bad for business. Really bad."

Our conversation was interrupted by two new customers.

Peevey and Lucerne greeted the husband and wife (or so they explained their relationship) politely, took their cover charges, and reminded them of the rule: No touching the girls unless it was to give them money. Once the newcomers headed for the show floor, Peevey fisted his hands on his hips. With a curt nod to Brawny, he said, "I get your point. Yeah. If your attacker is here, I'd rather have you bring him down and drag him out. So here's the scoop. Little Chuckie has all these weird rules. He comes up with them on the spot. If someone disobeys, he fires them. The owner hasn't caught on to Little Chuckie's problem. Not yet. We've tried to tell Mr. Esterhaus that his little nephew is a turkey, but he believes that Little Chuckie is the future." He put air quotes around that last word.

"Right, and global warming is a socialist plot," muttered Lucerne, picking up the thread. "The long and short of it is that there's a problem getting Kiki into the dressing room, although that would be the best spot for viewing the crowd. When Little Chuckie is here, no one can go into the back who's not a dancer. Seems reasonable, right? You'd think so, wouldn't you? After all, we don't want customers wandering around and harassing the dancers. But one night, the babysitter for one of the dancers had to drop off her two year old all of a sudden like. Under normal circumstances, that would be no problem. The girls would pass the baby around and entertain him while his mom danced. Everybody enjoys a little cuddle with the bambino, right? But Little Chuckie didn't see it that way. He fired the mother because the baby wasn't a dancer."

"That's outrageous," I said.

"Isn't it?" A feminine voice agreed with me as a woman pushed aside the flapping plastic curtain. She was wearing a ton of makeup, false eyelashes, a knee-length silk kimono, and a pair of six-inch tall high heels, but I would have known her anywhere.

"Susan!" I threw my arms around her and breathed in the

Chanel No. 5 she always wore. "I didn't realize you worked here!"

CHAPTER 64

Susan Tuttle is one of the many moms who show up regularly for my daytime classes. Tall, willowy, with dark blonde hair, she has a ready smile but troubled eyes. Soon after she started coming, I learned the reason why.

It's traditional for scrapbookers to pass their work around, reveling in the "oohs" and "ahhs" that accompany seeing each other's pages. Susan's work was always much appreciated by the others. From the start, it was obvious that she was particularly talented, with a knack for combining unexpected colors and textures that made her layouts particularly appealing.

Our first class together was one called, "Nature and the Art of Scrapbooking." Students were invited to bring in photos of the natural world, while I supplied objects from nature that could be added to a page. As an example, each fall I spent hours ironing colorful leaves between sheets of wax paper, so we could put the leaves onto pages. I also look for interesting bits of bark, especially the papery thin outer covering from birch trees. Twigs are a favorite of mine. They make terrific borders. Woven together with twine, they can be used as photo mats. My list of fun objects goes on and on.

During the class, I explained how we can take our cues from nature. For instance, most people balk at combining more than two types of green on one page, but look closely at a plant, and you'll see how many variations of green there are in each leaf!

Little ideas like that go a long way to blasting people out of their creative ruts.

Susan fit right in from the start. She seized upon the ideas I presented, and typically she took them to the next level. Her photos—a box turtle, a family of skunks, and a sunrise over a field in Illinois—totally wowed the rest of our group. But her close-up shots, like a zoomed-in picture of that box turtle's shell, inspired color and texture combinations that exceeded my wildest expectations for the class.

Next she signed up for a class called, "Families in Focus." Like most scrapbookers, she brought along photos of her child. I'd pre-kitted several pages for us to work on. When the time came to pass around our finished layouts, we did so. Susan had passed hers around reluctantly. My guests are normally very chatty after a session, but this time, each fell silent as she handled Susan's pages.

Curious as to why, I took one of Susan's pages out of the hands of a customer. Smack dab in the center was a darling boy propped up by a pair of crutches.

"That's Dallas," said Susan, quietly. "He's my one and only. He has Cerebral Palsy."

I can always find an honest compliment to pay my clients, and this time was no exception. Dallas was such a cute little guy. He had a heart-winning smile. But all my praise stuck in my throat.

Like the other guests, I was caught short by powerful emotions.

It had seemed like Susan had everything in the world going for her—good looks, money, a nice car, and a fabulous wardrobe. Because I'd heard their whisperings, I knew the other mothers were pea green with jealousy. But now we had a different perspective. I could only guess at how hard it would be to parent a child with a severe disability.

The silence that followed felt like it lasted forever. Many of my customers blushed with shame.

All of us learned a powerful lesson that day. Envy is a one-dimensional, shallow emotion. It roots in superficial soil and withers in the bright light of intimacy. Before we learned about Dallas, we might all have wished we were Susan. After meeting the child on paper, we were all humbled by our own good fortune.

I remember standing there, holding Susan's page and staring down at the picture of the little boy while I tried to decide what to say or do next. My goal is always to make my customers feel better after their visits to Time in a Bottle. I consciously look for ways to pump up their self-esteem, to show an interest, and to give them a sense that I care. Because I do. I really do.

But this time, I was flummoxed. I felt totally inadequate.

Susan rescued me by saying, "Look, I know all of you are feeling sorry for me. You're nice people and you're thinking how tough it is that I've got this kid who's messed up. Aren't you?"

A dozen pairs of eyes cautiously turned to her. Their expressions reflected their conflicted emotions.

"Don't waste your energy," she said, lifting her chin high. "Dallas is smart as a whip. He's doing real good in school. He's a sweetheart, and I'm lucky to have him. Every mother has her challenges. My son's CP is mine, but I'm glad to have him."

I think every woman in that class looked on Susan with new admiration.

I know I sure did.

CHAPTER 65

All this rocketed through my brain as Susan threw her arms around me. "Kiki! You're the last person I expected to see here. I heard you got married."

"Yup." I held up my ring finger to show off the band. "You might even call it a shotgun wedding. I started having Braxton-Hicks contractions, and Anya freaked out, so we threw a ceremony together at the last minute. I'll have some sort of celebration for everyone when the weather gets better."

"This is a strange place to come for a honeymoon. Where's that good-looking cop of yours?" She planted a big kiss on my forehead. With those high heels, she towered over me by nearly a foot.

Johnny interrupted by holding out a hand to our friend. "Hey, girl. You don't have one of those for me?"

Susan leaned in and hugged him too. "Johnny, you are such a rascal. You know just where to come for loving, don't you?"

"Yeah," he said with a grin. "By the way, this is Kiki's friend, Brawny."

"We've met. Brawny helped me knit a scarf for Dallas. It's so cool. Has a skull on it. He's so into pirates. I got it done in time for Christmas!" Susan extended her hand for a friendly shake. How odd the comparison looked. Brawny keeps her nails buffed and cut short. Susan's nails were two inches long and covered with sparkling faux gems.

"Susan, I'm here because I need help," I said. "It's about Detweiler."

Lucerne gave us a little shove toward the tables. "Kiki's got one whale of a story to tell. Why don't you find our guests a place to sit, Sassy? It's almost eleven and this place will be filling up. The two-for-one drink special is over. All our hardcore fans will be piling in."

I thanked Lucerne and Peevey for their help. They were appreciative of the coupons and vouchers for a free scrapbooking class.

"What do I owe you for the cover charge?" I asked, as the DJ did a sound-check with his microphone.

"Nothing. This visit is on the house," said Peevey.

Susan winked at the two bouncers and took us to a table. A beautiful Asian girl in a purple satin evening gown came over and asked if we'd like anything from the bar. I ordered a Seven-Up, while Brawny, Johnny, and Susan all had Cokes. While we waited for our beverages to arrive, I explained to Susan what had happened with the shooting.

"So you see, we think this man might be a customer here." As I'd been talking, more and more people joined us in the big open room. The lights had been adjusted to a dim glow. A bevy of women in colorful evening gowns crowded around the bar, waiting for their drink orders to be filled so they could deliver them to the tables.

"He might," agreed Susan, adjusting her robe modestly. "I vaguely remember Tunisia talking about a customer with a really hick accent. She pegged him as being from the Deep South. I can't recall if he had a problem with his arm or not."

She nodded her head pensively. "There's only one way you'll be able to spot him, Kiki, and that's from the stage. You could probably hang out in the wings. But you won't be able to stick around for long because Little Chuckie's scheduled to work tonight."

Johnny nodded. "The guys told Kiki about his silly rule."

"He usually shows up late," said Susan. "Really late. So we should be okay."

The drinks came. Johnny paid our bill and tipped our waitress. As we sipped our colas, I used the time to look around. More and more patrons were arriving. Susan had been right. Finding my shooter would be impossible unless I was up on that stage. I'm too short to see over most people's heads. Even if we changed tables, I'd still have trouble getting a panoramic view.

"What do you think?" I asked my friends.

"It's entirely up to you. I'll support whatever decision you make," said Johnny. "Brawny? How do you want to handle this?"

"Kiki, if you could get up there," and she nodded toward the stage, "or even if you can just hide behind the curtains on the side, you should be able to spot him—"

"And if I do?"

"Use the clock as your guide. Just yell out four o'clock or six o'clock. That will point us the right general direction."

"Once the creep sees her, he's likely to run," agreed Johnny.

But Susan added, "Or pull a gun."

CHAPTER 66

The lights overhead flicked on and off.

"Thirty minutes until show time." Susan smiled, but it didn't reach her eyes.

Since I might need to get in and get out fast, Johnny offered to take my coat and purse out to the truck. I started to hand over my things, but thought better of it. Instead, I reached into my wallet and tucked a twenty into my back pocket.

"You need fifty," said Susan.

"Fifty?"

Brawny handed me more cash.

Susan laughed. "You've got your own personal ATM? I like that. See, that's in case they treat you like us dancers. You can't even set foot in the back room without them charging you what we call 'rental fees.'"

"Rental fees?" I didn't understand. "For what?"

"They say it's to insure a clean dressing room and keep us supplied with cosmetics." Susan waved that idea away. "Really, it's a way of charging us to work here. See, the house makes money off the drinks, the food, the luxury boxes, and all of us."

"There's also the cover charge," added Johnny.

"Right." Susan nodded. "The rental fee protects the house because if a dancer isn't pulling good tips, she won't stick around. So you could say it acts as an incentive. See, sometimes dancers get fat or lazy. But if you have to pay to play, well, you tend to keep yourself sharp. Learning new moves. Updating your wardrobe."

"But you get a salary, right? Because you're house dancers."

"Nope. We only make tips."

"What if you don't make enough in tips to cover the cost of dancing?" I asked.

"Tough luck." Susan shrugged. "Featured talent, that's

different. Those girls tend to travel around, from place to place. Just so you know, in other cities, girls have taken club owners to court over the rental fees. They've even won. But the club owners keep coming up with new and creative ways to bill us for the privilege of performing. Ironic, isn't it? We don't get any benefits, and we have to pay to do our work."

Brawny frowned and handed me more cash. "You might need this to get past the house mother. As a bribe."

"House mother?" I echoed.

"She's the only non-dancer among us," said Susan. "Sort of a gatekeeper, although she's really a glorified stool pigeon for Little Chuckie. She makes sure all the girls are dressed properly, that we stay on time, and that we each take our turn in the spotlight."

I couldn't believe how complicated all this was.

Susan seemed to read my mind. "It's a business. What can I say?"

"Aye," said Brawny, "and now we need to figure out where we should be stationed. Susan, do ye have any suggestions?"

"Probably over there." Susan pointed to a set of stairs. "Those lead to the mezzanine and corporate luxury boxes. I don't know how they write them off, since I can't even write off child care, but they do."

"Lucerne and Peevey have the front entrance covered," said Johnny. "I need to watch the exit that's to the right of the stage. But there's a back door, too. It's off of the dressing room."

"Right," said Susan, "but you can't get into the dressing room without the security code. It's locked up tight, remember?"

"What about fire codes?" I asked. I was very familiar with these because I was buying the Time in a Bottle building.

Susan shrugged. "Let's just say our management is very friendly with the local inspector."

That really bummed me out.

"Okay, kids, its show time," said Johnny.

"Good luck," I said to my friends, and we went our separate ways.

I tagged along behind Susan as she wove her way through the tables. Our trip was interrupted numerous times by customers who beckoned her over. She was gracious to all of them, planting kisses on bald heads and freshly shaved faces. I hung back, feeling totally out of place.

Without Susan's help, I would have never found the door to the dressing room. It had been designed so that it blended in perfectly with its surroundings. The black fabric on the walls around it had been cleverly pleated to allow for the opening.

"This door used to be easy to spot, which was probably a lot safer, in case of a fire. But we had a big problem with customers who would try to sneak into the dressing room. As the night goes on and our patrons get drunker and drunker, a few of them start to believe they are invincible. They can do the dumbest things. After too many incidents, Mr. Esterhaus had the fabric panels made. He also put in the security lock. It's not high tech, but at least it's a deterrent."

After punching in a series of numbers, she pulled the heavy door open for me. We moved from the dimly lit show floor to a brightly lighted area that reminded me of my high school locker room. Except that the lighting was much, much better, and the boobs were much, much bigger. Since I'm so short, I hit most of the women at their bust line. I could feel my face turning red as I tried to find a safe place to look.

About a dozen women, all between the ages of eighteen and twenty-five, stood around in various stages of undress. Only a few were what I'd call beautiful, and the rest were merely pretty. Nothing spectacular. In fact, two of them were actually rather plain.

"Listen up, everybody," said Susan. Their faces turned toward her. "Remember that scrapbook I made? Those classes

I've been taking? This is the woman who taught me everything I know! This is Kiki Lowenstein. Remember? I've been talking about her!"

That led to a flurry of questions and comments. Seems the dancers all loved Susan's scrapbooks. Most of them were eager to do something similar for themselves. I decided to take advantage of their enthusiasm.

"Hi, everyone. My name is actually Kiki Lowenstein-Detweiler. I know it's a mouthful. I just got married, but my wedding was interrupted when two men shot at us."

"Whoa," said one of the older looking women. "I watch *Say Yes to the Dress* all the time on TV, and that never happens."

"Seriously?" asked a younger girl. She barely looked as if she was sixteen. "That's so rude!"

"Yup. Here's the deal. If you can help me find the man who shot my husband on our wedding day, I'll teach a special class for all of you, absolutely free. You'd have to pay for your supplies, but I'll provide everything else."

"Totally righteous," said a black woman.

Good. I had their attention.

"What's this creep look like?" asked a tall girl with enormous boobs that looked like they might cause her to take a headfirst tumble.

I gave them a description.

"Bubba," said a tiny girl with a mop of blond hair and huge eyes. She came over to where I was standing. "Do you know if he had a southern accent?"

"We think he might," I said, and I explained about the Walker County, Alabama, connection. "See, he attacked me and my kids, but I was too scared to listen for an accent."

"Attacked you? You being PG and all? That's so wrong," said another young woman, a stunning girl with strawberry blond hair. "Are the kids okay?"

"Yup."

"Walker County, Alabama? Who knew?" said a redhead cracking gum. "I grew up in the next town over from Gary, Indiana, and I always figured we had the corner on hit men."

"I guess not," I said.

"Hey-hey-hey, ladies!" The door flew open. In walked a short man with a big mouth.

CHAPTER 67

"Shoot," said Susan, under her breath. "It's Little Chuckie. For once, he showed up early."

The man swaggered in with his thumbs tucked inside his waistband. He probably weighed all of ninety-five pounds, after a big Thanksgiving dinner. His narrow shoulders gave his big face an impossible perch to sit on. At any minute, it looked as if his head might fall off and roll under one of the dressing tables.

The girls had been in various stages of getting dressed. But Chuckie's appearance caused all activity to cease. Most of the dancers grabbed robes and held them over their chests to cover themselves. All of them averted their eyes, hoping that Little Chuckie wouldn't pick on them. Their behavior said a lot about how much they despised the man.

I felt a shiver climb my spine, as he swaggered around the room.

"Girls, bad news. Anastasia is sick tonight. You'll have to do without your house mother. That's why I'm here early. To keep you all on your toes. Susan? I see you brought me a new dancer." With a smirk on his face, Little Chuckie waltzed over and looked me up and down. "Something for the perverts in the crowd, huh? So, Little Mama, you ready to make your dancing debut?"

"No," I said. "I'm a friend of Susan's and I came here to—"

"But Susan told you the rule, right? The only people allowed back here are performers and me. Let me spell it out for you." He poked a pencil-sized finger at my chest. "Either you get up there and do your thing, or Susan loses her job. It's that simple."

I gasped. I couldn't imagine how Susan would manage without this job. I'd overheard her talk about the expensive treatments and equipment that Dallas needed just to survive, much less to thrive. Afterwards, I'd looked it up. A child with CP costs ten times that of a child without CP. In fact, the lifetime care amounted to somewhere around a million dollars.

"You're kidding," I said. "You wouldn't do that."

Susan's eyes filled with tears. Her voice shook with panic. "Please, Chuckie, please don't! I brought her in really early, see? Before the place filled up. No one needs to know that a civilian is back here with us girls. I can tell the customers that she's my sister."

"Ah, ah, ah," he said, wagging his index finger and looking self-satisfied. "The rules were made for a purpose. If we allow one person back here, we've got no right to keep the rest of the patrons out. We're all clear on the rules, aren't we girls?"

To a woman, they nodded.

"You-all remember what happened to Delilah when her babysitter brought her kid here, don't you?" He had a mean grin that belied any kindness.

Cocking a hand to his ear, he said, "Let me hear the rule, ladies."

"No guests in the dressing room," they chanted.

"There you have it. Susan, start packing up your stuff. You've got fifteen minutes to get your butt—"

"Wait!" I shouted. "Stop! I'll dance. I'll do whatever it takes."

"Really?" He raised an eyebrow at me. "You'll go out there on the stage? This I gotta see. You know anything about dancing? Or are you planning to hop around like the fat cow you are?"

He snickered and glanced around to see if the others were laughing, too.

They weren't.

"Actually, I'm a terrific dancer. I've had ballet and modern jazz," I said, feeling my anger bubble up. How dare this pipsqueak fire Susan for being nice to me! What kind of a creep was he?

"Suit yourself, Big Mama." He sneered. "If you get booed off the stage, don't come crying to me."

"Don't worry," I said. "I won't.

Whatever embarrassment I'd felt previously was now replaced with raw fury. I had to restrain myself from giving this twerp a good kick in the shins. He and I glared at each other for what seemed like forever.

Finally, Little Chuckie threw back his head and laughed. "This I gotta see."

CHAPTER 68

The girls quickly introduced themselves and offered to show me the ropes, such as they were. "You can't go out there without a tan," said Candi, the tiny dancer. "If Annie was here, she wouldn't allow it."

I assumed she was talking about the house mother. "Um," I looked down at my winter white arms, "it's a little late in the game to worry about that, isn't it?"

"Heck, no," said Tunisia, handing me a foil package. "Inside are tanning towels. Wipe them all over your body. We'll get the parts you can't reach. Most of us are addicted to tanning beds, but this will do in a pinch."

Susan shook her head and said, "Kiki needs a costume. What do we have, ladies?"

That sent everyone scurrying. They dug through purses and bags, holding up bras and panties and bathing suits and garments I couldn't even begin to name. Tunisia hauled out a two-piece bathing suit. "This will work, if I glitz it up. Your belly will show. Is that okay? Good. Let me warm up my glue gun. I've got tons of fake jewels down here in my bag."

"That I can do. I'm a whiz with the glue gun." Finally, something I could relate to!

"Good," said Susan, "Because while you glue on the bling-bling, I need to get you all dolled up."

After seating me at one of the dressing tables, Susan hoisted a pink tackle box onto a bar stool and opened it up. Inside was the biggest collection of makeup that I've ever seen. In fact, it looked like someone had dumped an entire cosmetic counter into the box. Pawing through various supplies, she chose a bottle of foundation and a sponge. After smearing it over my face, she cautioned me, "This needs to dry. Do your gluing. I'll get my costume on."

All around me, women were disrobing, discarding plain cotton Victoria's Secret panties for tiny G-strings and bras covered with sequins and faux gems. I was glad for the job of gluing jewels to my two-piece bathing suit, because it gave me a place to look. Out of the corner of my eye, I could see that many of the women had chosen to be artificially enhanced. One of them, Foxee, smiled at me and nodded downwards at her own twin peaks. "Like 'em? I got a good deal from a local doctor. Still making payments on them, but with the extra tips I'm raking in they'll be paid off in no time."

"Oh," I said, feeling at a loss. "Then they were a good investment, right?"

"You betcha," said Dee-Lite-Full, a statuesque woman with a generous smile. "They can make the difference between earning a little and earning big. It's almost like an extra grand a week per cup size."

I'd finished adding sequins to the bathing suit bottoms. I picked up the top and started on it. Covering it with fake gems didn't take long at all. The cups were tiny. "Um, this won't cover everything. Since I've been pregnant, I've grown."

"It's not supposed to cover everything," said Susan, laughing. "That's the point."

"Or one of two points," said Tori, who introduced herself as Dr. Victoria Sanchez, "proud owner of a PhD in sociology."

"Right," I mumbled. *How on earth had I gotten myself into this?*

Tori came over behind me, so she could run her fingers through my chin length curls. "This will never do. I'll take care of her hair. Be right back."

Susan bent low to whisper, "Wow, she's really taken a shine to you. We all beg her to do our hair, but she won't. You're in luck."

While Susan attached false eyelashes to my lids—the trick

being to let the glue set up so it's tacky before you try to stick on the lashes—Tori skinned my curls back and pinned them into a tiny ponytail. Then she clipped on a large fake hank of hair. To cover the spot where the real and the fake hair met, she wrapped it with a glittery red band that matched the colors in my "costume."

I resisted the urge to giggle as Susan applied various brushes to my face, drawing in darker eyebrows and enlarging my lips. "Time for you to change. I can tell you won't feel comfortable baring it all in front of us. That's okay. The john is over there, behind the racks of costumes."

Most of the dancers were dressed and putting the final touches to their make-up. All whipped out bottles of fragrance and started spraying themselves. The back room smelled like the cosmetic counter at Dillard's. I covered my nose rather than sneeze.

Walking through a cloud of perfume, I headed toward a spare, utilitarian bathroom. No effort had been made to pretty it up. Because my belly was so big, I worried I'd get stuck in there. But somehow I managed to shed all my clothes and pull on the two pieces of the bathing suit. It did cover the essentials, but not much more. I breathed a sigh of relief. Next I wiped myself carefully with the tanning towel. Nothing happened.

So much for looking bronzed and healthy. I tossed the fabric square into the trash. Only then did I dare to look at my reflection in the mirror—and when I did, I gasped.

Who was that woman? She looked like a femme fatale!

"Yeah, I know who she is," I said, speaking directly to the reflection. "She's the woman who's going to save Chad Detweiler's life."

Leaving the safety of the restroom, I pushed past the clothing rack. But I came to an abrupt stop when I saw myself in the three-way mirror. I sure didn't look like me! If I hadn't given Johnny my purse with my cell phone, I would have taken a selfie.

No one was going to believe my total transformation. The tanning towel worked its magic, turning my skin a golden bronze.

Craning my neck this way and that, I admired my reflection. I looked like some weird participant in a TV reality show. There was just one problem. My baby bump was so advanced that my belly button stuck out.

Tunisia rolled the rack to one side and gave me the once over. She ripped open another pack of tanning towels and wiped down the back of my legs and shoulders where I couldn't reach.

I pointed to my navel. "This looks weird."

"When in doubt, add bling. By the way, you did a good job with the tan towel. See? It goes on clear, but now you're turning nice and brown." From her own red toolbox, she fished out a big fake diamond. Using a dab of E-6000 glue, she stuck it onto my belly button. Oddly enough, that looked just right.

With my baby bump leading the way, I stepped out of the bathroom and joined my new sisters, the Badda Bing Dancers.

CHAPTER 69

"Since you're so short," said Susan, "we decided you should follow Candi. She's first in line."

"But I was hoping to hide," I said. "I really don't want anyone to recognize me. I'd be so embarrassed!"

Tori pushed Susan aside and said, "Let me handle this."

Facing me, she put both hands on my shoulders. "Think it through, Kiki. If someone recognizes you, that means that he or she is sitting in the audience, right?"

"Right." I stared at her through a thick fringe of eyelashes.

"You're here to find the man who shot your husband, but why is the other person here?"

I stuttered, "To, uh, well, t-t-to..."

"Stare at half-naked and naked women," she said, calmly. "So which one of you should feel embarrassed?"

The logic stunned me. I felt my face relax into a smile. "You're right!"

She nodded. "I know I am. That's why you're going to get out there and dance. You're going to have a good time. Candi leads us onto stage. If at any point while you're dancing, you don't have a good vantage point, just strut on over to one of the spotlights."

"The spotlights?"

Candi nodded and smiled at me. "The spotlights are platforms all around the stage. Usually we take turns getting up on them, because that's where you collect the best tips, but we voted on it while you were in the john. We decided that you should have priority. Whenever you need to, just climb up on a spotlight platform and dance. Those offer the best vantage points in the house."

"But you've got to remember," said Sugar, a dark-haired beauty with a southern accent, "that the stage is a great big horseshoe. If you don't keep moving the rest of us will get all bunched up."

"At first, you might not be able to see a thing. Don't panic. Your eyes will adjust." Susan patted me on the shoulder.

"She's right," agreed Tunisia. "We're under these hot lights, and the crowd is kinda, sorta in the dark."

"But when you get up on the spotlight platform, then Phil will sweep the crowd with the baby spots," Susan said.

I was confused. "Sweep the crowd with baby spots?"

"Yeah, Phil handles all the lights. When a girl is on the platform, he pans the audience with smaller spotlights that encourage customers to come up and stick money in your bra and panties."

A new sense of panic filled me. "Stick money in my what?"

"Don't worry." Susan patted my shoulder. "If a patron touches you for any longer than absolutely necessary, Lucerne and Peevey will toss him out."

"Or toss her out." Tunisia rolled her eyes. "Remember that weird chick who tried to yank down my top last week? Geez, what a nut-case. She musta been high on something because she claimed I was wearing her clothes!"

Candi giggled. "Yeah, but Lucerne picked her up by the collar and carried her out like a mama cat grabs a kitten. He was so steamed."

"Not to worry," said Susan, as the music started up. "You'll be fine. Just pretend you're dancing by yourself in your kitchen, all alone."

That really, *really* put a scare into me.

CHAPTER 70

Here's my big secret, the thing I wasn't telling my new friends. I love to dance. Absolutely love it. When I dance, I close my eyes and get wild and crazy. Therefore, I rarely dance. At weddings, I allow myself the luxury of a couple of slow dances and that's it. And I never, ever drink and dance. It's just too dangerous.

I take that back.

I did do some drinking and dancing once. It was during a barbecue at Mert's house. I'd had a beer or two, and I started moving and grooving to one of my favorite songs, *Don't Cha*. I got so caught up in the tune that I lost all sense of where I was. My performance came to an abrupt end when I tripped over a planter filled with pink petunias.

Johnny helped me to my feet. He leaned close and whispered, "I think I better escort you home. For your own safety. Some of my sister's neighbors seem to have gotten the wrong idea."

I looked around and several men had their tongues hanging out.

"Come on, Anya," I said, and I stood up with as much dignity as I could muster. When we got into our house, she let me have it. "You were disgusting, Mom. I've never seen *anyone* act like that." She wouldn't speak to me for days.

A month after the party, Mert handed me a beautiful birthday card by Hallmark. The cover suggested that I should "dance like nobody's watching." But on the inside, she'd used a thick black marker to add, "In the privacy of your own home, please!"

One night over a couple of glasses of wine, I told Jennifer Moore about my dancing "problem." She quickly reminded me that Josephine Baker had been born right here in St. Louis!

"Maybe you're channeling her?" Jennifer added graciously.

Who knows? Maybe, baby!

Here's the bottom line: I love, love, love to dance. And this was a once in a lifetime opportunity, right? Besides, I had a good reason for doing my best. If I didn't, Susan might suffer the consequences for helping me.

I was revved up and ready to go when I took my place behind Candi. She gave me a once-over as the music built to a crescendo. "You look sexy, Little Mama," she said with a giggle. "Just get out there and have fun, okay?"

An announcer's voice boomed over the speaker system, "Ladies and gentlemen, let's give a warm Badda Bing Welcome to the Badda Bing Dancers!"

Polite applause and a few whistles followed, but we stayed put until the DJ started a fast-paced version of the Peggy Lee classic, *Fever.* The curtain parted slowly. It revealed nothing but darkness. Susan whispered, "Remember, your eyes will adjust."

I expected Candi to move forward, but she didn't. Instead, she stood there, posing cheerfully in the opening framed by the curtain. As the music swelled, she waved to the crowd. Peering around her, I tried to make out faces. First I was able to pick out the glowing embers of cigarettes. And then...the faint odor of cigar smoke drifted my way.

Was the shooter out there? I hoped so!

I wanted to race out onto the stage and look around, but I didn't. I had to wait for my cue.

Candi stepped forward, doing a slinky jazz walk. She'd taken about ten steps before pausing to do a slow body roll that drove the crowd wild. Two men rushed over and tucked bills inside the tiny band of her G-string. She blew kisses down at them but allowed them no further contact once the money was in place. Instead, she resumed her strut.

"Go, go, go," whispered Susan in my ear.

I hesitated. Candi had moved half-way down the stage. I could start to see faces. They were turned toward the curtain, expectantly. My heart fluttered in my chest and my mouth went dry.

"This one's for Detweiler," I whispered as I stepped out of the darkness and onto the stage.

CHAPTER 71

I let the music guide me. Over and over again, I told myself that I was all alone in my own kitchen. The image was a little hard to maintain, because the club smelled of sweat, fried foods, and men's cologne. But I reminded myself that I had people depending on me. If I didn't show a credible good effort, Susan might lose her job. If I didn't find the gunman, my kids and husband would be in danger.

Harking back to my dance classes, I did my own version of a sexy jazz walk. Shoulders back. Hips jutted forward. Chin up in the air.

The crowd did a collective gasp.

I guess they weren't accustomed to seeing dancers with a baby bump the size of a Mini Cooper. But the gasp quickly turned to applause and then the whistles started. Next came the cheers. But I paid the crowd no attention, because I was busy concentrating on my strut.

A few steps later, Candi did a body roll.

Okay, I could do that. Only I added a shimmy to my body roll. Thanks to my pregnancy, I was able to put a lot of bounce into the action.

The crowd went wild. I couldn't tell if it was for Candi or for me, but I didn't care.

It was still hard to see, but I reminded myself that I needed to scan the crowd. I shaded my eyes and glanced around.

A hand grabbed my ankle. I looked down. Bills were being waved in the air. Men were actually jockeying for the chance to give me money. No way was I going to let them touch me.

"Pssst." Susan hissed at me. "Grab the cash!"

Instead of letting them stuff it in my clothes, I reached down and plucked it out of their hands.

They didn't seem to mind! In fact, more men jumped up and

waved bills at me. I bent down again—and realized I was giving them a good view of my newly expanded cleavage!

Drat!

I changed my bend to a dip, a sort of half-curtsey. The new action worked, plus it gave me the chance to get a good look at the men's faces. My hands were full of cash, and it kept coming. And coming. And coming.

All of a sudden, I realized how exposed I was! The spotlight seemed to focus on me, bathing me in light.

What if the shooter whipped out his gun and decided to take me down? But just as quickly, I remembered that I didn't look anything like Kiki Lowenstein. Not even close.

Candi grabbed a handrail and swung herself up and onto a raised platform with a pole in the middle. Hanging onto the pole for balance, she leaned into a nearly perfect backbend. While she was performing, I had no choice but to stand in place.

To keep things going, I did a little side-to-side shimmy with a shoulder pop. That brought down the house. Voices yelled out, "Way to go, bay-bee!"

It was just the sort of encouragement I needed.

More and more hands shoved money toward me. In desperation, I stuffed it into my bathing suit.

Candi climbed down from the spotlight platform. The announcer said, "Let's hear it for Candi!" and polite applause followed.

I was up next. Slowly, I continued my jazz strut. Grasping the railing, I hoisted myself onto the platform. That wasn't easy because I had so much weight to lift. Once up on the tiny stage, I realized the girls had been right—I'd found the perfect vantage point. The tiny raised area gave me a 360-degree view of the club.

The spotlight nearly blinded me, but I couldn't shade my eyes and stare. That would just be too obvious. Instead, I grabbed the pole and leaned backwards like Candi had done. The crowd roared its approval. I took my time with my head hanging upside down, but I still didn't see my shooter. I straightened up and did a backbend in the opposite direction. Ever so slowly, I let my head drop. Fortunately, I was warmed up now and my muscles were more flexible. Lower and lower I went, balancing my need to look around against my body's ability to bend. I thought my back would snap as I scanned the crowd.

"Let's hear it for Kinky!" said the announcer.

Kinky?

A loud bass note caused the stage to vibrate. It raced up and down my body. I enjoyed the thrill of it. I closed my eyes and wagged my head slowly from left to right, letting the ponytail flip this way and that.

Suddenly, I caught a whiff of a familiar fragrance.

I snapped upright, stopped dancing, shaded my eyes, and stared out into the crowd.

"Cigar! Ten o'clock!" I screamed.

And pandemonium ensued.

CHAPTER 72

Brawny and Johnny hurdled themselves at a cigar smoking man to the left of the stage. Lucerne and Peevey abandoned their posts and raced over to help. The music kept blaring. Heads turned to watch the commotion, but most of the eyes stayed riveted on me.

"Kinky! Kinky! Kinky!" Voices started to chant.

Susan made tiny shooing motions with her hands. I thought she was signaling me to keep moving. If I didn't, the other girls wouldn't get their turns on the stage. But I was torn because I also desperately wanted to make sure that Johnny and Brawny had taken down the bad guy. As it was, I could see a minor scuffle happening. Fortunately, the crowd seemed to be mesmerized by our performance.

Scratch that.

By *my* performance.

My thoughts weren't based on egotism. I presented a novelty, that's all. As the music changed, to the thrumming beats of my favorite dance tune, *Don't Cha* by the Pussycat Dolls. The lyrics were so appropriate that I threw back my head and laughed.

That really got the crowd going. Again the chant started, "Kinky! Kinky! Kinky!"

Candi was prancing around in one place, blocking me from moving forward. I compromised by doing another slow shimmy and went back to my strut, this time taking tiny steps so I would move, but not go far.

Candi hesitated at the end of the stage, shaking her investment portfolio. I figured she planned to wave goodbye to the crowd. Instead, she reached behind her neck...and dropped her top.

My jaw fell open, and then snapped shut.

What had I expected?

This was, after all, a strip joint. Fists full of money waved in her direction. Stepping over her discarded halter, she collected the cash calmly, stuffing it into her G-string.

Meanwhile, other customers were franticly waving bills at me. Susan hissed, "Kiki, quick. Grab all this loot!"

I did my little half squat, which gave me the chance to watch as Brawny collared my attacker. Johnny winked and gave me a thumbs-up.

My heart soared with joy!

A half-ton of worries was lifted from my shoulders!

I couldn't help it. I broke into a little "happy dance."

Who cared if they thought I was a pervert?

We'd taken down the shooter! Whoo-hoo!

Detweiler and my children were safe!

A few more minutes of dancing and I could blow this popcorn stand. This whole evening would be a memory, one that I could easily forget. My husband would be able to come home from the hospital—and finally we could live happily ever after.

I lost the last of my inhibitions and thoroughly enjoyed myself, dancing like nobody's business.

When I opened my eyes, all I could see was green.

"Holy cow!" Tunisia was right up in my ear. "Kiki, grab that as fast as you can! The others are stuck behind us."

The announcer's voice boomed overhead. "Let's hear it for Kinky! Show her a little love, folks!"

I paused to wave at the people who'd made me feel so welcome. They screamed and stamped their feet.

"Kinky! Kinky! Kinky!" The crowd roared its approval.

That made me giggle. After blowing them kisses, I scooted off the stage.

"Oh, my gosh! You did great!" Candi, who was now wrapped up in a satin robe. She threw her arms around me and gave me a huge hug. To my surprise, I learned that artificially enhanced boobs are hard as rocks. But that didn't matter. I was caught up in the moment.

Next to Candi was a pile of cash, looking curiously like a big lettuce salad. "You've got money hanging out all over. Let's see how much you made."

I pulled it out of my clothes. "You count it while I change."

"You're changing? You aren't going out again?"

"Brawny and Johnny found the shooter! Didn't you see? They pounced on him and dragged him off."

"Nope. Stuff like that happens all the time. Just another day in the neighborhood." Candi organized the bills by denomination.

I stepped into the bathroom, peeled off the bathing suit, splashed water on my face, and changed back into my street clothes. "I need help removing this hairpiece," I said, as I pushed past the costume racks. Candi, Tunisia, and Susan were all waiting for me. Susan waved a thick stack of bills in my direction. "Kiki, you made $2,456! That's the most of any of us have ever made for one dance!"

"It's all yours."

"Seriously?" Candi blinked at me in surprise.

All activity in the back room had come to a halt. The dancers were staring at me. My heart went out to them. Whatever I'd thought earlier, I now had a new respect for them. They were good-hearted women, working their butts off to make a living in a tough, tough world.

And they'd accepted me, prepped me, and helped me out when I was facing a huge problem all alone. Tears prickled behind my eyes. Susan rushed over to hug me. She grabbed a tissue from a nearby box and handed it over. "Kiki, you earned that money. You can really, really dance, girlfriend."

I shook my head. "*We* earned that money. I couldn't have done it without the help of each and every one of you. Thanks to all of you, my family is safe. That cash is yours. What you've done for me tonight, well, it's priceless."

CHAPTER 73

The water hadn't done much to remove my makeup. I should have guessed it was impervious to moisture. Otherwise, it would slide right off the girls' faces when they performed. I decided that I didn't care. I was ready to go home. I handed my costume back to Tunisia, offering first to wash it.

"Girl, it's yours. You bought and paid for it several times over. Besides," and she winked, "you might want to show your husband some of those super-hot moves."

We all laughed at that. A respectful rap at the dressing room door cut our merriment short. Candi opened it and a disembodied hand offered up my cape. As usual Johnny was taking good care of me. I should have guessed Susan would have given him the security code.

In the pocket was a message: *Waiting out back*. With Dee-Lite-Full's help, I bundled up while Foxee put my bathing suit in a plastic bag. Tunisia unhooked the hairpiece. In short order, I was ready to leave. I gave all the women hugs and told them to call me so we could set up a special class just for them at Time in a Bottle.

With misty eyes, I left my new friends. They still had a long night ahead of them.

Susan walked me to the outside exit. I frowned, thinking about the fire code. Her smile was sad. "We live on the margins of the law, Kiki. People don't care much about strippers."

"Dancers," I corrected her.

"You have a good heart." She hugged me and gave me a little shove out of the building. As the heavy door slammed behind me, I blew out a long sigh.

Johnny helped me into his truck. The vehicle was warm and toasty as I slid from the driver's side to the middle. Brawny wore a look of pure admiration. "You did a fabulous job up there. I was amazed."

"I knew she could do it," said Johnny. "I've seen a sample of her skills."

I gave him a tiny arm punch. "Shh. That's our secret. Where's the shooter?"

"He's long gone by now." Johnny turned us around in the parking lot. "Probably halfway to Alabama."

"But we need information! What if he tries something again?"

Johnny threaded his truck between the rows of parked cars. The lights from the highway beckoned us home.

"He won't." Brawny sounded confident.

Too confident.

"How do you know that?" I felt panic rising. We'd gone through all this, and I'd made a fool of myself, for what?

Then it came to me. "He's dead, isn't he?"

"No." Johnny shook his head. "No, he's not. But Brawny was right. He's a professional."

"How do we deal with someone like that? Shouldn't he be locked up? Prosecuted? We can't just let him go free! What if he tries something again? We aren't safe!" I heard my voice. I knew I sounded hysterical, and I was.

Johnny patted my knee. "Settle down, girl. Brawny's got it under control."

The truck moved under a streetlight, and I noticed a red smear on the back of Brawny's hand. *Could it be blood?*

I felt sick. "You're keeping something from me. You didn't kill him did you?"

"No," said Brawny. "That was unnecessary."

"Then what did you do? Look, I won't stop asking questions, and I have a right to know."

The night crowded us, but the neon signage of convenience stores and the bright halos from local hotels kept the world glowing around us. Johnny stopped at a red light. Ahead were the red, white, and blue signs directing us to 270. He couldn't make a U-turn. Instead, he would have to take us down 270 and cut back over to Lindbergh. We had plenty of time to talk. Johnny and Brawny could stonewall all they wanted, but I had the right to hear what happened. I would not rest until I did.

And I said as much.

"You don't need to know how I encouraged him to talk." Brawny's tone was gentle. "Just know that I got what we needed from him. When he told us how much he was being paid, I doubled his fee. I explained that his employer would no longer be needing his services. I could guarantee that."

The adrenaline of my adventure was wearing off. I'd really exerted myself, and now I was starting to feel bone-deep tiredness creep up on me. I tried to make sense of what she was saying, but I couldn't. There was a message there. Partially obscured, but important nonetheless.

For once, the weather forecasts had been accurate. Snow was coming down in fat, fluffy flakes. This all seemed like a dream, a weird, surreal dream.

Brawny took note of the changing weather conditions, too. "This will turn to sleet in about an hour."

All right, so that's how it was going to be.

I squared my shoulders. "Look, I want to know what happened, and I expect you two to tell me."

The truck hummed along, gobbling up the pavement. Johnny reached over and took my hand. "See, a man like that does what he's paid to do. It was nothing personal. So Brawny doubled his salary. She explained that his employer is out of business. Or will be. That's it, that's all."

Brawny nodded. "He's never gotten caught before. This was a huge failure on his part."

"What else did he tell you?" I fought exhaustion, but I still wanted to know. "Is my husband safe?"

"He was always safe." Brawny spoke so quietly that I could barely hear her. Johnny exited at Page Avenue, so we could head south again.

My tiredness made me irritable. "What do you mean?"

I wanted to reach over and shake Brawny. We'd gone through so much to get to this point. Here she was, talking in riddles. I gritted my teeth. However long it took, I was going to get a straight answer out of her.

"I want to know what you two know—and I want to know it now. In fact, I *demand* that you tell me!"

Johnny said nothing. The quiet lasted an eternity. Finally, Brawny spoke up. "That's the point. He wasn't shooting at you. Or Detweiler. Or Hadcho."

"Quit playing games and tell me, Brawny. I have a right to know! If he wasn't trying to shoot me or Detweiler or Hadcho, who was he trying to kill? Was he after me? Was it Leighton? Or Lorraine? Or you? Who was it?"

"Erik," she said, with a hitch in her voice. "He was trying to kill Erik."

CHAPTER 74

"Erik?" I shook my head. "Are you joking with me?"

"Lorraine will explain everything to you tomorrow," Brawny said.

"Yeah. Sure. Right." I was so angry I wanted to slap Brawny up the side of the face. Instead, I text-messaged Laurel to say that we were on our way. Brawny would take over for her and Joe, while I checked on Detweiler.

Laurel messaged me back: *We've had a blast!*

I would have to come up with some way to thank her and Joe.

"Johnny? After you take Brawny to the house, please drop me off at the hospital." I planned to sleep in the recliner in Detweiler's room. If that proved too difficult, or if the duty nurse wouldn't let me sneak in, I'd sleep in the family lounge. Either way, I needed to talk to my husband. Maybe he could figure out what was really happening.

"Sure thing." Johnny was doing his best to sound upbeat, but I was too hacked off to care.

Lindbergh was practically deserted. Salt trucks vied with us for lanes on the road. In short order, we arrived at the house. A new blanket of snow gently rested on all the surfaces. The streetlight lit the inside of the truck. As Brawny climbed out, I noticed a wet spot on her sleeve. I touched it.

My finger came away bloody. "Brawny, you've got blood on your hand and your sleeve both. Are you hurt?"

"No. I'm as right as rain. Glad to have all that behind us. The children will be fine." She paused and studied my face. "We'll all be fine now. I know you are angry with me, and I canna do much about that. I'll tell you this: We accomplished what we set out to do tonight. We've solved the problem. If you have ever trusted me, trust me on this."

With that, my nanny shut the truck door and headed for the

house.

"I have no idea what she's talking about," I turned to Johnny. "Do you?"

"Nope." He pulled out of our circular drive. "But I will tell you this, that woman is a professional. If she's not worried, you shouldn't be."

"I saw the two of you jump the shooter."

"Huh. You saw *her* jump the shooter while I brought up the rear. It was scary-fast. She had his arm twisted up behind his back in nothing flat. That man was totally immobilized before he knew what hit him."

I stared at the passing scenery. Most of the houses were dark. Several had electric candles in the windows, beckoning the Christ Child to visit their homes. That got me thinking. *Was it possible? Could Erik have really been the target?*

It didn't make sense.

"What did Peevey and Lucerne have to say when all this went down?"

"First off, we were all standing around slack-jawed watching you dance. Golly, girl, you had it going on!"

I blushed in the dark. "Little Chuckie showed up. I had to dance or Susan would lose her job."

"I figured something like that had happened. He came out of the back room looking very pleased with himself. I'd love to give that creep a good pounding. I was torn between watching you and keeping an eye on the crowd. Then you yelled. Before I could peel myself off the wall, Brawny was on top of the gunman. Lucerne and Peevey were stunned. She was so fast, she moved like a blur. Peevey asked her later if she taught classes. She told them she'd meet with them on her day off and show them a few moves."

I gawped at him. "You have to be kidding."

"No, I'm not," he said, quietly. "Point being, if she thinks you're safe, you are."

That wasn't what I wanted to hear. "I can't believe that someone would hire thugs to kill my son. That just doesn't make a bit of sense. What sort of animal wants to bump off a five-year-old kid?"

"I dunno," said Johnny, drumming his fingers on his steering wheel. "But you can rest assured that the man who hired that thug is going to be roadkill before long."

CHAPTER 75

Johnny helped me as I trudged through the mounting snow and made my way to the hospital entrance.

The security guard gave me the once over.

"You got a problem?" I lifted my chin defiantly.

"Uh, no ma'am." His baby face flushed with embarrassment. I doubted he was much of a threat to any wrongdoer, and that ticked me off all over again.

"Boo!" I shouted. To my immense satisfaction, he jumped.

Johnny nearly wet himself laughing. He gave me a quick peck on the cheek, turned around, and chuckled his way into the night.

"Great, just great." I punched the elevator buttons so hard my knuckle cracked.

By the time I made it to Detweiler's floor, I was literally seeing red. The emotional roller coaster that had begun with my wedding plans had chugged up to a precarious peak and then plummeted into a valley.

They had dimmed the lights in the hospital hallway. Elva barely glanced at me as she looked up from her ever-present clipboard. "Your husband is awake. I just took his vitals. If you'd like to sleep in the recliner in his room, why don't you?"

I stepped under a buzzing florescent light—and her eyes snapped open wide. I opened my mouth to explain all the makeup I was wearing, but I couldn't summon up the energy. Instead, I gave her a nod and tiptoed down the hall to Detweiler's room.

"Kiki?"

"I'm here, my love," I said, leaning down to give him a kiss on the cheek.

"Wow. You smell like perfume. Cigarettes. What's with that? You okay?" He sounded groggy. Dark circles ringed his eyes.

His hair stuck out in a bad imitation of a bottle brush. I could see that his lips were cracked and chapped. I reached over for the small container of Vaseline. With my fingertip, I painted his mouth and then kissed him.

If Brawny was to be believed, Detweiler was safe. So was Erik. And Anya. Everyone who mattered to me. The shooter wouldn't be coming back.

"Never better. Scoot over." I cuddled up next to him. My eyes adjusted to the nightlight by his bed.

"Good." His smile came slowly. I relished every second of seeing it emerge, as I took his hand in mine and felt the warmth of his flesh. Leaning over, I tried to plant another kiss on his forehead. But what I saw on his pillow stopped me.

"Detweiler? Stay perfectly still. Don't move. There's a huge spider right next to you."

"Get it off of me!"

He's not afraid of snakes, or creeps, or bats, but Detweiler hates spiders. They absolutely terrify him.

I went looking for a weapon. Moving swiftly, I grabbed a copy of *Chicagoland Scrapbooker* that I'd left behind in the recliner. The magazine rolled up easily in my hand.

"Get that spider!" Detweiler rolled away from his pillow. I swatted the bug. Once, twice, three times. My efforts did nothing to crumple it up.

Elva threw open the door. She skidded to a stop when she saw me, holding the magazine like a club. "Stop it! Stop! What are you doing? Have you lost your mind? You can't whack at him. He's got stitches."

"Spider!" I pointed at the bedclothes.

"Get it off me!" Detweiler howled.

I hit the spider and it jumped.

"That's the biggest—" And then with two fingers, Elva delicately plucked up the hairy beast. "That's the biggest false eyelash I've ever seen."

"Oh, my gosh," I put a hand to my eye. "Must be one of mine."

"Yours?" Detweiler squinted up at me. "Since when did you start wearing false eyelashes?"

"Uh, since tonight. At the strip club."

"Strip club?" Detweiler and Elva repeated in chorus.

"Long story. Sorry, Elva. It was, um, work related. One of my scrapbookers. She needed my help."

But Elva had quit listening. She was clinging to the side of the bed, laughing so hard she could barely stand. "Strip club? False eyelashes? And you with a belly bump?"

Wiping her eyes, she continued, "Well, you beat that spider to death. You really did. That's a first."

"Yeah, I'm tough like that."

Detweiler shivered. "I hate spiders."

"Oh-kay. I'll leave you two alone. Try to keep it down in here."

I stuffed the eyelash in my pocket, but I didn't take off my cape. Not yet. I was happy to be wearing a lot of clothes.

"Well, that was exciting." Detweiler chuckled.

"Yup." I muttered, "You don't know the half of it."

"How are the kids?" He mumbled sleepily.

"Just fine," I said. "Everything and everyone is fine. We can talk about it in the morning."

CHAPTER 76

I woke up to the sound of the nurse, making her rounds and checking on Detweiler. Soon after, the breakfast cart came rattling its way down the hall. The scent of bacon proved irresistible.

I told my husband, "I'm going to run downstairs to the cafeteria. Your food has arrived."

"We need to talk when you get back."

"Right. We sure do."

All the exercise I'd gotten last night was causing me to feel extra-hungry. Detweiler wouldn't be happy to hear I'd gone snooping around while he was flat on his back. But the results would please him and put his mind at ease. Before I explained my nocturnal adventure, I wanted to pin down Brawny, but my cell phone was dead. I'd forgotten to plug it into the charger last night.

"Drat." My stomach growled. I decided to deal with the phone after I'd had my breakfast. Six pieces of bacon later, Hadcho showed up, moving gingerly and carrying a cup of coffee. "Is this seat taken?"

"Nope. Take a load off."

"Brawny text-messaged me to say that we can call off the armed guard," he said, easing into the plastic chair opposite of mine. A wince confirmed that he was still hurting. "You caught up with the second shooter."

"Yeah, I guess."

"What does that mean?" His coffee cup froze on the way to his lips.

"I identified him. Brawny and Johnny took him down. Supposedly, Brawny had a talk with him, but I have no idea what she learned. She turned him loose! Can you believe it? I would have choked that dude to death with my bare hands, but she lets him go. When I tried to find out why, she and I went around and around in circles. I couldn't get a straight answer from her. Some nonsense about Lorraine having to talk to me. What a load of bunk. Believe me, I am not a happy bunny."

Gulping the coffee and setting the empty cup to one side, Hadcho scowled. "Do you mean to tell me you don't believe her?"

"Oh, I believe her. She is totally convinced that we're not in any danger. All along this was a 'whydunnit,' and not a 'whodunnit.' From the get-go, I haven't been able to figure out why someone used us as target practice on my wedding day. Worse luck, I'm dealing with a so-called bodyguard who won't come clean on the details. All she kept saying was that she's got it taken care of. Terrific, huh?" I threw up my hands.

"And she didn't offer any explanation?"

"Only that the shooter was hired to take out Erik. Have you ever heard such nonsense? That is just plain silly. Who gets hired to kill a five-year-old boy? How dumb does she think I am?"

Hadcho's eyes are such a dark brown that you can barely tell where the pupil meets the iris. In the right light, they look like two dark lumps of coal. Now he stared at me, a muscle in his jaw twitching, as he asked, "Could she be right? Might they have been aiming at Erik?"

"How should I know? She wasn't exactly forthcoming about the details. If there's a Scottish version of the Sphinx, her name is Bronwyn." I was pouting as I picked at my seventh piece of bacon. I had three pieces left on my plate and I intended to eat every one of them. Maybe I'd even go back for more.

"Help me out here," said Hadcho. "I'm trying to remember the trajectory of the bullets."

After removing a paper napkin from the metal dispenser in the middle of the table, he fished for a pen from his pocket. He drew an octagon to represent the gazebo. Marking a series of Xs, he created a row down the middle from left to right. "This is

Anya, Erik, you, and Detweiler. Second row would be Lorraine and Brawny."

"You forgot Leighton. He wound up sort of behind Lorraine, helping her with the prayer book, remember? "

"Okay." Hadcho squeezed in an additional X. "Can you remember exactly what Erik was doing when we heard the first gunshot?"

I closed my eyes. I could see Detweiler's love-struck grin, Leighton's serious smile, and Hadcho's expression of concentration as we listened to Lorraine officiate the service. Letting myself relive the moment, I recalled how Anya had stepped back, and I reached down because Erik was—

"Jumping up and down, trying to catch snowflakes on his tongue."

"Right. I'd forgotten." Hadcho nodded enthusiastically. "Detweiler said something to me about this being Erik's first experience with snow. As soon as we walked outside, the kid started packing it with his bare hands. He asked where the flakes came from. Detweiler launched into this long-winded explanation of moist air versus cold air versus, and I don't know what else."

I picked up the thread. "When we got to the gazebo, Erik opened his mouth—"

"And started jumping—" Hadcho continued. His pen tip was touching the paper, allowing a black blob to grow at an alarming rate. But that didn't matter. We were onto something. Something big.

"I was worried about him toppling off the gazebo. I made a grab for Erik. He jumped up. I leaned down. The bullet went right through the hood of the cape I was wearing," I said. "Brawny's big on capes and hoods. She made mine bigger than my head, so it could be folded back on itself in layers. I was looking down at our hands, Detweiler's and mine. The fabric sort of blocked my view left and right. The way horse blinders would."

I hesitated and closed my eyes to help me dredge up more memories. "But out of the corner of my eyes, I could see Erik jumping up and down. We could feel it, remember? He shook the wooden floor of the gazebo. Because he was concentrating on the snowflakes, he didn't realize he was moving so close to the edge. Originally he was behind me, but after all that hopping up and down, he wound up slightly in front of me."

"That first shot went right through your helmet."

"Hood."

"Whatever." Hadcho capped his pen and took one of my pieces of bacon off the plate. He munched it thoughtfully. "I remember hearing the crack of the gunshot. I knew right away we were being shot at."

"Detweiler did, too. I felt him pull away from me."

"I must have been shot immediately. You don't always feel a gunshot wound. It cauterizes the flesh as it goes in. The adrenaline blocks the pain at first. I remember turning toward the noise. There was a shout when one of the creeps realized we were drawing our guns. It surprised them that we were carrying."

"They couldn't have guessed that Brawny was wearing a knife. Or that she'd throw a blade with such accuracy. Who invites a professional bodyguard to a backyard wedding?"

"Nobody," agreed Hadcho. "That's how come she was able to take out one of the scumbags."

I picked up the paper napkin. The black blot had grown to the size of an olive. A shiver swept through me. "Then Brawny had it right. Their target *was* Erik. That guy we found last night, he was really, really lucky."

"How so?"

"Brawny let him go. If it had been left up to me, I would have strangled him with my bare hands."

CHAPTER 77

Detweiler was asleep by the time we got back to his room. I didn't want to wake him, and Hadcho agreed.

"Look, I'll run over to the Webster Groves Police Department. They need to be filled in on what we've learned."

"Like they even care," I muttered darkly.

Jamming his hands in his pockets, Hadcho nodded. "Actually the Webster Groves guys have been working on this. I've been fielding phone calls. They're a good bunch. It's just that they don't want to tick off Prescott. It could look like they're doing an end run, see?"

Reluctantly, I admitted he had a point. Mainly, I was mad at the world. Sure, I was being unfair, but didn't I have a right to feel mistreated? Nothing that I'd learned made any sense. "Shouldn't you have a talk with Brawny? Get her to come clean?"

His smile was wan. "I tried. She stonewalled me like she stonewalled you. Kept going back to Lorraine Lauber. Something about this being Lorraine's call."

"Great."

We parted ways, and I slipped into Detweiler's room. There I hunkered down in the recliner, turning everything over and over in my head. My anger kept me awake for a while, but not for long. I woke up to Dr. Fizzio's voice. She was bent over Detweiler with her stethoscope on his belly. I waited impatiently for a report on my husband's prognosis.

"Your incisions are coming along," she said, with a smile for Detweiler.

She must have gotten a good night's rest, because she looked years younger than she had the night we'd first met. They always say stress ages you, and the proof was standing in front of me.

Her fingers moved rapidly over Detweiler's body, taking his

pulse, kneading his belly, and feeling his lymph nodes.

At long last, she pulled the stethoscope out of her ears and stepped back to study him carefully. "You are a lucky man, Detective Detweiler. Obviously, you were in excellent health when you got shot. You're recovering nicely. I think I'll send you home today."

A little cry of happiness escaped me.

"Provided, of course," she added with a stern glance my way, "that you promise to stay quiet. Can you do that?"

"I can," said Detweiler solemnly.

That brightened my mood considerably. After the doctor left, I called his parents with his cell phone. Thelma answered on the first ring. When I told her the news, she let out her own hurrah of happiness. "Louis is out in the barn. He'll be so tickled to hear this."

Then she paused. "But will he be safe, Kiki?"

"We tracked down the shooter yesterday. I have it on good authority that none of us will be bothered by him again," I said, as I hiked myself up so I could sit on the edge of his bed. "Here. Want to tell your little boy hi?"

After Detweiler finished his call, I phoned Brawny with the good news. "I'll come pick you up," she said. "Laurel and Joe will gladly watch the kids. Lorraine wants to speak to you."

"Yeah, well, I want to talk to her, too." When I finished, Detweiler patted the side of his bed. "Tell me all about it. How did you track down the second shooter?"

I explained about the matchbook. Although Detweiler scowled when he heard I'd gone to the strip joint, he didn't interrupt me. I recounted the kindness of Lucerne and Peevey. That brought a reluctant smile to his face. He had met Susan, aka "Sassy," and he wasn't surprised to hear she was one of my scrapbookers. Then I took a deep breath and told him about Little Chuckie's threat. That led to a summary of my brief career as a dancer at the Badda Bing Gentleman's Club.

He shook his head and smothered a laugh at the description of me strutting up and down the stage with my big belly sticking out. I explained how Candi's top-drop had taken me by surprise. "Believe it or not, when you're up on the stage, it can be hard to see out into the audience."

"Really?"

"I had to improvise when I did my pole dance." I got up and gave him a small demonstration. That got him laughing. But his stitches hurt when he did. He clamped his mouth shut rather than give in to the giggles.

"Unbelievable," he said. "I'm out of commission for a few days, and my wife is moonlighting at a strip joint."

"A gentleman's club," I corrected him. "By the way, I made tons of cash."

"Really? Show me the money." He demanded in a perfectly deadpan voice.

"I gave it all to the girls. They needed it, and they deserved it because they were so kind to me."

"They were nice to you because you were nice to them," he said. "Can I see your costume?"

I pulled it out of the plastic bag in my purse. In the bright light of day, it looked amazingly insignificant. Once again, Detweiler started to chuckle. I laughed, too. "Hey, buster. This is a customized outfit I have here. You'll never find one of these in your average maternity shop."

"You can say that again," and he beckoned me closer for a kiss.

In response, our son started kicking me.

I ran my husband's hand over my belly, allowing him to feel his child's enthusiasm for life. "Oops," I said, as my fingers hit a hard knot. "I forgot all about this." I flipped up my shirt and revealed the jewel in my navel.

"To think," he said, wonderingly, "I bought you a diamond for your finger. If only I had known."

CHAPTER 78

The hospital paperwork took longer than I'd hoped. Finally, Detweiler was officially released. As the orderly rolled my husband along in his wheelchair, I took deep cleansing breaths. Freedom was just around the corner. The crisp outdoor air felt good on my skin, especially after that stuffy hospital room.

As she'd promised, Brawny was outside waiting for us in the Highlander. She hopped out to open the back passenger door. More than a few visitors paused to stare at the sturdy figure in a tartan skirt, white blouse, knee socks and black brogues.

"The kids are really excited about having you both home." Brawny spoke to us over her shoulder. It felt weird to sit in the back rather than up front, but I wanted to be next to Detweiler. The hustle and bustle of getting him discharged had tired him out. All the way home, Brawny chattered like a tour guide. Remarking on traffic, the weather, and all sorts of stupid stuff.

"Brawny, we need to talk." I sounded brusque, but frankly, I was tired of playing games.

Her eyes sought mine in the rearview mirror. "I know we do."

"I'm still not sure that we're all safe."

"I give you my word. You are safe. Each and every one of you. I know I've been less than forthcoming, but I have to respect Lorraine's wishes."

"Respecting her wishes is one thing," I grumbled. "The safety of our children is another."

"*Aye.* I've planned for Detective Detweiler to take a wee nap. Then Lorraine and Leighton will come for dinner. When it's done, we'll all sit down together and chat."

She sounded conciliatory, but I was still ticked off. "Look, I know she pays your salary, but this won't work if I don't have any say in your actions."

"Aye." Brawny sounded perfectly agreeable.

That made me even more angry. I briefly considered firing her on the spot. Detweiler must have read my mind. He said, "Brawny, you're asking a lot of us. Especially given what we've just been through. I don't believe that Kiki is acting unreasonably."

"I totally agree, sir."

That respectful title was a sop. But I was still fuming.

"I've asked Hadcho to come to dinner," she said, almost as an afterthought. "I know he also has questions that are unanswered. I thought it best that we all put our cards on the table."

"How kind of you." The words came out so sharply that Detweiler squeezed my hand. I told myself that I needed to chill. Being mean to Brawny wasn't my style. Furthermore, she wasn't taking the bait. I decided to change the subject. "What about the kids? Are you planning for them to be there, too? I'm assuming I have no say in this matter."

"It might be best for you to hear everything first. Then it's up to you what you tell them. Mrs. Moore has invited them both to spend the night at her house. Nicci and Anya haven't seen each other in a while, so they're over the moon with excitement. Stevie is home from college, and he's promised to build LEGOs® with Erik. I guess he has two tubs of them that Jennifer has saved from when he was younger. Erik is thrilled with the adventure, too."

Okay, so she'd thought of everything.

I still wasn't happy.

CHAPTER 79

Anya and Erik squealed with excitement when Detweiler walked through the back door.

I walked Laurel and Joe to the foyer where they put on their coats.

"Thank you," I said. "I don't know how we can ever repay you."

"No, thank you," said Joe, as he helped Laurel adjust her scarf. "We had so much fun. We can't wait to have our own brood."

To my surprise, he gave me a quick buss on the cheek. Laurel did the same and added a hug.

I locked the front door behind them.

Meanwhile, the children were prancing around like Santa's reindeer on steroids. "Careful! Your father is very fragile. Let's get him onto the sofa so he can have a nice nap."

After we got Detweiler situated, they turned their attention on me. I accepted their affection gratefully. Next we were treated to "show and tell" as the kids dragged out one cool project after another.

Anya crowed, "Laurel and Joe are the best. Laurel says I can be a bridesmaid when they get married."

"I'm going to be an altered-boy," explained Erik solemnly. "If you say I can."

"An altered-boy?" Detweiler raised his eyebrows. "Wow, dude. That's amazing."

"I'm not sure you know what you're in for, little buddy." I gathered Erik in my arms. His legs were getting longer every day.

I let the kids have another ten minutes with their father, and then Brawny hustled them into the car for their trip to Jennifer Moore's house. After kissing them soundly, I waved them down the driveway.

While Detweiler slept on our sofa, I climbed the stairs to our bedroom. The minute my head hit the pillow, I fell sound asleep. I woke to the sound of voices in the foyer. Leighton and Lorraine had arrived.

Both of them hugged me. I suggested we move into the dining room. To my surprise, Detweiler was already there. Brawny had carried in a wingback chair. She had him propped up with pillows. Hadcho arrived soon after.

The meal was strained. We had three casseroles to choose from, but the food tasted like cardboard in my mouth. I did my best to be pleasant, but I was fed up with waiting for answers.

"How about if we take a pass on dessert," I said, folding my napkin politely.

That got everyone's attention. I never turn up my nose at dessert. But I was not in the mood, and my announcement put everyone on notice that I wasn't going to wait any longer for answers.

We moved into the living room.

"You also have every reason to be extremely angry with me," said Lorraine, in a quiet voice, as she folded her hands in her lap. She was seated in the second wingback. Brawny had dragged its twin back to its usual place. Detweiler was sitting in it, looking uncomfortable. I wanted to get this over with, because he needed his rest.

Lorraine continued, "After you hear the whole story, I hope you'll be able to find it in your heart to forgive me for being so stupid. This really is all my fault."

Detweiler reached down to take my hand, as I sat on the ottoman at his feet.

"This all goes back to a mistake I made as a young girl on a winter day in Waterville, Maine. I was supposed to be watching my younger brother Van, but there was this boy, a young man I had a crush on. His attentions distracted me. I quit watching Van as carefully as I should have. As a consequence, my brother fell through the ice. He was rescued by a boy named Roscoe Thornton. Thus began Van's lifelong friendship with Thornton, a man I've never liked."

With a sigh, she continued, "I always assumed that I disliked Thornton because he reminded me of my guilt. Van very nearly drowned, and it was all my fault. But I should have trusted my instincts better. Now I realize that I disliked Thornton from the start because he is a terrible person. I should have given myself more credit."

Detweiler frowned. "Is this the same Thornton who's Van's attorney? The one who sent me the paperwork when I brought Erik home?"

"Yes," said Lorraine. "He became my brother's right hand man. Thornton was Van's exclusive legal counsel. He set up and handled all of Van's trusts and his will. I only began to put credence in my instincts after Gina refused to work with him. They had one meeting, and she put her foot down. She told Van that she never wanted to see Thornton again. In fact, she hired her own attorney over Van's protests. You see, Gina was very perceptive. And she was also more courageous than I."

Lorraine paused to dab her eyes. "Her decision should have been a big red flag. I can't recall Gina ever questioning Van, except when it came to Thornton. She and I didn't discuss her decision. Oh, it registered with me, but I didn't think I had the right to question my brother's choice. Especially given my guilty conscience."

Okay, so this was interesting, but what did it have to do with our shooters?

I fought to hold my tongue. Maybe there was a connection, but I sure didn't see it. I shifted my weight and glared at Lorraine. She nodded. "Yes, I know I'm taking too long, but I want you to understand. I blame myself for what happened at your wedding.

As you hear my story, you'll see why."

Leighton was sitting next to Lorraine. Now he reached over to take her hand. She shot him a pained look, which he returned with a smile of encouragement.

"At Thornton's insistence, Van put him in charge of all his charitable giving. This occurred over my feeble protests. Gina's spunky decision was the push I needed to speak my mind. But Van wouldn't listen. After he and Gina were married for five years—during which she never asked him for a penny—Van changed his will. He took me into his confidence, but Gina never knew. Van left all his personal wealth, outside of the money already designated for the charities, to Gina, in the event that he preceded her in death. If they both died, or in the event of her death preceding his, Van's fortune was to go to Erik. It would stay in a trust until he reached the ages of eighteen, twenty-five, and thirty. At each milestone, a third of Van's fortune would be released to the boy."

Lorraine paused. I tried to take all this in. I had no idea how much money she was talking about, but I figured we were talking millions of dollars.

"I totally agreed with my brother's decision. Oh, people called Gina a gold-digger, but she wasn't. Van's choices made perfect sense, except for one tiny detail. If Erik died before reaching the age of eighteen, all of Van's fortune was to go to a variety of designated projects, charities, and institutions," and here Lorraine paused again. This time, she closed her eyes and shook her head. "Unfortunately, the person who would oversee all those gifts was Thornton."

It came to me in a flash. "And that's why Thornton tried to have Erik killed!"

"Exactly."

CHAPTER 80

Detweiler gave my hand a reassuring squeeze.

"Did you know all this?" I asked him. "About the money?"

"Some of it," he said. "Not everything. I wanted to discuss it with you after Christmas, but with the wedding, it fell by the wayside."

"I wasn't completely candid with your husband. I told him that some money had been set aside for Erik. He didn't know the source, and he's never been privy to the amount." Lorraine smiled at both of us. "In fact, Thornton was convinced initially that Detweiler would only take the boy if he knew there was money involved."

"No!" I said.

"Of course not. Your actions have made it perfectly clear that the boy was your priority." She blushed. "I must admit that when you needed a larger house, I nearly told you everything. However, Thornton can be very persuasive. He kept insisting that you two were expecting to improve your standard of living vis-à-vis, Erik's fortune."

Detweiler's face closed down. His amazing green eyes darkened with anger. "Lorraine, you know better."

"Yes, I do. And I should have been more forthcoming, but I secretly relished seeing what lengths Thornton would go to. He's said the most outrageous things about both of you. Laughable."

From across the room, I saw Brawny fighting a smile.

"That's one reason I sent Brawny along with Erik."

I flushed with anger. "You were spying on us."

Brawny quickly shook her head. "No. I was watching over my wee tyke. Lorraine and I had done our due diligence early on. We knew the child was a lucky boy to come live with you."

"When I fell in love with Leighton, all the pieces clicked into place. I didn't want anything to change. Money changes everything. It's a poison."

That last word blanketed us like an evil spirit. I could see that she was right.

Hadcho spoke up. "You're telling us that these two assassins were hired by Thornton?"

"*Aye.*" Brawny nodded.

"Again," said Lorraine, "I have to take the blame for all of this. Kiki, your husband wanted us all to sit down and discuss the finances, at least what he knew of them, but I hesitated. You have to forgive me, Kiki. I've never been part of a family. It's always just been Van and me. Detweiler pushed me to tell you these details, but I was enjoying our time together over the holidays, and I didn't want to ruin it. I wasn't sure how you'd react. Quite frankly, this amount of money is a burden. If Van had talked to me about it, I would have suggested that Erik inherit a modest sum, and that the rest go irrevocably to charity. But my brother could be very hard-headed. Of course, Thornton wanted the money to be earmarked for charities, at a point in the future. I suspect he's been playing with the investments for some time now."

"Lorraine has been worrying over this," said Leighton, putting his arm around her. "We have our own news, too, and that distracted us as well. Lorraine and I have decided to get married."

"Congratulations," I said, but I didn't hop up to give them both a hug. I was still feeling too raw, too ill-used.

"That's terrific news," said Detweiler.

"I understand now how love makes one fuzzy-headed. In my excitement, I quit thinking strategically," said Lorraine. "I didn't worry about Thornton doing anything so quickly, because I had my own timetable. Again, I'm responsible for what happened, because I pushed Thornton into making a desperate move."

"How do you figure that?" I asked.

"Right before the holidays, I made out checks to all my various charities. It's something I do every year at the same time. They've come to expect it. As usual, the heads of the groups called to thank me. Two of them mentioned that my money was particularly welcome because the funds from my brother's trust hadn't arrived yet."

My stomach tensed. I could guess what was coming. Lorraine closed her eyes and shook her head. "I knew right then and there that something was wrong. I immediately hired a forensic accountant to look into Van's financial arrangements. Sure enough, stocks had been moved around, repeatedly, in a sort of Ponzi scheme to cover up withdrawals."

"Tripwires," said Hadcho.

"Yes." Lorraine opened her eyes and blinked back tears. "Even though the forensic accountant was excellent, he spooked Thornton. I should have waited until after Christmas. We could have discussed all this and planned ahead. But I felt bad for those charities that had depended on Van's support. Especially with the holidays upon us."

"This creep was so desperate that he hired not one but two assassins to kill a child?" Hadcho's mouth curled in disgust. "You're sure about that?"

"Absolutely. That's exactly what he did."

"How could you be so sure?" I asked.

"Because he also hired a man to kill my brother and Gina."

CHAPTER 81

"What?" I almost fell off the ottoman.

"You're sure?" Detweiler asked Lorraine. "Do you have hard evidence?"

"No," said Lorraine, turning toward my husband. "I don't. After you shared your suspicions with me, I hired a private detective. He quickly discovered, just as you had, that the accident report on the car crash was incomplete. Tracking down the California Highway Patrol officers who'd written the report provided futile. When the investigator went to look at Van's Porsche, it wasn't at the shop. It had been released to a junk yard, and already crushed. This happened despite my specific instructions that the car was to remain intact. Also, when my investigator poked around into the report, he discovered that there were no recreations of the car's trajectory. In fact, the authorities did none of the normal investigative work that's supposed to be handled when there's a fatality."

"My heavens," I said. Suddenly, I didn't feel so angry with Lorraine.

"As you can imagine, all of this has been overwhelming." She paused to wipe her eyes.

We dispatched Brawny to bring tea and coffee. All of us kept silent until she returned with a heavy tray. Besides the hot drinks, she brought us lemon custard and shortbread cookies.

The tea seemed to fortify Lorraine. "The private investigator kept at it. Finally, he told me that the crash was suspicious not because of what he found but because of what was missing. Someone had meticulously removed or destroyed any telltale evidence. That's not normal. Especially under the circumstances. While he couldn't point to specifics that proved tampering, what he did say that in his thirty-plus years as an investigator, he'd never seen a vehicle fatality with so little left to review."

"Lorraine," I said, "I am so sorry."

"So am I." Her emotions swamped her, and she began to cry softly. Leighton pulled her to his chest, rocking and patting her. At last, she pushed free of him. "I have to go on. There's more. In the aftermath of the accident, I'd forgotten one important fact."

"Forgotten what?" Detweiler asked.

"Erik was supposed to be in the car with them that day. It was a fluke that he wasn't."

I felt sick. "Who kills an entire family? What sort of monster is this man?"

"A desperate one," said Leighton. "He's been siphoning off money from Van's trusts for years. Thornton has a string of ex-wives, and he likes to live high on the hog. When the economy took its downturn a couple of years ago, he'd invested heavily in mortgage backed securities."

Lorraine raised her head. "I let my brother down not once but twice. That day at the pond, and again by not speaking out more firmly against Thornton. As a result, I let that animal kill my brother and my darling sister-in-law. And he very nearly killed Erik, Detweiler, and Hadcho. In fact, if Kiki hadn't been so brave, that hired hit man might have wiped out all of you. Please, please forgive me."

"I've heard enough," said Hadcho, getting to his feet. "That lawyer is a dead man. I don't mind getting my hands dirty. That's the kind of filth that doesn't deserve to live."

"That's very noble of you," said Brawny. "And I would be right there beside you. But we don't need to trouble ourselves."

"Why not?" growled Hadcho.

Lorraine smiled at us. Her eyes were bright and her jaw determined. "Such sad news. Late last night, Thornton was killed in a carjacking."

CHAPTER 82

"Another cup?" I offered Jennifer Moore a second helping of tea from my Christmas gift, a Clarice Cliff teapot she'd purchased for me on eBay. Although I'd never heard of the artist before, my friend had made a wise choice. I immediately fell in love with the colorful images on the clay.

Watching me as I poured, Jennifer stretched her arms over her head. She leaned back in one of my kitchen chairs and smiled at me. "I'm so glad you like it. By the way, Stevie and Erik had a blast. There were LEGOs all over the great room floor. Let me show you what they built."

She flipped through photos on her smart phone. When she came to a picture of the two boys next to their creation, she handed the gizmo to me. I stared at a castle built from tiny plastic bricks.

"Wow, could you send that to me? It would make a dynamite scrapbook page."

"Sure thing. By the way, have you heard any more from Sheila?" Jennifer hit a few buttons and was rewarded by the iconic "flush" sound that signaled the picture was on its way.

"Not exactly." I used a spatula to dig out pieces of cherry pie for her and for me. "But I did hear from Robbie. I guess Sheila isn't allowed to phone anyone for the first two weeks."

"How's she doing?" Jennifer took a ladylike nibble of the pie. I loaded my fork with a honking-big bite.

"She tried to back out of the whole rehab scene somewhere north of Dallas. Robbie actually handcuffed her to the steering wheel."

"You have to be kidding!" Jennifer's eyes widened. She had a tiny red smear of cherry filling at the corner of her mouth. I dabbed it off. Jennifer is such a lady, and I'm usually the one who wears her food.

"I kid you not. I guess he drove the next two hours with her smacking at him. Can't fault the man for his determination." Although the scene sounded funny, it was really a sad commentary on his determination and her denial.

"Gee." Jennifer stood up, went to my refrigerator, and helped herself to a glass of cold milk. I love it when my guests feel at home. It's easier on me, and it means they feel welcome in my house. She stood next to the kitchen counter and took a long swig from her glass. "That's love, isn't it? He's willing to incur her wrath than to give up on her."

"It sure is love. That or pig-headedness."

Jennifer cocked her head at me. "Speaking of which, you seemed pretty miffed with Brawny when I picked up the kids the other night. Is everything all right?"

I used my fork to stab a cherry. "Yes. Now it is. But I had a good reason to be upset with her before."

After checking that the kids couldn't overhear, I told her the backstory on the shooter. "See, I made a fool of myself, dancing half-naked, and then she let the guy go. I couldn't understand it."

"But I still don't understand. Why did Brawny let the gunman go free? That doesn't make any sense. How could she have been so sure he'll never come back?"

"Um..."

"Come on. You can tell me. My lips are sealed," and she pantomimed zipping her lips, locking them, and throwing away the key.

"Brawny showed me a little souvenir she took. I didn't get to see it until after Lorraine explained that Thornton wouldn't be hiring a new assassin. Ever."

"Souvenir? Another matchbook?"

"Nope. Brawny finally showed me a baggy she'd been carrying around. Inside was the gunman's trigger finger. She cut it off with a knife."

Jennifer's mouth fell open. "You have to be kidding me!"

I shook my head. "According to Brawny, to be an effective shooter, you actually have to slowly squeeze the trigger so you don't jiggle the gun. It's that slow steady motion that keeps the barrel pointed at your target. When she deprived him of his index finger, she effectively put him out of business. Forever."

CHAPTER 83

Jennifer stood there with her mouth open. She shook her head, "Unbelievable."

"Yeah," I said. "Tell me about it. That night after I did my turn on the catwalk, I saw a dark stain on her clothes and a smudge of red on her hand. I knew she'd done something, but I didn't know what."

"Gee, and I always thought a pink slip was cruel and unusual punishment."

"Brawny wouldn't have shown it to me, but I kept nagging her. It was both gross and somewhat reassuring to see that hairy digit inside a snack-sized baggy."

"You're sure that lawyer is dead? Van Lauber's cheating attorney?" Jennifer sat down and picked at the pie.

"Yup." I opened the screen on my cell phone and pulled up a news article. "Roscoe Thornton, a local attorney, died yesterday morning in a failed carjacking attempt. Mr. Thornton was leaving the apartment of an acquaintance when he was accosted by a man wearing a black ski mask, according to photos taken by the parking garage security cameras. A brief scuffle ensued. Thornton was pronounced dead at the scene."

"What a coincidence." Jennifer handed my phone back to me.

"That's not the only co-inky-dink. Get this," I said, as I put it in my pocket. "Lorraine's driver Orson decided to retire. Suddenly. As of yesterday. And he moved to Costa Rica. Brawny once told me that Orson served in Special Forces."

Jennifer shivered. "Is there a draft in here?"

"Nope."

CHAPTER 84

Lorraine and Leighton got married on New Year's Day in my formal living room. Father Joe did the honors. Detweiler was Leighton's best man. Brawny gave the bride away. I was the matron of honor and Anya was a bridesmaid. Erik performed admirably as the ring bearer.

For the event, Lorraine wore a gauzy blue-green cocktail dress. A light shawl in sea foam green was draped over her shoulders. Leighton looked fabulous in a navy blue suit with a green tie. Paolo and Gracie wore green and blue ribbons around their throats.

I cried with happiness, seeing our former landlord and his bride.

"You didn't cry at our wedding," Detweiler whispered to me.

"I didn't get the chance," I said. "I was too busy fending off bad guys."

If we all acted a "wee bit skittish," well, we had good reason. But the happy ceremony went off without a hitch. The bride and groom kissed each other, and I'm pleased to report that no shots rang out.

Afterward, we sat down to a huge meal in the dining room. Brawny had cooked a standing rib roast, caramelized brussel sprouts and mashed potatoes. She also heated up several of the casseroles in our freezer. While the others toasted the new couple with champagne, I sipped carbonated apple juice.

"Are you planning to stay here or move back to California?" asked Anya. "Because we all want you to stay here. You said you would stick around, but I'm just checking."

Lorraine blushed prettily. "There's nothing for me back in California. Leighton has asked me to stay here, and I'd like that, if you don't mind."

"Of course we don't," said Detweiler. "Although we might

change our minds, if you two insist on hosting loud parties."

That brought a laugh from all of us. Leighton and Lorraine both loved the blues and jazz. Occasionally if the wind was just right, we could hear the strains of a saxophone or a clarinet, but you really had to be listening hard. Actually, the sounds were rather pleasant.

"No loud parties unless you two are invited," said Leighton. "How's that?"

"Perfect," I said.

"Oh!" Anya jumped to her feet. "I almost forgot, Aunt Lori. I brought the mail in today. There was a postcard for you."

As soon as Anya left the room, Lorraine had turned teary eyes to me. "I always dreamed of having a family. Thanks to the two of you, my dream has come true."

Anya returned to the dinner table with a postcard in hand. Lorraine glanced over it. "It's from Orson. He's so happy down in Costa Rica."

I smiled to myself, thinking how handily he'd managed to remove himself from the long arm of the law.

"He always wanted to live there." Lorraine passed the card around.

"Where are you two going on your honeymoon?" asked Anya, smiling at Lorraine and Leighton.

"My bride and I have decided to sit tight until after the baby is born. She tells me that she's never had the privilege of holding a newborn," said Leighton.

"Never? Well, we can certainly fix that," I said, as the doorbell rang.

Anya hopped up. "I'll get it."

We heard the door open. Anya sang out, "It's Aunt Amanda!"

"Amanda?" I got up from my seat to meet my sister halfway.

"It's Mom," said Amanda, as she ran straight to my arms. Between sobs, she managed, "I just can't take it anymore."

~The End~

Kiki's Story continues in the next book
in the series --
Glue, Baby, Gone
(Book #12 in the Kiki Lowenstein Mystery Series)

Bonus Excerpt
from

GLUE, BABY, GONE

BOOK #12 IN THE
KIKI LOWENSTEIN MYSTERY SERIES

January 10, Friday
Five days before Kiki's due date

~*Kiki*~

Time slows to a crawl when you're nearly nine months pregnant. Every day is a struggle, because you feel like a klutz. A fat klutz at that. Your joints loosen up, your balance shifts, and your feet become a distant memory. With the first baby, you're excited and scared. With the second, you just want to get the delivery over with. My little passenger must have felt the same, because the baby struggled to get comfortable, turning and twisting and kicking against me as though my skin was a set of covers he could knock to the floor.

Added to our joint misery was the weather. I stayed indoors as much as possible, out of the brutal cold. A beautiful dusting of snow totally hid a mirror-slick frozen surface. With subzero temperatures the norm, even a short walk could prove hazardous.

Yes, January had slammed Missouri like a boxer dealing a knock-out blow. An overnight ice storm turned the bleak winter landscape into a crystal wonderland, broken by the fluff of snowflakes here and there. Light bounced and reflected off of every bush, branch, and broken blade of dead grass. The landscape twinkled as if it had been salted with a handful of diamonds. Although the world outside my window was breathtakingly beautiful, I knew that it was also very, very dangerous.

Shards of tan stuck out on one of the branches of our sugar maple. The crack proved that the limb was going to come down any minute. Tracing it with my eyes, I could see it would take a power line along with.

"We need to get out there and grab that thing before it takes out our power," I said, turning to my children's nanny, Bronwyn Macavity, affectionately called "Brawny."

"No, we don't," she said, in that deep voice of hers. Her Scottish accent always seemed heavier in the mornings, leaving me to wonder if she spent the night dreaming in her native Gaelic tongue. "You are going to stay right here. I can get that down in no time. If I hurry, I can get it done before your husband wakes up."

"I agree. The last thing we need is for Detweiler to get out there and pull out his stitches."

"Aye, and sure he would. He's not taking well to the doctor's orders to rest up and heal, is he? Do you really think he should be going back to work so soon?"

I turned away from her so she couldn't see how worried I was. "Of course I think it's too soon for him to be going back. He's still weak from all that blood loss, and he's not supposed to lift anything heavy. But with Robbie Holmes out on leave, Prescott Gallaway is acting police chief, and Prescott hates Detweiler."

Brawny sipped her coffee. "I'll finish my cup and then take down that branch."

She drinks hers strong, black, and unsweetened. Mine is decaf mixed with almond milk and two packs of Truvia. I'm a big believer in trying to give my babies their best start in life, so I avoid caffeine, artificial sweeteners, and any food additives that might be harmful. That doesn't leave much.

A few sips later, Brawny was more awake. She asked me, "Why would Prescott hate Detweiler? That makes no sense. Detweiler's one of the best detectives on the force. His close rate is brilliant."

"Ah, but it does make sense in Prescott's pea-sized brain. Think of it this way: Detweiler is loyal to Robbie Holmes. Prescott knows that Detweiler has got his number. So he hates my husband, pure and simple."

"Got his number? What does that mean?"

Every once in a while, American slang confuses Brawny. So do references to popular culture. I'd considered saying, "Detweiler is Team Edward, and Prescott is Team Jacob," but that would have totally thrown Brawny for a loop. I doubt that she's heard of the Twilight series, much less Edward the Vampire and Jacob the Werewolf. Her choice of reading material seems to be strictly non-fiction, books on history and biographies. Each time I see one of her heavy tomes, I think, I really need to read material that's more educational. Then I pick up a cozy mystery, or a women's fiction title, and happily lose myself for hours. And guess what? I usually do learn a thing or two.

I explained, "Detweiler knows that Prescott is incompetent—and worse luck, Prescott knows that Detweiler doesn't think much of him."

"I see," she put her coffee mug in the sink, rinsed it, and grabbed her boiled-wool jacket from the back of the kitchen chair. Pulling on a pair of scuffed suede gloves, she headed for the back door.

"You aren't going outside in that? You'll freeze." I stood up and stared out the window at the frozen, skeletal shapes of trees and shrubs.

We live on a prime piece of property in a charming community called Webster Groves. The lot is nine-tenths of an acre, complete with mature trees and a garden most people would give their eyeteeth to grow. My former landlord, Leighton Haversham, the author, sold us the property with the proviso that he be allowed to live in the garage he'd converted into a small cottage, when we moved into what was his former family home.

"Ach, this is more covering than most of my clan wear even when they're outside on the heather all day and all night. Don't be worrying your sweet self about me, Kiki. Sure and I'll warm up the car and drive you into the store later when you get yourself dressed and ready. There's no need for you to set your bahookie on a freezing leather car seat. A happy mum makes for a happy baby. You are feeling all right, aren't you?"

"Perfectly fine," I said. "I wish this baby would hurry up and come. I'm tired of being pregnant. I'm so uncomfortable that I barely get any sleep these days."

"Is that what's bothering ye?" asked Brawny. "You're certainly not your usual happy bunny self."

"That and the weather." I stopped myself from complaining about my mother-in-law. Thelma Detweiler, who'd once been my biggest fan, had turned against me. She thought I should have quit working at my store. According to Thelma, I was putting my baby in jeopardy.

Each time I thought about how she was carrying on, I fought the urge to snicker. Did it occur to Thelma that sitting at home would send me out of my pea-picking mind with boredom? Now that would definitely put my baby in danger. Working, not so much. At the store, all my employees treated me like a fragile blown glass vase.

But Thelma? She was treating me like I was her personal piñata.

My patience with her was wearing thin, while the ice outside was growing thicker and thicker.

The storm had added yet another coat of frozen wet stuff, a menace so undetectable on the roads that you think you're driving on dry pavement. One minute you're traveling along, and the next your car is spinning out of control, thanks to what we call "black ice." Despite the warmth in the house, I shivered violently. Ice storms scared me. When Anya was an infant, she came down with an ear infection the morning after a bad ice glazing. My first husband, the late George Lowenstein, was at a conference, so I had no choice but to pop her into her car seat and head for the pediatrician's office. I crept along, gaining speed as the car seemed to have good traction. Halfway there, on a busy stretch of Highway 40, my car spun out of control. The change of direction snapped my head left to right, disorienting me. For a second, I thought I was on a carnival ride. Then my car hit a guard rail. I remember thinking, "I've killed my baby!" I unbuckled my seat belt and climbed over the console, so hysterical that I couldn't even see for my tears. In fact, I tumbled onto the floor behind the passenger seat. The whiplash of the car had messed with my sense of balance, so I then had to do a somersault to right myself. When I did, Anya was staring at me, those denim blue eyes wide with surprise.

"Anya, honey, you okay?" I whimpered, sure that I'd hurt her so badly she was paralyzed.

Then, blessedly, she began to cry.

As I did now, just thinking back on it.

Brawny shook her head at me, setting that thick gray ponytail of hers swinging this way and that. *"Aye,* the dark and the gloom gets to some people more than others. Seasonal Affective Disorder, it's called. Or maybe it's the lack of sleep, but you certainly aren't yourself these days."

"No. No, I'm not," and I blew my nose on a paper napkin.

~ To Be Continued~

Kiki's story is part of a thirteen book series. Her story continues with
Glue, Baby, Gone:
Book #12 in the Kiki Lowenstein Mystery Series.

E-book and paper copies are available at Amazon.com

The Kiki Lowenstein Mystery Series

Every scrapbook tells a story. Memories of friends, family and … murder? You'll want to read the Kiki Lowenstein books in order:

The Cara Mia Delgatto Mystery Series

A new series that's a spin-off of the Kiki Lowenstein books. If you believe in second chances, you're going to love Cara Mia and her friends. Here are those books in order:

1. ***Tear Down & Die***
2. ***Kicked to the Curb***
3. ***All Washed Up***

Author's Note for *Shotgun, Wedding, Bells*

In each of my books, I ponder a social issue, hoping to educate myself and my readers. For *Shotgun, Wedding, Bells,* I researched the world of strippers, or as they prefer to be called, "dancers."

Many years ago, my husband took a credit application for a new piano from a young couple who were shopping with the man's parents. When it came time to fill in the application, the couple asked if they could speak to David privately in his office. There they explained that the man had an office job and made a fair salary, but the woman was an exotic dancer and pulled down six figures! The young man's family was not aware of how their daughter-in-law earned her income. That piqued my interest.

I was surprised to read about the varied background of dancers, the work expenses levied on them, and other small tidbits. If you, too, are curious, I suggest you read *Strip City: A Stripper's Farewell Journey Across America* by Lily Burana.

~Our Gift to You~

Kiki and I have a special gift for you. We have a file filled with instructions and patterns so you can create the projects mentioned in this book. Just send an email to SWBBonus@JoannaSlan.com, and our computer guru will automatically send the file to you.

Furthermore, we will add you to our online newsletter mailing list at no charge. Each month we send you a list of free and discounted books and other goodies. You'll see why people can't wait to get it! If you have any trouble accessing the free bonus or with the newsletter, contact my assistant, Sally Lippert, at SALFL27@att.net

With gratitude from your friend,

Joanna

P.S. If you enjoyed this book, I hope you'll consider writing a review and posting it on Amazon, Barnes & Noble, Kobo, or Goodreads. In today's crowded marketplace, more and more of us turn to reviews to make purchasing decisions. (I know I always read all the reviews before I buy. Even the bad ones, because they are enlightening.) Your opinion matters. In addition, I read reviews to get a better understanding of what you, my readers, like and enjoy. So…thanks in advance.

P.P.S. I'd like to introduce you to a few of my author friends. Go to http://bit.ly/2HH, and you'll be able to download a copy of ***Happy Homicides 2: Crimes of the Heart*** absolutely free. It's a collection of short mysteries by a variety of authors.

About the Author

National bestselling and award-winning author Joanna Campbell Slan has written 30 books. Her first non-fiction book, ***Using Stories and Humor: Grab Your Audience,*** was endorsed by Toastmasters International, and lauded by Benjamin Netanyahu's speechwriter. She's the author of three mystery series. Her first novel – ***Paper, Scissors, Death (Book #1 in the Kiki Lowenstein Mystery Series)*** – was shortlisted for the Agatha Award. Her first historical mystery – ***Death of a Schoolgirl: The Jane Eyre Chronicles*** – won the Daphne du Maurier Award of Excellence. Her contemporary series set in Florida continues this year with ***All Washed Up (Cara Mia Delgatto Mystery #3).*** In addition to writing fiction, she edits the Happy Homicides Anthologies. When she isn't banging away at the keyboard, Joanna keeps busy walking her Havanese puppy Jax or making miniatures. Her husband, David, owns Steinway Piano Gallery-DC, so he provides the class in the family while she figures out how to turn trash into treasure. The Slans make their home in Jupiter Island, Florida.

- Visit Joanna at – http://www.JoannaSlan.com
- Email her at – JCSlan@JoannaSlan.com
- Ask her questions and share quotations at --- http://www.Goodreads.com/JoannaCampbellSlan
- Join her community of readers for fun, special offers, contests, and more at – http://bit.ly/JCSGroup
- Like to color? We do too at http://bit.ly/JCS-ColoringClub
- Send her mail through the USPS at –Joanna Slan / 9307 SE Olympus Street / Hobe Sound FL 33455

Do You Like Free and Discounted Books?

Who doesn't? Be sure to sign up for Joanna's free online newsletter, *Deals and Steals*. Each month she features free and discounted books, recipes, and other freebies. Go to http://www.JoannaSlan.com to sign up.

Thanks!

Many thanks to the wonderful people who've helped me with this book: Allyson Faith McGill, Amy Gill, Amy Goodyear, Dru Ann Love, Lynn Tondro Bisset, Marla Husovsky, Tricia Yifat Cestare, Nena Hanna, and Frances Walker.

Special thanks to my dear pal and Author Assistant, Sally Lippert, and my Queen of All Proofreading, Wendy Green.

64288808R00157

Made in the USA
Middletown, DE
14 February 2018